Smoldering Lies

Maddie Castle

Book 5

L.T. RYAN

with

C.R. GRAY

For information contact:

contact@ltryan.com

https://LTRyan.com

https://www.instagram.com/ltryanauthor/

https://www.facebook.com/LTRyanAuthor

The Maddie Castle Series

The Handler

Tracking Justice

Hunting Grounds

Vanished Trails

Smoldering Lies

Field of Bones (Coming Soon)

Want a free copy of the Maddie Castle prequel novella? Sign up for my newsletter and download a copy today:

https://liquidmind.media/maddie-castle-newsletter-signup-1/

Love Maddie? Noble? Cassie? Hatch? Get your very own L.T. Ryan merchandise today! Click the link below to find coffee mugs, t-shirts, and even signed copies of your favorite thrillers! https://ltryan.ink/EvG_

Chapter 1

UGH. SHE HATED THE SMELL OF THIS SHIT.

She pitied mechanics and other people who had to work with it daily. Even when she was careful, like she was now, using a nozzle to gently pour the gasoline on the dusty old hardwoods, the smell still clung to her. She had kept a spare change of clothes in the car but putting them on didn't help much. It was like the vapors had absorbed into her skin. Scouring her flesh in the shower with as many perfumed products as possible was the only thing that did the trick.

So why was she doing it?

Why drench this multimillion dollar mansion in gasoline? Why disable the alarm, make certain each room was contaminated, and tiptoe backward into the several thousand acre property with the jug of gas in hand?

Why strike the match?

Standing outside in the manicured grass, she stared up at the mansion. Each of the ten columns supporting the porch stood as strong and proud as those of the White House. Each window sparkled in the bluish light of the moon, allowing the slightest view inside. A view past the perfectly staged designer curtains into rooms adorned with the highest quality furniture.

Every room inside was like that. Perfect. Move-in ready.

As though someone who could afford a house at this price wouldn't bring in their own designer.

But that wasn't why she was doing this.

She hated the rich bastard who owned this place. Hated him more with every breath she took. Hated him like flames hated water.

That wasn't the right metaphor. Not really.

He was not water. She may have been fire, but he was not water. Water was peaceful. Safe. A life source for all who breathed, all who were parched and needed quenching.

He was a tsunami. He tore through all he touched. He killed, destroyed, gave the world nothing. He only brought pain.

This wasn't because he was rich. It was because he was evil.

Still staring up at the house with a taut jaw, she released the trigger on the nozzle. With flames in her blood, she walked thirty yards from where the trail of gasoline ended. That's what the internet had said to do. If you wanted to set a fire with gasoline, get as far from it as you could.

There, a hundred or so feet away from where the gasoline trail ended, she shined her flashlight on the grass. There it was. A large stick with an old rag tied on the end.

She chucked the empty jug in that spot and lifted the lighter from her pocket. She flicked it with her thumb. The flame burned. She held the rag to it using her other hand.

Once it erupted in fire, she held it as far from her body as possible. The stick was at least four feet long. Not much of a buffer in terms of flammable gases, but it would be enough.

God, she hoped it'd be enough.

Stepping closer to the trail of gasoline, her heart banged against her ribs.

She didn't want to die. She didn't want this to backfire.

So why risk her life for it?

When she reached that damp spot in the grass, the one drenched in gasoline, she swallowed the lump in her throat.

Lower it slowly to the gas? she wondered. *Or should I just...*

She threw the flaming stick and ran.

A *whoosh* sounded in her wake.

She ran as fast as she could.

A bright orange light flared.

It overtook the dark field.

Now, she could see her car in the distance.

She grabbed the gas can.

She ran.

She ran, and ran, and ran.

She didn't turn back until she reached her car.

Winded, finally at the driver's side door, heart pounding in her skull, she stared at the mansion one last time.

Flames burst through the windows. Glass shattered, spraying outward in a shower. The flames ran faster than she had. All the way to the second floor, shining with the light of a thousand suns.

So why? Why do this? Why risk her life, her future, her freedom, just to start a fire?

Because no one else was doing a damn thing to stop the swine named Brandon Adams.

Chapter 2

I HATED MEN LIKE THIS.

Brandon Adams.

Wealthy. Powerful. Important.

So important. At least, that was how he saw himself. I saw him as a paycheck.

Standing before a large plate-glass window that overlooked the city, he sipped from a crystal glass of scotch. Never mind that it was noon.

The suit and tie that hung off his sculpted physique probably cost more than my car. Hell, the Italian loafers he stood in atop the marble floors easily cost as much as my house. Wasn't saying much, since I paid five grand for my trailer, but the fact remained.

Even his office was a statement of status. Take the large glass desk for example. It was probably bigger than my kitchen table, which made little sense since it was bare of any paperwork or other personal touches.

I could understand spending a lot of money on a desk of mahogany with structured dovetail drawers. Something with exquisite detail, hand carved by an artist in Italy. But only a computer sat atop the sheet of glass, perched on four black metal legs.

Aside from that, the place was hardly decorated. The glass

windows overlooking the Pittsburgh skyline were the showpiece of the room. The marble floors, glass desktop, black modular sofa in the corner, and sparkly chandelier overhead weren't the important parts. The view out the window, the social status the appearance commanded, was.

Modernist style. People who enjoyed it were the same as the man who stood before me. Status mattered more to them than family photos. Hadn't seen a single one of those since I'd entered this building. Money mattered most to Brandon, and that's what his office showed.

"I'm sorry." Brandon gestured to the bar cart by the window, the only other piece of furniture. "Would you like a glass?"

Aside from the fact that I was sober, what normal person drank at noon? If my trailer trash ass in jeans and a faded T had a glass, I'd be a lowlife. It was only socially acceptable if you were someone as wealthy as Brandon and looked the part.

"No, but I'll take that seat." Plopping down in the low back swivel chair, I gestured around. "Nice place, by the way."

"It gets the job done." He crossed his arms and leaned against the windowsill. A half smile spread across his lips. Almost charming. Maybe it was. Maybe he was a decent guy. But I'd learned to trust my instincts with men like him. He had skeletons in his closet, and that's why I was here.

"So tell me about the fires." I re-situated myself in the seat, attempting to get comfortable. Not possible in this modern, high-end furniture. "They started last month? And no one's been hurt?"

"No, no one was present at the first. But yes, the first one happened last month. I thought it was a gas leak. Then the fire marshal gave us a report, and they confirmed it was arson."

I reached into my purse for my notebook and pen, found both, and started jotting notes. The recorder was doing its job in my pocket, but notes were easier to glance at. "You're a real estate developer, correct? All these fires have been on your properties?"

"Yes, ma'am." Brandon eased in the leather office chair on the other side of the desk. "The first was a luxury home I had just finished. From the ground up, every inch had been redone. It was a mansion. One of those old ones time neglected. But the bones were good, and it was on almost a hundred acres of land. I figured I would start with that home, and then build all over. Turn it into a gated community. I'd already broken ground on the other fifty houses. The walls were up, structures sound, and we were using the mansion as a showplace for buyers. Then I got the call. Insurance won't cover the million I dumped into the place, and the cops aren't doing a damn thing."

I almost had to laugh. Cops neglected many cases. Of all of them? Yeah, I preferred it was this guy and his million-dollar mansion that took lowest priority.

"And what was your reaction to the fire?" I asked. "When the cops didn't do anything, when it was confirmed arson, did you plan to take the hit?"

Sighing deeply, Brandon leaned back in the leather chair. His gaze fluttered around the room and his tongue traced along his pearly whites. "At first, yes. There wasn't much more to be done. I figured maybe it was a prank or a couple kids sneaking in to get high. Surely a onetime incident that wouldn't repeat. Unfortunate to lose so much work and money, but worse things have happened."

Worse than losing a million dollars? Phew, this guy must've had it rough.

"But I did wonder if the descendants of the previous owners did it." Brandon raked a hand through his salt-and-pepper hair. "I had the police look into them, and aside from vengeance, none of them had a good reason, nor the means, to burn the place."

I cocked my head to the side. "Why would the previous owners want to get vengeance? What did you do?"

Apparently, he didn't appreciate the way I said that. His jaw tightened, and he squared his shoulders. "There was an estate battle. I don't know the details. One grandkid wanted to sell, another didn't, but ultimately, they all got paid. They decided on their own that they wanted to surrender the property, and I bought it. Guess it was sentimental. They didn't want to see it go, so I wondered if they had something to do with it. But the granddaughter, Emily Foster, she was the only one dead set against selling, and she wasn't in town when the fire occurred. Anyway, that doesn't explain the following three fires."

Fair enough. "How far apart were they?"

"The first was mid-July, the second was two weeks later, the third was a week into August, and the fourth, just a few days later. August thirteenth. All at different locations, none of which are connected to the mansion."

Still, I would do a deep dive on Emily Foster. If she had been blackmailed into selling by her siblings, or even by Brandon, I could see it. She *may* have set out on a mission to destroy Brandon Adams's empire.

Or somebody else hated him. They wanted to see him burn. The mansion was just the costliest building to begin with.

"Tell me more about the other three locations." I flipped over the notebook page and labeled the details as *fire one, fire two, fire three, and fire four*. "Were they all worth as much as the first building?"

"No, certainly not." Brandon clicked around on his computer and turned the monitor to face me.

Another historical building. A Victorian on a half-acre of land, smack dab in the middle of a small town nearby. Not far from me out in Somerset, in fact. It was decrepit, covered in vines with boarded-up windows. With enough effort, I could see the place selling for a pretty penny, but it was no mansion.

"How much did you pay for this?" I asked, noting the address on my pad.

"Thirty thousand dollars," Brandon said. "It was condemned by the city two years ago. I hadn't even finished demolition. All in all, less than sixty thousand worth of investment. I can get that just selling the land. In a way, the fire almost helped me. Controlled burns are hard to arrange, you know. And that's what this place needed. Not ideal, but no, not a major investment."

That alone gave me another avenue to explore. "Mr. Adams—"

"Oh, Brandon, please."

A tightlipped smile. "Brandon. Have you stirred any pots with historical associations? Historical properties like these, tearing them down to the ground, then rebuilding them from the foundation up, I could see that pissing some people off."

He rolled his eyes. "Sure. I piss plenty of people off. That's the nature of this business. But historical associations are easily paid off."

Openly admitting bribery. Nice.

"Environmental activist groups, they're the ones who picket my building sites. Usually doesn't go past that, but..." Brandon chewed on his lower lip. "Is that who you're looking for? Enemies of mine?"

"If a serial arsonist is burning your empire to the ground, yeah. I'm assuming somebody's pissed off."

A quiet harrumph escaped him. Giving that devilish smirk again, he lifted his glass of scotch. After a long sip, he wagged a finger. "Touché, Miss Castle. Touché. In that case, yes. I can think of somebody who hates me and cares a whole hell of a lot about the environment. I got some backlash for the following two buildings as well. The second one was a historical home, the third was a historical office building, and the fourth fire was my new suburb. I had to cut down about ten acres of trees just to break ground. The hippies weren't happy." He spoke that last line with a certain smugness. As if people were horrible potheads and lowlifes for caring about the world around them.

"And who is this enemy?" I asked. "The environmental activist?"

"Autumn. Autumn Adams." Catching my look of confusion, Brandon took another long sip of his drink. "My daughter. We fell out while she was in college. Before that, even. But if anybody wants to see my empire burn, it's her. Look at Autumn before you look into anyone else."

* * *

I ASKED BRANDON FOR MORE DETAILS, BUT HE WOULDN'T GIVE ME any. All he'd say was that I should talk to her. When I'd agreed to but had still wanted a better explanation as to why his daughter may have set out on a serial arson mission to get back at him, he had to rush off to a meeting. Very convenient for him.

So, with that smidgen of information, I returned to the sitting area, which was just as bland and modern as Brandon's office. A few modern chairs, a black modular sofa, perched in a circle around a glass coffee table. The only character in this place was the receptionist's desk.

Behind the chest high, mahogany secretaire, Olivia—Brandon's assistant—sat on the floor with Tempest. She did her best to remain modest in the pencil skirt and blazer, scratching the big German shepherd's head with manicured fingers. She was more my kind of people than Brandon. Assistants, janitors—blue collar folks altogether—always were. Although she wore makeup, the dusting was light. Just enough to correct any redness in her peaches and cream skin. Her long black hair was slicked back in a tight ponytail. Professional enough, but low maintenance.

"She wasn't bad for you, was she?" I asked.

At the sound of my voice, Tempest perked up and spun to greet me. Bending down, I ran my fingers through her hair and roughed up her scruff. Full of excitement, Tempest rolled onto her belly, letting me scratch every inch.

"Oh, no. She's an angel. I wish my dog was this well-behaved." Olivia reached out and scratched Tempest's flank. "I'm so sorry again she had to stay out here with me. Mr. Adams, he's just not a real big fan of dogs."

Typically, I would have argued with Mr. Adams. But he was offering a hefty retainer for my labor. Pissing him off was the last thing on my mind.

Before the meeting had even begun, Brandon handed me a check for a thousand dollars. May not have been all that much in today's economy, but that was for one day of work. If this case lasted two weeks? I would be sitting pretty by the end of it. Although Ox's life insurance policy had cleared my bank account a few weeks prior, I hadn't decided what I wanted to do with it yet. My personal savings were drying up, and I needed money.

"As long as the check clears, I'll get over it." After giving Tempest one more scratch on the head, I straightened. "Weird how much she likes you, though. She doesn't usually like strangers."

"Aw, she's telling stories on you." Voice raising to a sweet falsetto, Olivia massaged both of Tempest's ears. Tempest coiled closer into her. "You're the sweetest puppy I ever did meet."

"Yeah, until you try to take her bone away." My knee throbbed from that squat to greet Tempest, so I leaned against the desk for support. "Hey, do you know anything about Autumn? Brandon's daughter?"

"Just that I sent her a card at Christmas." Olivia stood up as well. "Why do you ask?"

"He asked me to look into her. Said that if anybody wanted to burn his empire, it would be her. You don't know anything about her?"

"I know they have very different values." Frowning, Olivia shook her head. "A few years ago, Brand—Mr. Adams asked me to deliver a gift for her birthday. He didn't even know her address. I did some digging online and found it, but it was in Philadelphia, and I know she lives local. It turns out that's her business address. She's very private, so getting any information out of her won't be easy. But in her line of work, I can't blame her."

"What's her line of work?"

"Environmental law." Olivia leaned in a bit closer, lowering her voice. "A few of her cases have been against Brandon. So, yeah. I agree with him. Look into her."

If his own daughter had sued him, I couldn't begin to imagine what I would uncover in this investigation. "Can you tell me anything about those cases?"

"I really shouldn't. I don't know much anyway. I'm just a secretary." Her eyes darted down the hall and she stayed close, keeping her voice quiet. "Mr. Adams, the work he does, there are plenty of people who hate him because of it. But his daughter, she has more reason than most to—"

The slam of a door sounded.

Olivia jolted.

Brandon's footsteps sounded down the hallway, his voice getting closer.

"Sure," I murmured. "Thanks for your help."

I could've dived deeper. I could've stayed and kept questioning her. But someone like Olivia was probably living paycheck to paycheck. I wouldn't ask her to risk her job just to help me with mine. She'd given as much as she could without compromising her livelihood.

Walking down the winding hallway, Tempest close to my side, I stared out at the cityscape beyond the glass. While I waited for my elevator, pieces of the puzzle began to click. All that infrastructure, all that land, all those buildings—they were dollar signs.

When an environmental lawyer interfered, telling someone like Brandon that a piece of land they planned to build upon, or an old building they planned to tear down, was vital to the ecosystem, it was a threat.

Brandon was a vulture. An environmental attorney? A crow.

Who did a crow think it was to poach the resources of a beast like him? What would a vulture do to a pest who swept into their hunt?

Autumn Adams was clawed by a predator far fiercer than she.

Maybe she bit back.

Chapter 3

It was almost two o'clock by the time I made it home. My house wasn't close to Pittsburgh, and if there was anything I could count on along the way, it was traffic. The weather was nice, however, so when I got there, I tied Tempest to her leash, ran inside for my laptop, and settled in my lawn chair. The sun all but blinded my screen, but the heat on my bare arms was refreshing. The blue sky overhead lifted my spirits, feeding my motivation to get this work done.

But no sooner than I had opened my browser did a familiar voice call, "Hey, girl!"

Barreling toward the trailer beside mine, Tempest all but tore her lead from the ground. At its end, standing on her hind legs, she howled with excitement at the girl walking her way.

"Down," I told Tempest. When she did, only to bounce up again, I turned my wagging finger on Grace. "Don't you pet her until all four paws are on the ground."

She waved me off, as if to say that she knew the routine.

And yet, she had created the routine.

Grace was my boyfriend's teenaged daughter. And one of my best friends. Her bubbly smile, framed by bouncy brown curls, always raised my spirits. And it did the same for Tempest.

Tempest was in rough shape when I'd gotten her. Defiant, burdened with resource guarding and an aggressive attitude. But almost a year later, her behaviors had largely improved. Except for the jumping. Which hadn't even been an issue when I got her.

But every time Grace came over, or I took Tempest to Bentley's, Grace would raise her voice to that adorable pitch every woman used when addressing a dog. Tempest would get so excited, she'd jump and nearly barrel Grace to the floor, and Grace would laugh about it as she stumbled.

In Tempest's mind, that was a positive reward. So she would do it again. And now, Tempest—all hundred and some pounds of her—thought it was just darling to tackle anyone she came across in greeting.

With my experience in dog training, I knew how to handle this problem. Make certain nobody greeted her until she settled down. When she was calm, and all four paws were on the ground, then she could be greeted. But not a moment sooner.

Of course, Grace had already greeted her with the, "Hey, girl!" so part of the damage was already done.

Grace did wait, however, for Tempest to sit before she scratched her ears and settled into the grass beside her. "Was that good enough?"

"Would've been better if you hadn't gotten her excited in the first place," I said. "But that part's fine."

"How am I not supposed to say hi to this ball of cuteness?" Grace rubbed her ears more and planted a kiss on her forehead. Which I also wasn't a fan of, but Tempest never minded when Grace did it. "What are you up to today?"

"About to dive into some research. Your dad still at work?" I asked.

"Yeah, he doesn't get off until five." Standing back up, she nodded to the lawn chair beside me. "I was hoping to get some reading done, though. Mind if I join you?"

"Have I ever minded?" I patted the seat beside me.

* * *

Environmental hero.

Autumn Adams wasn't just an environmental *activist*. She was a *hero*. A quick Google search told me that much. Two years ago, she'd won a massive case against Apex Fuel—a natural gas conglomerate. That was her most well-known case, at least.

A rural town, not far from the West Virginia state line, was a natural gas cash cow. The town and neighbors had protested when the local farmers had sold their land to Apex. But, as most things worked in the world, money won.

The farmers had been struggling, and Apex had offered a hell of a lot of cash. Couldn't blame them for taking it. Especially because, for the first eight years that Apex had fracked there, it'd been fine. Their rigs may have been an eyesore to the rolling farmland, but no harm came, and it'd created a lot of jobs.

Until something *had* changed.

Dozens within a mile of the fracking site had fallen ill. Two children—a boy and a girl—had developed leukemia. One survived, and one didn't. Many of the other neighbors had complained of respiratory symptoms that'd developed around the same time as the children's cancer. Another man had developed cancer as well. And leukemia. While he'd survived, he'd racked up hundreds of thousands in medical bills.

A mass exodus had begun. The town was almost empty by the end of Apex's decade reign. Those who'd left reported symptom improvement after a month in their new homes.

The article I'd found didn't go into extensive detail on how it'd been revealed, but Autumn had built the case on a leaking wastewater tank. Apparently, the hazardous materials from fracking had been stored inside it. The company had been aware of the leak in the wastewater tank and had done nothing about it. Not until just before Autumn began her suit against them.

Once that part came out—that they'd been aware of the leak and had waited to repair it—Autumn had them by a landslide. All residents nearby had received a small settlement, but the ones with serious health conditions got millions. That man who'd developed leukemia? 2.3 million. The children? 5.4 million, and 6 million for the family of the one who passed.

At the end of the article was a video clip. Its cover photo was of Autumn and two families. The one who'd lost their daughter, and the one whose son was still battling. That little boy, only six years old, stood beside his mom and Autumn with a Batman scarf wrapped around his bald head. I noted his posture, though.

Although he stood close to his mother on the right, he tucked himself just as comfortably against Autumn's hip. Maybe a small thing, but certainly worth noting. Children knew things. And if that little boy trusted Autumn, maybe I should, too.

While I could see the resemblance to Brandon, Autumn radiated a beauty that his cold eyes lacked. Big red curls speckled with gray and silver dangled around her strong face. Rather than a fancy pantsuit, she wore a blue paisley dress that brought out the blue in her eyes with a black blazer. Her jaw was sharp and strong; her nose and cheekbones were no different. Still, there was an undeniable warmth in her gaze.

Brandon had the same strength in his appearance, but there was almost a foxy edge to it. Conniving. Twisted. There was fury in Autumn's face, but no mischief.

When I clicked the play button, her voice was just as powerful as her demeanor. "We may have won today, but each time a corporation pays 6 million for a child's life, *they* win. 'This was a mistake,' they say. 'We didn't realize the wastewater tank was leaking. We need the natural gas, but we would never take it at the expense of a life.' But they did."

Autumn gazed out at the small audience where a handful of reporters huddled together. "When it's nuclear power, when an explosion could take out a town like we saw in Chernobyl, we execute careful protocols. One mistake, and a town gets wiped off the map. But when it's toxic chemicals, when it is poisoning us slowly, we pretend it isn't happening. That's what Apex did.

"They knew their tank was leaking for at least *eighteen months* before they repaired it. They tried to sweep it under the rug. They pretended they didn't know all the way up until this week in court, when we showed proof that they did. They manipulated, they lied, and they killed.

"No bomb went off and destroyed the town. But bit by bit, day by day, they poisoned us so they can get richer. So they can make trillions every year. And then give this family 6 million for their dead daughter." She wrapped an arm around the woman to her right. A woman whose cheeks were red, eyes the same, snot streaming from her nose, just like every other grieving mother I'd ever met. "6 million dollars does not bring that little girl back. 6 million dollars didn't save her life. That is how much Apex believes McKenzie's life was worth. But we all know that there's no price tag on a life. Especially not an innocent three-year-old child.

"It doesn't repair the damage they did. It's hush money. And we'll take this money, but we will not shut up. We're not going to sit idly by while these corporations get rich on the suffering of innocent people. We won today, but the true win is legislation. Laws preventing the gross exploitation of our environment. These companies are destroying our planet, but now we know they're destroying the future of the human race.

"We will not stop until *they* stop the willful destruction of our world." If I didn't know better, I would've sworn fire ignited in her eyes. "Clean energy. That's what those 6 million, and 5 million, and 2 million dollar settlements should've been invested in. Not hush money. So I urge everyone watching this to yell, *scream*, for better. Demand laws that protect our planet, but more importantly, protect *ourselves* from the havoc these people are wreaking on our health."

As the video ended, I rubbed the goosebumps on my arms.

There was no denying Autumn's fire. I was sure she would be a force in a courtroom. She was blunt. Blatant in her opinions. Loud. As fiery as she may have been, she didn't seem the type to burn an empire in silence.

But Brandon had insisted. My job was to investigate where he felt I needed to. So I continued down the Google rabbit hole.

Like I expected, finding Autumn's address was no easy task. Given the way she'd decimated the multitrillion dollar company, I didn't blame her for being secretive. My address was easy to find, but my enemies were few. Autumn must've had many, and in high places. People far more powerful than even her father.

While it was almost impossible for me, a civilian, to find Autumn's address, I had a handful of connections in high places, too. That was, if you considered the Pittsburgh Police Department a high place.

I reached out to Ashley Harper. A quick text, asking if she could find me an address. Five minutes later, I had it. I told her I owed her one, and she responded with, *Nah, this just docks one of my IOUs.*

I chuckled at that, then continued down my rabbit hole. Who was Autumn Adams? Well, after digging through her accolades, the ads with her company phone number, her lack of social media, there was only one place left to look. A standard background check. Which had a heavy charge on it.

Autumn was a felon.

In 2002, she was arrested and charged with rioting.

But I was suspicious. How did a felon become a renowned environmental lawyer?

Another quick Google search filled me in there, too. I searched *riot* and the date that Autumn was arrested. And there it was. An article dated two days after her arrest about an unlawful residential development on Native American territory. That's what she was protesting.

The timeline put her in law school—maybe having just graduated—around her arrest. Meaning that a fellow environmental lawyer may have looked at that charge and applauded her for it. And, despite the rioting charge, those protests *did* prevent the development.

It gave me some perspective. While I believed in the American right to protest, riots carried the potential to become violent. Even if it was twenty-some years ago, maybe Autumn's passion had more fire to it than

I realized. Maybe she wanted to take her father down for something, but he'd been able to cover his tracks well enough to prevent it, and she'd decided it was time to find vengeance outside of the courtroom.

Beep-beep!

I jumped. Grace did too.

She dropped her book. My computer stayed in place on my lap. I did, however, knock over my drink on the side table that sat between us.

In the driveway, Bentley grinned through the windshield of his pickup truck.

Flipping my laptop shut with one hand, I flicked him the bird with the other.

Laughing, he hopped from the driver's side. He wore his usual garb—a navy blue paramedic uniform and a boyish smile. "I just couldn't help myself."

"You're gonna pay for that, mister." I wagged a finger at him. "If I'd dropped my laptop, you'd have been buying me a new one."

"Good thing you've got good reflexes." He bent down to greet Tempest. Who did not jump on him, much to my relief. Standing back up, he nodded to his trailer. "You guys hungry? Did you eat yet?"

I stood as well, set my laptop on my chair, and stretched my arms overhead. "I am. But Sam's bringing dinner. Unless you want to have two meals."

"Pssh." He huffed. "I will definitely eat a dinner I don't have to cook."

"How about a walk, then?" Stretching each of my legs out, yawning, I nodded to the street ahead. "It's a nice day, and I've spent way too much of it sitting."

"Sure. Let me get changed real quick." He pecked my cheek and turned to Grace, who'd already gone back to reading. "You want to come with us?"

"Not really." She turned the page in her book.

Pressing his lips together, he eased out a careful breath. As frequent as his smiles were, they'd gotten more and more fleeting in Grace's presence these days.

"Oh, come on." Leaning down, I stretched my arm out beside hers. "If my pale ass is darker than you, you're not spending enough of your summer in the sun. Just a quick one."

With a dramatic grunt, she stood. "Fine. But I'm making dessert when we get home."

"No complaints here." Smirking, I raised my hands in surrender. "Go get some sensible shoes."

"Yeah, yeah," she grumbled, heading past me to the door.

Once she was out of sight, and the front door shut behind her, Bentley met my gaze. The smile was back, but it was weak.

Chapter 4

Tempest enjoyed the walk more than the rest of us, in spite of the nearly hundred-degree temperature. Even if we hated the heat, exercise was never a bad thing. I needed it to manage my pain. Grace's therapist had recommended it for her mental health, and Bentley needed as much time with his daughter as she'd allow.

We talked a little along the way, swatting at mosquitoes, but mostly just trying to catch our breath in the humidity. After listening to Grace groan for twenty minutes, Bentley got fed up with his thighs rubbing together and agreed it was time to head home. Tempest wasn't too happy about it, but I needed out of the damn heat, too.

Only a few strides from home, a familiar old pickup rolled past us. He honked his horn and waved our way as his tires crunched into my driveway. Stepping from the driver's side, a shit-eating grin spread across his lips. Sam reached into the passenger seat and said to Grace, "Guess what I found at the flea market."

Still panting from the walk, she squinted inside. "I don't know. You tell me."

He kept on with that shit-eating grin, looking far too much like a devious child. "Guess or you don't get it."

She crossed her arms and leaned against his truck. "Something vintage?"

"You consider anything from before the year 2000 vintage," I said, paying mind to Tempest at my side. Despite wagging her tail, she kept the leash lax, waiting patiently for Sam's greeting. I rewarded her with a scratch behind the ears.

She shook my pets off, as if to say, *Yeah, yeah. I know I'm a good girl. Now let me say hi.*

Bentley chuckled at my side, still a few strides behind Grace and Sam.

"It's vintage, alright," Sam said.

Grace slumped. "Give me a hint. Something I can actually guess."

"Remember the custard incident?" Sam asked.

The custard incident had occurred when they'd put custard in what they'd believed to be heat-proof dishes that shattered once inside the stove. The custard had spilled onto the heating elements, the house had filled with smoke, the alarm had gone off, a dozen fire trucks had showed up, and Bentley had promised he would get Grace a set of ramekins for her birthday. She'd been absolutely devastated that her custard had failed.

Grace's jaw dropped. "Ramekins?"

"Not just ramekins." Sam held out a brown paper bag. "Limited-edition Pyrex ramekins. The original, *real* Pyrex."

Grace gasped, almost jumping out of her skin. "No!"

Sam only smiled.

Giddy, all but squealing with excitement, Grace dug around in the bag, lifted out a small ceramic bowl, spun around, and began a lengthy rant. Apparently, this was the most magnificent cookware find she could imagine. Most teens got excited about concert tickets and high-end makeup. Grace? Vintage cookware got her blood pumping.

Somewhere in her lecture on the difference between *PYREX* and *pyrex*, she lost me. I just wasn't passionate about culinary arts.

Bentley wasn't either, but he listened to every word. Asked about the history of the cookware company, what made these pieces so unique, which ones she wanted to add to her collection the most. Despite his sweaty pits, the mosquitoes buzzing around both our faces, that blinding sun shining in his eyes, and his growling stomach that even I could hear, he listened. He didn't care about the cookware. His comfort didn't matter either. His daughter was excited, wanted to share something with him, and he held onto that like his life depended on it.

"This is dessert," she finished her rant, wagging a finger at us. "This is gonna be the best custard you've ever had."

"I can't wait to try it, kid," Bentley said.

After another squeal of excitement, Grace skipped into the house with the brown bag.

"Thanks for grabbing those." Bentley walked closer to Sam, reaching into his back pocket for his wallet. "How much were they?"

"Don't worry about it. I was getting all kinds of dishes and stuff for myself, and I saw them, and I knew she wanted them. But I could use some help with this." He gestured to the floor of the passenger side. Several foil pans were stacked almost as high as the seat. "We finished that house we were working on today. The family got us a catered lunch. I was the last guy still there, so I got to take it home. That's our dinner. And it's damn good too."

"Are you sure?" Bentley made his way around the truck. "Those couldn't have been cheap."

"The lady selling 'em had no idea what kinda treasure she was sitting on," Sam said, reaching over the center console to grab a few of the foil containers. "Gave me a whole box of shit for thirty bucks. Really, don't worry about it."

"If you insist." Standing with the remaining pans, Bentley peeled back the lid and peeked inside. "Ooh, Italian?"

"Rigatoni, stuffed shells, and salad," Sam said. "Dinner for a few days, at least."

"Cool, I'll go heat it up." Bentley kicked the passenger door shut and started toward the house. "Thanks again, man."

"Any time." Following behind, Sam stepped from the driveway onto the path. "Oh, and—"

"Before you take another step toward that house, you better greet this dog." I nodded to Tempest, whose whole butt was wagging back and forth now. "She's been waiting very patiently for you to say hi."

"Aw, I'm sorry, Tempy." Sam bent down with his arms outstretched for her.

I released the leash, half expecting her to pummel him over. Once she reached him, though, she looked back at me, as if to say, *Is this okay, Mom?*

"Good girl," I told her.

She spun back to Sam and sucked up all the loving he'd give her, keeping all four paws on the ground as she did.

Still on the ground, roughing up her scruff, Sam looked up at me. That almost skittish look returned to his eyes. "Hey, was that okay?"

I propped my hands on my hips. "What's that?"

Glancing behind him to make sure Bentley was inside, he kept petting Tempest. "Should I have given those to him to give to her? I didn't even think about it until just now when I saw his face, and—"

"I think he's just happy to see her happy," I said. "But I'll ask him about it later if that'll make you feel better?"

He nodded quickly. "It would."

When Sam had first reentered my life, I wasn't sure how he'd fit into it. If I wasn't working, I was with Bentley and Grace. Having him around could've put an awkward wedge in our dynamic.

But it hadn't. Sam's presence filled in a gap I hadn't realized existed.

He loved to cook, and so did Grace. Every time he came over, the two of them were perfecting some new recipe together, hence the custard incident. Grace seemed to be a sort of surrogate daughter for Sam, since he'd missed out on watching me grow up.

I'd asked Bentley if Grace enjoying spending time with Sam bothered him. "It's better that she's baking fancy desserts with your dad in my kitchen than doing the shit we did at her age," he'd said.

Which I couldn't disagree with.

* * *

SAM ONLY HAD SALAD, SAYING HE WAS SAVING HIS SUGAR FOR dessert. I followed suit, and so did Bentley. Having a diabetic in the house had made us all a bit more cautious with our carb intake.

Bentley and I cleaned up afterward, making room for Sam and Grace to assemble their masterpiece. While they were hustling in the kitchen, Bentley, Tempest, and I settled in on the sofa. Bellies full and the scent of cream and sugar filling the air, Bentley watched some TV while I studied on my laptop.

I had gathered just about everything the internet could tell me about Autumn Adams, but I needed to know more about Emily Foster. The woman who hadn't been too happy about Brandon Adams purchasing her family home. Finding information on her was a hell of a lot easier than learning about Autumn.

Emily was a trust fund baby. Her family came from old money. Her great-great-grandfather invented some important part for a vehicle a century ago, got rich, and passed it all down to his descendants. So Emily was used to wealth.

Her social media showed it. She attended a prestigious private school, then Harvard University. She got a degree in art history that she didn't use. Now she was a stay-at-home mom of three boys. That much was clear from all of her *#BoyMom* posts on Facebook and Instagram. Colton, seventeen, Bradley, twelve, and Abraham, eight. Her husband was Joshua.

They were one big, happy, blonde, perfect American family. Their status made them beautiful by society's standards. They drove around in Mercedes and Audis, toting Louis Vuitton and Chanel bags when they flew first class several times a year to obscure destinations all around the world.

There was an image of her and her boys watching the sunset on a vineyard terrace, looking out at the French sunset. "We found this cute little town last time we went to France, and now we go each year! I'll #gatekeep the name 'til the day I die!"

Of course, posts like that weren't hard to find. Because she posted every single moment of her life. What she had for breakfast. Her gym routine after breakfast. Her lunch. Her afternoon coffee. Her "greens." Even the new lingerie she had bought to wear for her husband.

Honestly, as an ex-cop, the lingerie was less concerning than her public record of her precise routine. That much personal information was a stalker's, burglar's, rapist's, or murderer's dream. Sure, the digital age made my life easier, but people were idiots for sharing so much of their personal life online.

Especially when I found the posts about her brother Evan.

Eight months ago, Emily had posted almost daily, ranting about her brother. Things like, "It's funny how family is supposed to love you the most, but they treat you the worst! #imdone #bloodisntthick-erthanwater."

That was one among many of her long, rambling rants. She hadn't disclosed any of the details. Only that she'd wanted to keep the house because of all the family memories there. Evan had wanted the money. Their mother had agreed with Evan.

Emily had refused to buy them out of her share in the mansion until seven months ago. That was when the *#imdone* post had appeared.

Despite her obnoxious, constant social media posting, she didn't seem the type to fight fire with fire. She seemed the "Let me go make a Facebook rant about it," type. She also had never said anything about Brandon, only about Evan.

"I guess I can't blame her for that," Bentley said when I explained what I had found so far. "I can't see me and Phoebe being on the best of terms if she tried to force me to sell Mom's house."

"That's crazy," Grace said, shaking her sugar-coated apron onto the powder-covered kitchen island. "You wouldn't bash Aunt Phoebe online like that."

"Well, no." After grabbing his empty glass off the coffee table, Bentley walked to the fridge behind Grace. He held his glass to the dispenser on the door. As it filled with water, he said, "But Phoebe and

I wouldn't let our relationship fall apart over something so stupid. Family comes first."

"Exactly." Grace held the bowl she had made the custard in toward me. "You want to lick the bowl?"

Rarely did I turn down a chance to lick the bowl.

I stood, headed that way, and dipped my finger inside. After a lick, I said, "I don't know, though. I need to talk to her in real life. I'd like to think that if I had a brother, that relationship would matter to me more than anything, but I don't know what the guy did to her. There's got to be a reason she ended up relinquishing her rights. He could've black-mailed her. Hell, Brandon may have."

"Wait." Sam slowed his wipes on the kitchen counter. Head tilting to the side, he squinted at me. "What did you just say?"

I took another lick of custard batter. "About Brandon?"

He shook his head, confusion still riddling his face. "You said if you had... Ah, shit."

"What?" I asked, setting the bowl down and leaning against the counter. "What are you 'Ah, shit'ing about?"

The color trickled from his face. Exhaling, he ran a hand through his hair. "Since she didn't tell you anything else, yeah, this makes sense."

Now it was me cocking my head to the side and looking at him like he was crazy. "Mom? What else didn't she tell me?"

Another deep breath escaped his nostrils. Dropping his rag to the sink, he swallowed hard. He leaned against the counter across from me, massaging a hand through his beard. "You do have a brother, Maddie."

Chapter 5

For a few heartbeats, I just stared at Sam. His eyes creased, worry pulling his brows down into them. That greenish hue remained in his light skin, now paler than usual.

To my knowledge, I was an only child. It was best that way. Some parents shouldn't have been parents, and my mom was one of those.

But I had a brother?

"What do you mean?" I crossed my arms and leaned against the island. "What—Did you knock Mom up again? She gave him away for adoption?"

Frowning, Sam shook his head. "No, Dylan isn't your mom's."

There was no stopping the scoff that made its way up my esophagus.

Could I blame Dad for cheating on my mom? No, of course not. I hated the bitch as much as he did. But now I understood the reason she hadn't told me. Why would she want to inform me of his love child? She had probably wanted to forget he existed.

"It was after I left," he said, voice soft and tinged with shame. "A month or so after I left here, I met Andrea while I was working for Russel. She was a secretary, I was a guard, we went out for drinks once, and then there was Dylan."

The room was silent, aside from Tempest panting in the corner. Grace and Bentley exchanged a few glances. The kind that said, *Should we give them the room?*

And I didn't know what to say next.

Sam broke the silence anyway. "She brought him in to meet me a few times when he was little, but he didn't really want contact with me." He wet his lips and scratched his head. "Can't really blame him for that. Andrea died a couple of years ago, and that's when I stopped hearing about him. When I got out, I stopped on the way here to see him. He didn't want to talk to me then either. But I know Andrea reached out to your mom to connect you two. I didn't talk to her all that much, but when I was in, she said once that she tried to get you two together. I guess I thought Nat would've told you about him, at least. I didn't know you didn't know about him, Maddie. I'm sorry I'm just telling you now."

Chewing my lip, I turned my gaze to the floor. A few drops of custard speckled the new hardwoods. I was surprised Tempest hadn't come to lick them up yet. The sugary scent of the custard in the oven filled my nose, and I'd been craving it a moment ago. I'd never had freshly made custard.

Now, my appetite was gone. So was my desire to spend time with my father.

Clearing my throat, straightening, I called for Tempest to join me at my side. When she did, I grabbed her leash off the counter. "It's only six. Emily lives pretty close. An hour or so. I think I'm gonna go interview her. Get that out of the way. I don't think she did this, but just to cross it off my to-do list."

"Honey, I'm so—"

"It's okay," I said. Fixing Tempest's leash in place, I forced a smile for him. "It is what it is. I just need to get some work done."

Sam swallowed hard. "You don't want to talk about it?"

"Nope. I'm good." I walked around the island to Bentley and gave him a kiss. "Let me know how that custard comes out."

His eyes were sympathetic, but he followed my lead. "I will."

Because he knew this was how I worked through things. When I wasn't sure how to feel, when I was trying to accept some piece of new information, I couldn't focus on it. I had to let it drift in the background while I focused on something else.

Today, that something else was a serial arsonist.

* * *

A BROTHER.

I had a brother. Almost all my life, I had a brother.

As I drove, that's all I thought about. My brother. The sun was still high, birds chirping in the treetops. With the windows down, going slowly on the back roads, coasting through the potholes rather than swerving around them like I usually did, I tried to process that. It was a beautiful day, and I had a brother.

If Sam got Andrea pregnant when I was seven, that would put him in his early twenties. Twenty-two? Twenty-three? Either still in college or having just graduated. Was he one of the lucky ones who'd gotten to do that?

What had his mom been like? Better than mine, I hoped. Wouldn't take much to be better than mine, but I hoped she was *far* better. I hoped he'd had a good life so far.

She must've been somewhat decent if she'd attempted to connect Dylan and me. But if that were so, if she had tried to connect us when we were children, did that mean he knew about me? Did he know my name? Had he stalked me on social media? Or at least attempted to, since I didn't have many of those and wasn't active on the ones I did have.

If he knew about me, why had he never reached out? He didn't want contact with Sam. Most people didn't want an ongoing relationship with a felon.

Did he think of me the same way? Had he googled me at some point only to realize that I was the same trailer trash as my father? Was that why he hadn't reached out? Sure, if he googled me, he'd see my many accolades, my association with the Pittsburgh Police Department.

Maybe he hated cops. God, I hoped it was because he hated cops and not because he thought I was trailer trash. The latter said something about his character, and the former suggested he was my kinda people. Not because *I* hated cops, but because I came from a world where they were rarely the heroes.

What if he didn't know about me? What if his mom hadn't told him? My mom had refused to let us meet, so maybe she'd never talked about it again?

I liked having my dad around. I liked having a family. Sam was far from perfect, but there was a certain bond between blood. Maybe I could reach out to Dylan, and after a few months, or maybe a few years, we could be best friends, like Bentley and Phoebe were.

Maybe that was wishful thinking.

I didn't know. But I didn't want to think about it anymore.

Luckily, I was approaching Emily's house as that thought ran through my mind. Contrary to what her social media had made me believe, she wasn't as wealthy as it'd seemed. At least, not judging by the front of her home.

Although it was nice, it was nothing spectacular. Two stories high, a large lot with no acreage, and a large, attached garage. Rich brown stone framed all four walls. There were a few windows on each floor, each decorated with a pretty set of curtains. While all the bottom floor ones were identical, different curtains covered each on the top. Baseballs, footballs, and basketballs on one, the Hulk, Spider-Man, and the rest of the Avengers on another, and the last was a simple pale blue. Emily may have had a certain style in mind for her home, but she cared enough for her children's preferences to decorate how they would like. I found that endearing.

Houses in this neighborhood must've sold for half a million, but in today's society, that really wasn't rich. It was middle-class poor.

After shifting the car into park against the curb, I stepped out and tapped my hip for Tempest to do the same. Once she did, we walked up the winding cobblestone path. The grass was well-maintained, and mulch framed a bed of azaleas and lilies beneath the windows. At the door, I lifted the golden knocker and tapped a few times.

It took a few moments for Emily to come to the door. Although not identical to the way she looked in her social media pictures, she was still beautiful. Her skin wasn't as clear without the filter, wrinkles pulling the corners of her eyes downward, but her eyes were the same soft brown as they were in the images. They were gorgeous against her bright blonde hair. She wasn't as well-dressed as she had been online either, wearing a pair of faded blue jeans and an old bleach-stained T-shirt.

"Can I help you?" She peered past me onto the road, noting my Subaru covered in flowers and butterflies. Then she glanced down at Tempest, who only panted at my side.

"I really hope you can." I extended a hand her way. "My name is Maddie Castle."

She looked me up and down and decided to shake my hand. "How can I help you, exactly?"

"I'm a private investigator. I was just hired for a job, and your name came up. I just thought I'd come talk to you and see if you could give me some information. Primarily about the man who hired me."

Still, she stared at me with confusion, not fake confusion, but, *You're freaking me out. Should I call the cops?* kind of confusion.

"Brandon Adams," I said. "He hired me, and he mentioned you as a possible enemy. Someone has been burning his properties to the ground, and I know the cops already talked to you, but I'm just wondering if you can tell me more about the type of person Brandon is. Knowing more about him, how he does business, might make figuring out who is responsible a little easier."

Emily snorted. "Believe me, plenty of people have good reasons for hating the guy. But you're right. The police ruled me out, so if you don't mind." She started to shut the door in my face.

I reached for the handle and propped the door open with my foot. Emily opened her mouth to speak, probably to tell me to go screw myself, but I spoke first. "Did he blackmail you? Is that the kind of business Brandon runs?"

Emily hesitated. She looked at me, then deeper into the house, and blew out a deep breath. "Walk around back. Have a seat in the garden. I'll be there in a minute."

* * *

The garden was what I expected. Off the rear deck, a few white, wrought-iron chairs sat beside a pond framed with flowers of a million hues. Hummingbirds fluttered between the leaves, and orange fish swam in the water to my right.

What I hadn't expected was Emily's kindness. When she came out the back door, she had a tray with a few glasses of water and some cookies. As she sat, she invited me to take however many I wanted. It was a rare occasion that I turned down a cookie.

Fabulous recipe, in fact. I made a mental note to ask Emily for it before I left. I'd give it to Grace as soon as I saw her again.

With a deep exhale, Emily hunched slightly over the breakfast table that sat between us. "Yes. He blackmailed me."

As I had suspected then. "Do you mind if I ask what he used against you?"

"By nature, blackmail is information that you don't want to share with others."

"I'll sign an NDA if you'd like."

Squinting, she cocked her head to the side. "How is this relevant to your investigation? I had nothing to do with this. Do I feel bad for the guy? No. He's an asshole. As far as I'm concerned, he deserves whatever he gets. But knowing what he did to me isn't going to help you."

"If he blackmailed you, he no doubt blackmailed others." I wiped some crumbs from the corner of my mouth. "Knowing how he did it, where he got that information, the way he runs his business, will help a lot more than you realize. Did he hire a private investigator? Did he hack into your personal files? Did he threaten you with violence?"

Emily frowned. "No, no, and no. My brother told him."

That explained why she hated him so much. "What did he tell him?"

Rubbing from her eyes down the bridge of her nose, she slouched further. "You're going to keep this confidential?"

Unless it was something heinous, like rape or murder, I had no reason to repeat it to anyone. "Swear on my life."

One more deep breath. She avoided my gaze, propping her elbows on the table, likely weighing if this was worth the risk. Eventually, she must've decided that it was. "It was my son," she said. "My oldest, Colton."

Maintaining my poker face, I scratched Tempest's head at my side. "What did he do?"

"He's a smart kid, he really is. And he has big plans. He wants to *be* somebody. He wants to save the world." She laughed, shaking her head a bit. "All he's ever talking about is what's wrong with it. The ways we're destroying the planet, all the hate there is, all the ways we can fix it. He wants to go into politics. Not for the money, but because he wants to really change things, you know?"

I didn't know many politicians who cared all that much about what was wrong with the world and wanted to improve it. But hey, maybe Colton would be the exception. "Sure."

"But he's—he's not good at tests." She scratched her head, only sparing me a shameful glance. "He wants to get into Harvard, like I did. And his grades are good enough. All straight As. He has all the extracurriculars, and he's on the football team, and he doesn't do drugs, and he doesn't drink, and he's done everything right. But he failed every practice SAT he took. His anxiety, it's just so intense. And he knows how important those tests are. He can't get into any decent university if he doesn't pass with flying colors. But he did. He passed them. That's what his results were, anyway. That's what we thought."

I had the feeling I knew where this was going. "He cheated?"

Unable to meet my gaze again, she sighed. Eventually, she nodded.

"How did your brother find out?" I asked.

"He was my accountant," she said. "He found a weird cash advance on one of my credit cards. At first, I thought maybe my husband was having an affair or something. Then Evan did a little more digging, realized it was withdrawn from the kids' credit card, and I put two and two together."

Damn. A teenager with a credit card.

"I didn't know what to do about it, but I explained it to my brother because he was worried my husband was cheating on me. We were already fighting about the house. It was civil until then, really. But then we were all together at a picnic, things got heated, I left, and a few days later, Brandon shows up at my door." Emily massaged her temple. "Says that if I refuse to sell, he's gonna report it to the education board. Colton is already in his freshman year of college. He's doing great. Top of his class, brilliant, kind, and I just—" She took in a sharp breath. Finally, she looked at me. "He cheated, and that was wrong. But he deserves what he has right now. He works so hard. His anxiety is just really bad. He couldn't get that test done on his own. The pressure of it was crushing him. And I love that house. My granddaddy's house, I mean. But not more than I love my kid. So, I sold."

Honestly, I wasn't sure where I stood here. Cheating was bad. But the schooling system was broken. Maybe Colton could've passed that test when he was home alone, but he'd blanked under the pressure.

Of course, the kid was more privileged than many others trying to get into that prestigious university. He may have taken the spot of somebody who deserved it more, someone who hadn't cheated.

That wasn't why I was here, though. People had been blackmailed for far worse. I just needed to know how low Brandon was willing to stoop.

"Why was the house so important to you?" I asked.

"Because it was so important to my grandpa. He's rolling over in his grave about what that son of a bitch did to his land. Turning it into a development, come on." Gritting her teeth, she rolled her eyes. After a heartbeat, she retained her composure. "I know I live a nice lifestyle and everything, but money shouldn't come first. Every time somebody like Brandon buys out farmland, it's doing more harm than good. He's just a greedy bastard. And men like him piss me off. But not enough for me to throw away my life. I'm not burning his buildings. I'm just stewing in silence."

Someone had stewed in silence for too long. The problem was still figuring out who.

Chapter 6

On my way home, I ironed out my findings. Which wasn't much. But I had no doubt about one thing.

Emily didn't do it.

It just didn't make sense. She didn't like Brandon, as the majority of people who crossed his path surely didn't, but she was a suburban mom with too much to lose. The friction he'd caused in her family wasn't reason enough for her to throw her life away.

That interview taught me something, though. The vibe I had gotten off him was accurate. I didn't dislike him because he was a rich son of a bitch. While that played a part, men like him just weren't my kind of people. He was shady. He conducted business illegally. He blackmailed a boring, suburban mom who he'd known wouldn't fight back.

But that didn't mean he hadn't messed with a bull with big horns.

Someone was pissed, probably for just reason. If my interview with Autumn tomorrow also proved fruitless, I had to interrogate him for another lead. His past was undoubtedly littered with conspiracy. So long as he was honest with me, I could find this person. Even if I had to dig through every horrible thing he had done.

I had a feeling that would be the problem, though. Admitting to the things he'd done would mean admitting to felonies.

When I got inside my house, I checked my phone. Bentley texted to inform me that the custard was phenomenal. I sent back, *Did you save me any?*

After unclipping Tempest's harness, I flicked on a lamp and sat on the sofa. I continued through my notifications. Grace had sent me roughly a thousand Tik-Toks, which I had no interest in leafing through at the moment.

A text from Sam read, *I'm so sorry I didn't tell you sooner, kid. If you want to talk about it, give me a call. I could even come by tomorrow.*

A deep sigh reverberated from inside me, ending in a trill from my lips. That sound got Tempest's attention. She cocked her head to the side, as if to ask whether that was an invitation to play.

I smiled at her. Scooting off the couch, I held out my hands. "Get your toy."

She wagged her tail and pounced to the basket of them in the corner. Fishing inside, she landed on a pink, chewed up rope. She barreled back to me, planted it in my hands, and all but pulled me over in a ferocious game of tug-of-war.

For a few minutes, I laughed and pulled and roughed up her ears. My phone dinged a few times, but I paid it no mind to it until she tuckered herself out. Plopping to the floor at my feet, she panted up at me with the biggest grin.

"What do you think, Tempest?" I rubbed her black, silky ear. "Should I talk to Sam?"

She stopped panting and looked at the door. Likely expecting him to walk through it.

"I mean, what's the worst thing that could happen?" I asked. "Say I reach out to Dylan, and he tells me to go screw myself. What difference would it make? I didn't even know I had a brother until today."

Tempest turned her gaze back up to mine, waiting patiently. As she always did. Who needed therapy when my dog would listen to everything I had to say? At least she didn't tell me to "feel my feelings."

"But if he wants to be involved in my life, that could be kind of nice, right?" Working my fingers down into her scruff, I shrugged. "I think it would've been nice for you to have gotten to meet Bear. You might've tried to bite his face off, but he would've loved you. Then again, that might be why Dylan hasn't reached out to me. If his mom knew anything about mine, she probably warned him to stay away from me."

My tone must've gotten a bit emotional there, because Tempest stopped panting, jumped up onto the couch beside me, and nuzzled her head against my thigh. I scratched her ears some more and leaned back on the cushions.

A picture of Sam and me hung on the wall beside the TV. If someone had told me a year ago that my father would reenter my life and I would frame a photo of the two of us together, I would've laughed in their face. But now, I treasured every dinner we had together, every text we sent, and every phone call we shared.

Maybe it could be the same way with Dylan. What was the worst that could happen?

I picked up my phone again and glanced through the notifications. The first was Bentley apologizing for having eaten the remaining custard, for which I quickly called him an asshole. I texted a tongue sticking out emoji, so he knew I wasn't truly angry.

Then I typed to Sam, *Dylan Castle? Is that his name?*

Before I even had time to put the phone down, Sam texted back, *Yeah, that's his name.*

Do you think he'll be mad if I reach out?

I don't think so. All he did was shut the door in my face.

There were few things I couldn't handle. A shut door in my face was not one of them.

So, I did what any millennial would do and opened Facebook.

But nothing. There were Dylan Castles, none of whom could have been my brother. And then the obvious occurred to me. "Only old people use Facebook, Maddie," Grace had told me once when I was working a case. "Gen Z use Instagram and Tik-Tok."

To Instagram I went. As expected, there were thousands of Dylan Castles. Sam hadn't specified Dylan's race, nor his exact location, so I had to scroll through a dozen or so Dylans to eliminate them from the result.

Eventually, I found him.

He looked like me, like Sam. But more put together than either of us. The same blond hair and blue eyes, and rather than my dog fur-coated hoodies and sweatpants, or Sam's mud-covered blue jeans, he wore button ups in all of his selfies. Even a tux in some of them.

Those were few and far apart, however. His social media wasn't a shrine to himself, but his life. He liked to cook. Much like Emily Foster, he posted almost every meal he ate. Difference was, he featured the recipes in the captions.

It seemed like he had a passion for photography, too. Or maybe just nature. There were dozens of artistic shots of mountains, waterfalls, ocean waves, and sunsets. They made up most of his account. He'd tagged the location in each photo. Some were nearby. He'd taken one of his forest photos at the same national forest where I had been held captive, in fact.

Others were across the country, like his photo series of the redwood forest. Another was titled, "The Beauty of Yosemite." He'd captured the most immaculate photo of a geyser erupting there beneath a pink and yellow sunset.

Most of his Instagram was only that. But once in a while, he'd tossed in a picture of a computer with a caption that read, "office setup" or something of the like. It looked nice. A big, curved monitor atop a standing desk and a treadmill beneath. LED strips lined the wall behind the screen, blue in one photo, green in the next, and purple in another. That wasn't nearly as beautiful to me as the nature shots, and his following didn't seem to think so either, considering those got a few dozen likes while the rest got thousands.

It interested me, though. What did he do for a living? He worked from home, evidently, and those jobs weren't easy to come by. Especially not for somebody who had just gotten out of college.

Where had he gone to college? He had to have. What twenty-three-year-old got a job that required a fancy home office without a college degree?

So I kept scrolling. Somewhere in there, he must've mentioned his career. Most people did on their social media. But not Dylan. Nowhere did he mention his job aside from the occasional photo of his office.

Eventually, I clicked on his tagged photos. There, I found an image of him with a few other guys holding beers at a bar. He wore a U-Penn sweatshirt, and so did one of the others.

Damn. University of Pennsylvania. That was no easy college to get into. In fact, it was Ivy League.

He must've been smart. Which explained why when his felon father had shown up at his doorstep, he'd slammed the door in the man's face. Not that I condoned it, but I understood it. Dylan had a lot to lose. A designer life, so to speak. He didn't want the drama and chaos that came with someone like Samuel Castle.

The chaos was what I knew best. The idea of living a life like Dylan's was nice, but I would always feel out of place in it. People like Sam were the ones I belonged with.

It wouldn't shock me if Dylan felt the same about me as he did about our father. I had to try, though. Even if Dylan wasn't the type of company I usually kept, maybe Emily was wrong. Maybe blood *was* thicker than water. Maybe we could give each other a shot.

Holding my breath, I typed out a direct message.

Hey, I don't know if you know about me, but my name is Maddie Castle. My dad's Sam Castle. I think that makes you my brother. Weird as hell, since I grew up an only child, lol. But I guess I was just wondering, would you want to meet up for coffee sometime?

Then I stared at the message. Was that weird? It was. Reading it over and over again, I searched for a better way to phrase it, but I couldn't think of one. There was no how-to book for this. Nobody told you how to contact a long-lost half-sibling.

It was the best I could do, so I held my breath and pressed send.

Just as my front door slammed open.

I reached for my gun on the table out of reflex. But Grace's head bobbed around the edge before I could grab it. I pulled back my hand and put it to my chest, willing my heartbeat to slow down. "Jesus, Grace."

"She posted." Wide-eyed, she hurried to the couch beside me and held her phone screen to face me. "Daisy posted another story."

Chapter 7

Daisy Miller had disappeared almost two years ago.

I had been looking for her for the last three months. Daisy was a writer and posted her stories on fanfiction websites. One of her stories was an obvious self-insert. It'd led me to believe that a man she had fallen in love with had kidnapped her. Shortly after, I'd found a poem she had published during her disappearance—*Bird in a Cage*—which was an obvious allegory for her captivity. It was the only evidence I had that she was still alive. Also the only evidence suggesting someone was holding her against her will.

Although I had a couple of contacts in the FBI, they said this was below their pay grade. The Columbus PD, the jurisdiction for Daisy's disappearance, didn't believe a poem was evidence of anything. "The girl wrote sci-fi and paranormal romance," Detective Conroy had said. "How am I supposed to believe this is anything more than one of those stories?"

That was if I could prove it was Daisy's work at all. She posted her stories online under a pseudonym, so proving they were hers was just about impossible.

And even if they were hers, that only proved she was alive. It didn't prove she was being held captive. It didn't prove she had been kidnapped. She was a runaway foster kid turned tweaker, turned prostitute, after all.

"Girls like that disappear," Detective Conroy had said. "You haven't found her because she doesn't want to be found. Same reason *we* haven't found her. Not because somebody is holding her captive, Miss Castle."

"She ran away from foster homes where she was beaten and sexually assaulted," I'd snapped. "She ran to the only family she had left. If she were on the run, she would run to them, not *from* them. She's out there somewhere, and if I could just get a little bit of help, maybe I could find her."

Conroy had snorted and chuckled a bit before ending our call without another word. Just like every other official did in a case like this. The junkies, tweakers, and whores, they were the enemies the suburban families needed protecting *from*. Criminals. Criminals didn't deserve help from the cops.

But this time, maybe I had something.

i've got a new friend,
a pretty bird, just like me,
with blue eyes of ice,
and raven black hair

SHE DOESN'T TALK MUCH,
she won't be here long,
just like the last 3S

AS BEAUTIFUL AS THE ATLANTIC,
TALL as a tree,

BUT SHE'LL BE GONE SOON.
i'm sure she is by now.

if i can't save her,
i'll at least avenge her.

I MURMURED THE LAST LINE TO MYSELF.

"What?" Grace asked, turning my way. "Do you know what it means?"

"I'm not sure." I grabbed my laptop off the table and flipped it open. "But I think it's a description."

She squinted at me. "I don't understand."

"'A pretty bird, just like me,'" I quoted, running my finger along the screen. "'She'll be gone soon.' 'If I can't save her, I'll at least avenge her.'" Still, Grace looked at me with confusion. "He has another girl. I think that's what she's telling us. He kidnapped somebody else, and he's going to kill her."

Grace's eyes widened. "And she's trying to tell us who she is so that we can save her."

Doubtful. Daisy posted this today, but that didn't mean she had written it today. She could have written it months ago. It wasn't a cry for help, but a trickle of information. She was just trying to give us a hint.

But that was too solemn to tell Grace. So I said, "Maybe," and opened my browser.

"Why wouldn't she just tell us where she is?" Grace asked, shaking her head. "That's what doesn't make sense about all of this. If somebody's holding her captive, why not just say that? Why not just reach out online somewhere?"

"She can't." Clicking around on my screen, I headed to the database for missing persons. "He could be reading what she writes. Or monitoring her internet activity. Maybe she doesn't have internet at all. Maybe, on occasion, he takes her out into the world, lets her use a computer somewhere in public, and lets her upload her files."

That was the theory I had landed on shortly after finding *Bird in a*

Cage. And why I couldn't blame the cops for saying I was grasping at straws. I was.

"But *why*?" Brown eyes twinkling in the light of the end table lamp, her forehead scrunched up. "Why would he let her post her stories? If he's this evil villain, he would want her under his complete control. If this is a code that could get him caught, why would he let her share it?"

"I've been asking myself that question for months." I had an image of Daisy displayed in one browser window. The database was displayed in another. With every missing person, an image was attached. So what was I doing? Leafing through all the most recent missing person images displayed. If any of the many people reported missing every day looked a hell of a lot like Daisy, it could be a lead. "In that story she wrote, *Sins and Silk Ties*, Mr. Deluca was obsessed with Lily, right?"

"Right." Grace said the word slowly.

"And something Mr. Deluca liked about Lily was that she was a writer. It fascinated him."

"Like in that chapter where she reads aloud to him."

I nodded, still sifting through the images on my screen. "For all we know, that could be why he's kept her alive. She could remind him of someone he knew before. Maybe his mom was a poet, or his high school girlfriend entered writing competitions. Maybe he's kept Daisy alive because of her passion."

"But I still don't understand why he would let her post them. Write them, sure. But she's giving us messages through them. That could destroy him."

Snorting, I raised a shoulder. "In theory. But so far, we don't have close to enough evidence for that."

Grace huffed, propping her chin in her hand and watching over my shoulder. "If they do go out in public, and that's how she posts her stories because she doesn't have access to the internet otherwise, why hasn't she asked someone for help?"

Two possible reasons for that. One of them Grace wasn't going to like. "He's holding something over her head. Threatening someone or something she cares about."

"But all she really had was us. Me and Dad. No strangers have come in and threatened our lives."

"True." After sliding over to my email, I jotted a quick note for Harper, along with the link to inform her of what I was doing with the database. "But when you're in a situation like that, when an abuser has control over you, fighting back is terrifying."

"I did it." She tightened her jaw. "Daisy can, too."

Once I finished up my email, I swiveled to face her. And I frowned. "It's not that simple, kid."

"Yes, it is. If he takes her in public, all she would have to do is shout for help, and someone would."

My frown deepened. "It's different when you love the person who's hurting you. Even if you hate them, if you once loved them, it's not that simple."

"How can you say that?" Her face screwed up in some combination of disgust and fury. "You think he's going to kill this other woman he's holding captive? And it's just okay that Daisy has done nothing about that because she loves him? Maybe? You don't even know what the relationship is like and—"

"I know what that situation is like better than you do." I didn't mean to take the tone that I did, but there was no dialing it back now. "I asked for help after my dad left, and I became my mom's punching bag. Where did I end up? Foster homes where I was just somebody *else's* punching bag. The hell I ended up in was worse than the hell I started with. And my mom knew that. After she got me back, any time I would stand up for myself, she would threaten me with foster care. So, I stayed. I stayed because I had no choice. Which could very well be the position that Daisy is in right now."

The dim glow of the lamps around the room and the bluish light of the moon pouring in from the windows contributed to a grim atmosphere. Crickets chirped outside, filling the silence.

A hard swallow bobbed in Grace's throat. "You think she tried to escape before? Then something bad happened? That's why she can only ask for help in code?"

"I hope so."

The face Grace gave me told me she didn't understand. That was okay. She didn't need to.

Because the alternative was far worse.

Either Daisy couldn't ask for help because it would compromise her safety, or the police were right. We couldn't find her because she didn't want to be found.

But I didn't believe that. I believed the theory I had just explained to Grace. Somehow, Daisy was stuck. It wasn't that she didn't *want* help. She just didn't have a way to get it.

"Why she can't give us more hints doesn't matter." I minimized the email browser and went back to the missing persons database. "If we find her, she can explain then. But for now, we work with what we have."

"Looking at missing persons, you're hoping we find somebody who looks like her?"

"Exactly."

Grace sighed. "Alright. Let me get my laptop."

GRACE CAME BACK NOT ONLY WITH HER LAPTOP, BUT ALSO WITH Bentley. He had been in the shower when she'd found that poem, and he wasn't happy Grace had told me about it before she told him. He stayed quiet about it, though, only making a few passive-aggressive comments under his breath.

Hair still dripping wet, having apparently grabbed the first set of clothes he could find in his frenzy, he sat on the couch with his laptop as well. Then, for the next three hours, we scoured the missing persons database together.

Much to our dismay, there was no algorithm to sort through people based on their hair color, eye color, or facial features. The most we could filter for was state, date, and gender. We checked Ohio first.

In the last six months, there were fifty missing women who were similar enough to Daisy. Dark hair, light eyes, and light skin. Every time one of us found a woman who resembled her, I started a file for her. Researching each individual person would take me hours, days, maybe even weeks. But if this is the only lead I had, then I would dissect it until only mush remained.

For now, we focused on categorizing.

By midnight, Bentley started nodding off. Grace made it until around 2 a.m. Sometime after that, I must've fallen asleep as well. I woke at 7 with my neck bent on Bentley's lap, one leg on the floor, and the other turned against the back of the sofa. My laptop was on the floor beside me, having fallen in my slumber.

After lifting it onto the coffee table, I nudged Bentley awake. He muttered, "Shit, shit, shit," rushed to his feet, asked if I could make sure Grace got up before noon, and kissed me goodbye.

I wasn't the best person to task with waking up a teenager. If it were up to me, I would sleep until noon myself. But Daisy's case wasn't the only one that needed handling.

So I let Tempest out, took a shower, shoveled some granola into my face for breakfast, brewed a cup of coffee, and woke Grace around 9:30. She grumbled a bit but got to her feet.

From there, with Autumn Adams' address in my GPS, I set out to find a serial arsonist.

Chapter 8

NOW *THIS* WAS THE DREAM.

Autumn's house was about an hour's drive from mine. After venturing through miles and miles of farm hillside and deep verdant vegetation, I found myself on a small country road. I had to slow to fifteen miles an hour to not screw up my alignment on the gravel, but it was worth the slower pace. It was like a vacation drive, dodging chipmunks and bunnies and what seemed like a thousand other little woodland creatures.

Hers was the only house on the road but calling it a house wasn't the best descriptor. It wasn't much bigger than my trailer. Barely more than a cabin, really. Four wooden walls of logs made the frame. Big, shuttered windows let in light and fresh air on each side. Window boxes overflowing with foliage sat below each one. Their vines climbed all over lattice ladders. A thatch roof protected all of it, and that made me smile. I'd never seen a thatch roof in real life, but it was the cutest thing.

The front yard was an oasis of wildflowers, fruit-bearing trees, and plants. Not a massive garden, but one that looked like it had manufactured itself through nature. What wasn't covered in flowers had clover instead, where little bumblebees and butterflies buzzed about.

The path of cobblestone traveled from the gravel driveway to the teal, arched front door. Stepping from my car and walking up it with Tempest at my side felt like stepping into a storybook. The wind blew all those floral scents to my nose. A creek trickled in the distance, giving me an odd sense of tranquility. From the open windows came quiet laughter, but not like that of a party. It was a sweet, innocent baby giggle followed by the indistinguishable but endearing tone of a mother playing with her child.

As much as I loved my job, it was rarely this lovely.

Once I made it to the landing, I knocked on the door a few times. The adorable baby laughter ceased. Footsteps padded on the other side, then the door creaked open. But Autumn's face wasn't the one that greeted me.

She was a pretty woman, around my height, with warm brown eyes coated in muted brown eyeshadow and thin wings. The onyx hue of her skin popped against the orange sundress draped over her frame. Her curly black hair was swept into a tidy bun at the back of her head.

On her hip sat an adorable little boy, about a year-old. His skin was a few shades lighter than the woman's, but the resemblance was still undeniable. He wore only a cloth diaper and a pair of sandals.

"Can I help you?" she asked.

"I hope so." Giving a smile, I extended my hand. "My name is Maddie Castle. I'm a private investigator. Is Autumn home by chance? I was just hoping to talk to her for a few."

The woman's brows furrowed. "Can I ask what this is about?"

"Her father." The way she tensed told me I was about to get the door shut my face. Before she had the chance, I continued, "He insisted I talk to her. I've done my research. I really don't think she's done what he thinks she's done, but I want to rule her out so that I can move on to actual leads."

She snorted. "And what does he claim she's done?"

A deep breath escaped from my nostrils. "There's been a series of fires on his properties. I asked him if he has any enemies, and he pointed at Autumn. Said I should check her first. Like I said—"

This time, it wasn't a snort, but a scoff. "Oh, sure. And they're enemies because of her, right? She's the villain, and he's innocent?"

I knew where this was going, and I didn't like it. Before this conversation could go any farther downhill, I said, "Look, I don't like the guy. He's a rich, entitled asshole. And I'm sure he's got a lot more enemies than just Autumn. She's a humanitarian, an ecological hero. I can't see her suddenly becoming a serial arsonist. But if I don't talk to her, he's gonna hire another PI who will. I'm just hoping she can point me in another direction."

Clenching her jaw, the woman looked behind me. The tension in her posture softened when she saw my butterfly-and-flower-covered Subaru. Her tone was still firm, however. "How did you find our address?"

"I used to be a cop," I said. "Still have a few friends at the PD. With civilian software though, I couldn't track it down."

Again, her attention relaxed. She looked me over for a few heartbeats, then sighed. "She'll be back soon. Let me give her a call and let her know you're here."

JANINE HARRIS. THAT WAS HER NAME. AUTUMN INFORMED ME OF that as we sat in the wooden rocking chairs out back, nestled between a pond and a small field of solar panels. "I considered having my surname changed to hers after we got married," Autumn explained. "But I've already built up a reputation as Autumn Adams, so I kept it. Autumn Harris does have a nice ring to it, though, doesn't it?"

"That it does." Leaning forward on the rocking chair, I propped my elbows on my knees. "Always makes sense to keep your surname as a woman in business. I wouldn't change mine if I got married either. Too much work to change it back if it doesn't work out."

Autumn chuckled, adjusting the baby in her lap. "That's what I'd advise all young women do."

Since she had arrived, her demeanor was much like it was now.

Relaxed, laid-back. She was a lawyer, of course, which meant that she was a good liar. But this didn't seem like a show to me. It seemed like an average person who came from a shit family and was used to them making her life hell. Like she'd learned to deal with it with a smile.

"So." She set the toddler on the ground and held his hand to keep him steady as he toddled to the clover nearby. "What's going on with my dad?"

"You haven't seen it in the news?"

"I don't have cable." She nodded to the house. "I read the paper at lunch, but I have controversial opinions about journalism. Staying up to date on current events is great and everything, but you can't convince me that humans are meant to hear about catastrophe after catastrophe day in and day out, every day."

That was fair. Closing your eyes to the reality of the world to make it go away didn't help anyone except yourself. But how could I judge Autumn? She had done more good for the world than most. If she had to protect her peace along the way, so be it.

"Well, a few of his buildings have burned down. They thought it was accidental at first, but there've been too many. Someone's doing this, and he hired me to figure out who."

"And he thinks it was me?" Arching a brow, she gave a half smile. "Of course he does."

"When I asked about enemies, he only mentioned you." I gave her the same expression she was giving me. "But he wouldn't explain why. What caused your falling out?"

"Death by a thousand cuts." She shrugged. "I hated him as a kid. Which sounds crazy, right? How can a kid hate their parent? But I did. I never respected him. Hated the way he treated my mom. Resented that other kids had dads who were around, and mine was always on a business trip, or in a meeting during dinner, or nowhere to be found on my birthday.

"When my mom died, that was when the real hatred began. I blamed him for it. Still do, in some ways. Then when I went to college, and I became more politically aware, more environmentally aware, I hated him even more. Then I fell in love with a woman, and he hated me just as much. Went no-contact on advice of my therapist when I was in law school. I've only seen him a few times since then."

All that, she spoke so casually. It was a vulnerable disclosure, but she said it like she was ordering lunch. One part stuck out though. "Do you mind if I ask why?"

"Why I went no contact?"

"Why you blame him for your mother's death?"

"Because he's a piece of shit." She reached to help the toddler onto his bottom in the grass. When she looked back up, she must've read my expression, because she sighed. "My mom's death was ruled a suicide. Accidental or intentional, nobody ever confirmed. She didn't leave a note though, I know that."

A knot wadded in my belly. "You think he killed her?"

"That's a question I've spent the last twenty years pondering." Autumn raised her shoulders again. "He wasn't in town when it happened. But even if he had nothing to do with her actual death, he led her to the bottle. Also why she developed insomnia. That's how she died. Alcohol and sleeping pills."

I saw the point she was making. "Was he abusive?"

"Physically? No. Never put a hand on me or her. To my knowledge, at least." Autumn pushed a handful of curly red hair from one side of her face to the other. "But psychologically, twenty-four hours a day, seven days a week. When he wasn't absent, when he wasn't neglecting his family, he was critiquing us.

"Mom gained a few pounds. That was the end of the world. Mom didn't make sure his suits were organized in his closet or picked up from the dry cleaners, and he'd throw a tantrum. Tell her she was worthless, that he deserved better. She had no idea how lucky she was to have him, blah, blah, blah. The man is a psychopath."

Many successful, intelligent businessmen were. Not all psychopaths were murderers though. Some of them were just selfish, master manipulators. "I'm sorry you went through that."

"Don't be. That shit made me who I am." A smile. "Who I am quite happy to be, by the way."

"As you should be. You have an astounding career," I said. "I read about the settlement you got for those people against Apex. That's really impressive."

"I like to think so." Crossing her arms, she turned to face me better. "What are you getting at here, Maddie?"

She was a lawyer. She worked with cops all the time. Of course she knew I was going to follow-up that compliment with a crowbar. "Given how passionate you are about your work, I just have to wonder if any cases you've worked against your father made you particularly angry."

"I've been angry with him my entire life." She huffed a laugh. "And yes, I have sued him directly—on behalf of clients—several times. Some I won, and some I lost. As is the nature of the law. But when I'm working on those cases, when I get so angry and passionate, it's because there's right, and there's wrong. I'm angry about the wrong itself. Not at him exclusively."

I understood what she was saying, but surely she had more to add there. So I waited.

"Alright. You're trying to get a feel for me, the type of person I am, right?" Autumn leaned in and propped her elbows on her knees. The same passion I had seen in that clip returned to her voice. "When I won that case against Apex, it wasn't about the money. It wasn't even about taking down the corporation. It was about these kinds of people. That's why I got into this business. That's why I practice environmental law, because our world is on fire. You told me how beautiful you find my yard when we sat down, did you not?"

"I did."

"And this place is nothing special." Holding out both arms, she gestured around. "Every plant here is indigenous to this land. I'm far enough away from civilization where I don't have to worry about air pollution and water pollution the way that most do. And I'm so incredibly privileged for that opportunity, but make no mistake, this is the bare minimum."

I didn't disagree with that either. Autumn lived a modest, yet beautiful life. "I agree. And I respect that."

"Then you respect my work. Because all I'm doing is asking for the bare minimum. A little less greed, and a little more decency." She tucked a curl behind her ear. "You know, after World War II, the steel mills were running strong in Pittsburgh. That's how we got the nickname. Steel City?"

Every Pittsburgher knew that story, so I nodded my understanding.

"But the city was so polluted that at ten o'clock in the morning, you had to have your headlights on to drive through it. The smoke was like the thickest fog you can imagine, just sitting on the city. Constantly, it destroyed buildings. People couldn't breathe, for crying out loud. But you know what people thought about it?"

"I bet you're gonna tell me."

"It was a sign of prosperity." She snorted. "The steel mills were creating jobs. They made a meaningless little city important. It wasn't that they didn't care if it was harming people. It was that money won. No one really enjoyed looking outside at a smog-covered city, but people were desperate for money after the Great Depression. So they chose the jobs over lives."

It was one of the few things I remembered from high school history. I just wasn't sure how it connected to my questions. "And that's why you do what you do."

"Exactly," she said. "My point here is that time and time again, humans screw up. Because of the modern way of life, the fact that money rules, we step on each other and our own to survive. Even dogs don't shit where they eat." Autumn gestured to Tempest, napping at my feet. "And nine times out of ten, people like my father are the ones responsible. The world will be a better place without men like him. But in the grand scheme, he is one flea on an infested dog.

"Burning his buildings, destroying his business, wouldn't do me any good. Fighting in court, taking class-action suits to the Supreme Court, *that's* how I win. I might be passionate, but I'm not violent. And if these dates and times are correct"—she pointed to the notes I'd shown her when I'd arrived—"I have alibis for all of them. Out of town for this one, in court during this one, and home during this one. Which my security cameras can prove."

Damn. Now I saw the point. I also wished I were working for her instead of Brandon. But the fact remained. I was hired to find the arsonist.

"That makes sense," I said. "You wouldn't mind sending me proof of your alibi, would you? I believe you, but I need it for Brandon."

"Of course."

"If you wouldn't do something like this, can you think of anyone else your dad has screwed over who might?"

"Give me a bottle of whiskey, and I can probably get you a list of fifty within the hour." Leaning back into the chair, she rocked on the ball joint of her feet, posture and tone softening. "But the first that comes to mind is Greta. She has damn good reason to want to destroy him."

I clicked my pen and opened my notebook. My phone was recording the interview, but the vital stuff, I liked to have on paper. "Who's Greta?"

"She was his mistress. The only one I know about for sure, at least," she said. "A couple months before my mom died, that's when we found out about Greta."

Shit. No wonder she blamed her dad for her mother's suicide. "Why would she want to destroy him?"

"He knocked her up. He told her to get rid of it, and she told my mom." A certain sadness crept into Autumn's eyes. "Few months go by, shortly before my mom's death, and Greta gets T-boned in a hit and run. She survived, barely, but she lost the baby. After she was released from the hospital, she showed up at our door. She was hysterical. Claimed my dad hired somebody to scare her off. Or maybe to do exactly what happened."

A tightness squeezed my chest. "Do you think he did?"

"Eighteen years of child support with the kind of money he makes? Oh yeah, he'd kill to get out of it." Another shrug. "I have no evidence that he did. But there are few things I would put past him. And either way, I could definitely see her coming back for revenge."

"What's Greta's last name?"

"Moris, I believe."

Onto the next lead, then.

Chapter 9

Greta Moris was next. But I needed to talk with Brandon first. What other enemies had he failed to tell me about? I couldn't do my job without all the information.

So that was where I headed.

It was almost a two-hour drive without traffic. With traffic, it came to about three. My knee was killing me by the time I stepped out of my car to head into his office. Stretching in the elevator helped, but not as much as I would've liked.

This was the worst part about living with chronic pain. Not the pain itself, but how difficult it made the simplest tasks, like driving a car or doing my job. All I wanted was to do my work, and do it well, but the pain made every step a chore.

By the time I was on Brandon's floor, I was wincing each time I bent my knee to lift it for the next step. Which pissed me off.

Learning what I just had about Brandon left me less than impressed with the man. The pain only made that irritability harder to conceal. Especially when I asked Olivia if I could head into Brandon's office, only for her to tell me he was in a meeting. He would be out in fifteen minutes.

Sure enough, fifteen minutes later, he and a few other people in suits walked out of his office. When the others fanned out, I opened my mouth to ask if we could talk. But before a word could leave my mouth, he held up his pointer finger to silence me and said, "I've gotta run across the street and grab a coffee. Hold that thought."

Considering I had called on my way here to ask if we could meet, and he had said yes, I found that rude. But I was willing to work around it. "We can walk and—"

"I'll be right back." He kept walking, not so much as looking my way, only held that pointer finger up to silence me. "Just sit tight."

I bit my tongue and gritted my teeth. Wasn't this what men like him had assistants for?

Rude, sure. But I was getting paid for this. I was getting paid *well* for it, even if that meant I was being paid to be treated like shit.

So I waited. I leaned against the wall in his waiting room. Olivia suggested I have a seat. Sitting made the pain worse, so I thanked her but declined. Ten minutes passed, and I started pacing, hoping that would alleviate some of the pain. It didn't.

Another twenty minutes ticked on, and my irritation was growing. Partially because Brandon was an asshole, but mostly because the pain was worsening, and I needed relief. After popping a fistful of ibuprofen, I asked Olivia where the restroom was. She pointed me down the hall.

It was one of those family restrooms, so I had some privacy. Which I greatly needed for what I was about to do. The floors were the same marble as Brandon's office. Well-maintained and, I hoped, clean. Because I laid on them with Tempest at my side and started through my stretching routine.

It wasn't the first time I'd needed to do my physical therapy in public. It was the first time I had done them on the floor of a public restroom, however. Un-hygienic, I knew, but it was reaching a six or seven on the pain scale, and I had to do something before it tapped out at ten.

After twenty minutes of doing those exercises two times over, I got it down to a manageable three on the pain scale. With the handicapped railing and Tempest's support, I made it to my feet. Walking out of the restroom, I noted the small line that had gathered. I kept my gaze on the ground as I limped past them to the end of the hall.

Behind her reception desk, Olivia gave a sad smile. "Are you okay?"

"Living the dream." I propped my elbows on its top, bearing as much weight as I could on my arms rather than my legs. "Is he back yet?"

"Just came in a minute ago." She nodded to his office door. "I'm sorry again about the wait."

"Why should you apologize?" Heading toward Brandon's office, I spoke over my shoulder. "That wasn't your fault."

Panic set into her big brown eyes. She grabbed the phone off her desk and held it to her ear. "Let me let him know you're—"

"Don't worry about it," I said, grabbing the door handle and letting myself inside. Eyes meeting Brandon's on the other side of his desk, I propped my hands on my hips. "He knows I'm here."

He traced his tongue along his teeth, lips working into an expression I assumed was supposed to resemble a smile. It looked more like a snarl. "No knock?"

"Seeing as how I waited,"—I glanced at my watch—"almost an hour and a half for you to squeeze me into your busy schedule, I figured I should act fast."

Brandon tightened his jaw. "Sure. Leave the dog with my secretary and have a seat."

"She's a service dog, and she's helping me walk, so unfortunately she's gonna have to stay with me." Kicking the door shut behind me, I took a few steps into the office. "I interviewed Emily Foster last night. She hates you, but the cops were right. Her alibi's concrete. And I just don't think she has the balls. This morning, I met with your daughter. She has an alibi too. She's not responsible for the fires. But I've got another lead. I just need more information from you before I look into it."

"Is that right?" He leaned back in his chair, locking his fingers together and looping them behind his neck. "And what might that be?"

"Greta."

The smugness in Brandon's expression vanished. He sat upright in his chair, tightened his jaw, and shook his head. "That's none of your business."

I huffed. "Let me get this straight. A serial arsonist is burning your properties, likely for vengeance because of something you did to them. You hire me to find that person. I learned that a decade ago, your mistress shows up at your door claiming that you tried to have her killed —that you succeeded in killing her unborn child—and it's none of my business?"

"Greta is a very sick woman." He spoke that with confidence. "She made all of that up. The accident was tragic, but—"

"You aren't on trial, Brandon." Even if he should've been. "Don't spout the hysterical woman bullshit. Whether or not you had anything to do with that car accident is irrelevant to me. What matters is if *she* believes you did. Because if she does, she has damn good reason to destroy your life."

Tracing his tongue along his teeth again, he crossed his arms against his chest. "Fine. Look into her then. But what do you need from me?"

"I googled her, and I couldn't find her. Any idea why that might be?"

"She changed her name." An eye roll. "She's married now. I believe she lives in Ohio. Greta Jenkins."

Part of me considered asking why he kept tabs on her if she was just a hysterical woman who meant nothing to him. But I doubted he would answer honestly, anyway. I had the name now, and that would be enough.

* * *

I COULD'VE GOTTEN IN MY CAR AND DRIVEN HOME, BUT MY KNEE was still aching, and I wasn't ready for another hour's drive. My laptop was still in the car, so I stopped to grab it and walked across the street to the coffee shop. A nice place with warm brown walls, quiet jazz music playing over the speakers, filled with the aroma of java and pastries. But most importantly, big wraparound booths. None of which were taken.

I grabbed my usual at the checkout counter and cozied up in one both with my right leg stretched out to rest on the opposite side. The relief came instantly. I felt bad for taking up the entire booth, so I overcompensated with a sandwich, a cookie, and a twenty-dollar tip for the barista.

Then I got to work. Greta Jenkins. Who was she?

No one, according to my Google search. Not to say that she didn't exist. There just wasn't much on the public record about her, aside from what I already knew. She was a woman in her thirties. Married. And she lived in a small town outside of Columbus, Ohio.

Which was convenient. I'd been looking for an excuse to go to Columbus while investigating Daisy's disappearance, but I just hadn't had the time with juggling my other jobs. There were a lot of people I wanted to interview. The police department, who couldn't hang up on me if I was standing in front of them. Her ex-boyfriend and former pimp. His family of meth dealers.

This was a good excuse. If I needed to interview Greta anyway, why not kill two birds with one stone?

With that in mind, I shot Bentley a quick text. *How would you feel about a day trip to Columbus with me?*

Then I went back to research. Greta didn't have a criminal record, had never been featured in a news article like most thirty-year-olds, and she was active on social media. And—like many stupid individuals—she made my job easier by keeping all of her profiles public.

Her Instagram showed an average woman her age. She was pretty, but not in a narcissistic, show off kind of way. Unlike Emily, who had posted thousands of her pictures of herself, Greta had a handful of selfies. Nice brown hair peppered with gray. Hazel eyes that she often framed in black wings. The center of her social media were her two kids. A boy and a girl, both under five. She'd posted several quaint family photos. Some taken herself, others done by professionals.

Whatever Brandon had done or hadn't done to her, it didn't show in her social media. She seemed normal, happy, or, at the very least, content. Could I see her on a path of vengeance to ruin Brandon's life? That depended on what she believed he had done to her. Which I was going to have a hard time finding out on the internet.

There wasn't much more research I could do with the information I currently had, but arson was a particular crime I didn't know much about. Narcotics and cop dogs were my expertise. But I knew there was an intricate psychology to it, so I headed to Google.

There were different classifications of arsonists, apparently. One was called a firebug. They liked fires, so they set a lot of them. If that was what we were dealing with here, Brandon's buildings wouldn't be the only ones affected.

Alternatively, there were arsonists for hire. That could very well be the case here. And could send me back to square one. If Emily or Autumn had hired an arsonist to get back at Brandon, the only way I would know is if I had access to their bank records. Although I was a private investigator, I was not a hacker. So I wasn't sure how I could go about that.

The last was the obvious pyromaniac. These people had often lived harsh lives. They were loners, came from broken homes, and often had a history of mental illness. Sometimes, they set fires because of untreated personality disorders, possible sexual deviancy, but rarely with the intent to kill someone.

The objective for these arsonists was what I expected. Revenge. Fury. They had been burned, and they wanted to burn back. I was ninety-nine percent sure that was the case here. The problem was the fact that Brandon was such an ass. He had too many enemies for me to count, as Autumn had told me this morning.

This research helped a bit, however. Because from the people I had interviewed so far, neither of them had harsh lives, were loners, or had a history of mental illness. That's the type of person I needed to look for in potential suspects.

While I couldn't find much of Greta's family history online, I could ask if any of those depictions describe her when I saw her in person. I spent roughly half an hour tracking down Greta's address.

Right around the time Bentley texted back, *For what?*

I have a lead on this case. She lives close to Columbus. Figured I could interview some people about Daisy while I was at it?

Which gave me another thing to do. It was after 5 now, and I probably should've started home. But my knee was finally feeling better. I wanted to bask in the relief for a while.

Since I had just about all I could gather on the arsonist, I opened my phone and went to Daisy's stories. Reading her work was getting me back into reading for fun. Mostly because that was how she was sending us messages, so I needed to comb through each and every story she had ever posted.

But I also enjoyed the hell out of her writing.

I got caught up in one of her Sci-Fis about humans discovering life on another planet, only for a war over resources to begin. It had an *Avatar*-esque vibe to it. As always, there was a romance subplot, but the main plot was more detailed. That was something I enjoyed about Daisy's writing. It never fit cleanly into one genre but pulled bits and pieces from several to create a multidimensional story.

At about halfway through, the barista jarred me from the fantasy world I was lost in. Standing beside my table now, she said, "We'll be closing in about half an hour. Is there anything you want me to grab you before we shut down?"

I glanced outside. My eyes widened at the sunset, and then the clock that read 8:25. "Shit. No, I'm sorry." Wasn't sure if I was apologizing for cursing or for taking her table all night. I set my leg down and scavenged all my notes and devices into my backpack, then dropped another twenty on the counter. "Thank you, though."

She smiled at me and said, "Thank *you*."

As I stood, pain stretched from my knee up my thigh, but it was a bearable ache rather than the sharp stab it had been earlier. At least now I could make it home. And I felt accomplished. I had gotten a fair amount of work done, even if most of it did feel like lounging in a café.

With Tempest by my side, backpack around my shoulders, I started outside. When we made it to a patch of grass near the garage where I had parked, Tempest looked up at me with the saddest puppy eyes. As if to say, *Can I? Can I pee now, Mom?*

"Go ahead." A wave of guilt moved through me. I'd gotten so lost in my work, and then that book, that I hadn't even thought to take Tempest out. "Go potty."

She frolicked to the grass, stretching out her lead. I chuckled at the relief on her face as she did her business, then looked away to give her some privacy. And my eyes fell on Brandon's building.

It stuck out on the street. Most of the others were old brick or stone buildings, while his was like a metallic skyscraper. Just on a smaller scale. There was no taste to the design, only glass windows six stories high, tucked in a small township outside of Pittsburgh. You could see the skyline from Brandon's office, but this wasn't downtown. Probably cheaper property than it would've been down by the rivers with all the benefits of the city nearby.

But I had noted this before. It was nothing special. For some reason, though, I couldn't look away. Something in my gut said, *Pay attention. There is something important there, and you're missing it.*

A few hours ago, while I was on my third cup of coffee, I had watched everyone fan out of the building while my computer buffered. That was around 5 o'clock. Which made sense. Most office buildings shut down around that time.

Now, all the lights were out. All except for one on the top floor. Brandon's office.

I stared up at it a moment longer, expecting to see Brandon behind the glass with whiskey in hand.

Instead, against the glass, I saw letters. Bright red letters. I had to squint and cock my head to the side, almost impossible to decipher from here. I may've mistaken it for advertising of some kind if I hadn't been inside that very room earlier today.

Blinking hard, the lettering became a word.

MURDERER

Only then did I notice the silhouette behind the graffiti.

I couldn't make out the face, not even their body type. But they were looking at me. We were making direct eye contact, even if I couldn't decipher who those eyes belonged to.

It was like I could hear them screaming, *This is why! This is why I'm burning his empire! Just look! Pay attention!*

I wanted to yell back, "I'm trying! Tell me where to look! Tell me what he did!"

But they couldn't hear me from here.

So I ran toward them.

Chapter 10

WHEN I RAN, SO DID THEY.

They were on the sixth floor, and I was on the ground. Surely after spray painting Brandon's windows, they were ready to rush out of there. They weren't going to hide out in the building somewhere. So long as I got to the ground floor before they did, I'd catch them.

What would I do with them? I didn't know. Also didn't know if the arsonist was even the villain of this story.

That didn't matter right now. What mattered was finding out what they meant.

A car horn blared. Couldn't blame them. I'd jumped out in front of them. But they stopped, and I kept going.

Tempest jogged beside me, waiting for a command. I didn't have one for her yet.

Sprinting up the sidewalk, I reached for the handle on the glass door.

Locked. I yanked the other.

Again, locked.

I'd come through the side door yesterday. Maybe that was how they had as well.

The warm summer wind whistled past me as I jogged around the building. I didn't even feel the pain in my knee anymore. All I felt was that wind and a desperate yearning to know. To know what he had done.

And there it was.

A small rock jutted between the service entry door and its frame. Propping it open, holding it in place.

I grabbed the metal door, tore it open, and started up the stairs. The adrenaline soared through my veins as my feet pounded the concrete steps. Heavy breaths panted in and out of my lungs. Nearly falling a dozen times, I eventually grabbed a handrail. But I didn't slow down. I used the leverage like a launchpad, helping me move from the first floor to the fifth in heartbeats. It felt like only heartbeats, anyway.

But when I made it to the sixth floor, I'd yet to cross another person's path. Whoever they were, they had to be in the stairway. They couldn't have gotten out before me. They wouldn't have had enough time. Had they taken the elevator?

I hurried through the doorway with the big "6" written on its steel frame. Feet squeaking against the marble now, I ran to the elevator midway down the hall, midway to Brandon's office. The big down arrow overhead glowed green.

Shit. They had taken the elevator.

I spun to run back to the stairway, but Tempest looked to my left. She whimpered. I followed her stare, and I smirked. One of those plastic signs on the wall with a stick figure atop a staircase. "Good girl."

Grabbing the door handle, Tempest all but barreled through me.

"Do you smell them, Tempest?" I asked.

Her bushy black tail wagged.

Taking the first step, I said, "We'll get him."

Only problem was, the burst of adrenaline was wearing off. I'd run all the way up here, expecting to find the assailant somewhere along the way, only to now realize we had taken alternate staircases. They'd realized I was on their tail and decided to take another. So I waited for that next burst of adrenaline, but it didn't come. The pain was returning.

Going down steps was always harder than going up them with my knee as it was, and I really could have used that burst of adrenaline.

Especially as Tempest kept looking back at me like she was saying, *Come on, Mom. Hurry up. They're going to get away.*

And I tried. I tried to move faster, but I was disabled. Without the natural painkillers, I just couldn't move as fast as I wanted to.

Just as we reached the fifth floor, a door banged below.

I stretched over the railing.

There they were. Two floors below me, moving much faster. I still couldn't make them out. Not in any detail. Only the top of their head, covered in a black hoodie. Could've been a woman, could've been a man, could have been a monster in disguise. But I had the feeling it was more of a vigilante.

"Hey!" I called, doing my best to pick up speed. "Stop! Stop or I'm going to send my dog!"

A glance over the railing. They only moved faster, taking two steps at a time now.

There was no way I was catching up. But Tempest could.

I snapped my fingers for Tempest's attention. She looked up. "Take him down easy." I released the leash.

With a big smile, tongue flapping out of her mouth, she stampeded down the steps.

Only then did I smell it.

I should've thought of this sooner. I wasn't sure why it hadn't occurred to me yet. Maybe I'd hoped I wasn't the villain in their mind. Maybe I'd hoped they would have known I was on the side of justice, not the side of Brandon.

But it was too late to hope. The smell of smoke seeped from the top floor, and more from the fifth-floor door as I passed it. A glance over the railing, watching Tempest soar to the third floor, showed more smoke drifting from below that door as well.

"Shit," I said, hurrying faster down the stairs. "Shit, shit, shit—"

I missed a step.

I stumbled.

A flash of concrete.
A bang against my temple.
The smell of smoke.
The color red.
Blackness.

Chapter 11

THIS WASN'T SUPPOSED TO HAPPEN.

Maddie wasn't supposed to be here. Neither was the dog. *No one* was supposed to be here.

But they were. Tempest pinned the woman to the ground, smoke filled the stairwell, and Maddie had just fallen down. She assumed that was what the sound was, anyway. The *thump... thump* of Maddie's steps had stopped. That's how it'd sounded when she walked. A thump, a moment of quiet as she adjusted her bad leg, and another thump.

She liked Maddie. She admired her, even, for doing such a physical job with a disability. She hadn't wanted to hurt her. She didn't want to hurt anyone, aside from Brandon. But that bastard deserved it. He deserved a special reservation in hell.

Yet here she was. Laying beneath the hundred-pound German Shepherd, struggling to get up from beneath her, with an ache in her stomach and a drumming in her chest.

That had been a hard fall. Maddie wasn't coughing, wasn't groaning, wasn't cursing. That meant she was either unconscious or dead.

Unconscious, she told herself. *Please let her be unconscious.*

She wouldn't know until she could get up to check. But all she could see was the big, fluffy German Shepherd over her.

She reached up to run her fingers through Tempest's fur, but Tempest bared her teeth. Of course she did. Maddie had told her to take her down.

"It's okay," she said, keeping her voice soft. Very gently, she held out her hand for Tempest to sniff. "It's okay. I won't hurt you."

Tempest's ears floated backward in submission, allowing the arsonist to stroke her scruff, but she kept her stance firm.

"Where's your mom?"

With her nose, Tempest pointed up the steps.

"Is Mom hurt?"

Maddie must've taught her what the word hurt meant, because she cocked her head to the side.

"Help Mom?"

Tempest didn't understand that one. She just looked at the arsonist like she was stupid.

So close to the second-floor door, the black smoke thickened, filling her lungs. There wasn't much time. And the alarms weren't sounding. She had disabled them before she started the fire, wanting them not to do their job and destroy this place before the fire department could put it out, but she was really wishing she hadn't right now.

Biting her lip, she tried to remember the phrases her dog trainer had used in that doggy boot camp she'd gone to years ago. Nearby, the trainer was working with a blind person and their dog. The trainer had the owner get on the ground, as if they had fallen, so that the dog could help them up. What was the command?

It stood to reason that the trainer would've used the same commands for that disabled person as Maddie used for Tempest, since she was also a service dog. But what was the damn command?

Not help, apparently. Support, maybe? Lift? No, that didn't sound right either, but she said it anyway. Aid? A —

"Assist!"

Tempest stood up quickly. Her jaws, big enough to tear out the arsonist's throat, were still only a few inches from her face. But that was the word. That was the correct command.

"Assist Mom," she said quickly. "Mom's hurt. Assist Mom."

Tempest looked down at the arsonist, then up the stairs again, then back down at the arsonist. She turned up to the stairs one more time, then barked. Maddie said nothing in response. Tempest whimpered.

The arsonist understood. She wasn't the owner. That was who Tempest took commands from. But Tempest was scared too. Mom wasn't around to give her command. What was the first priority? Helping Mom, or doing as Mom had said and taking down the arsonist?

"Mom's hurt," she repeated. "Assist Mom."

Tempest studied the arsonist for a few more heartbeats. Heartbeats that turned into crackling smoke, heat rising from beyond the metal door.

A loud thwack sounded behind the door.

Tempest jumped.

Through the glass, the arsonist watched a flaming ceiling tile fall from the drop grid.

Tempest did too. Then she glanced at the arsonist one more time.

And she hopped off her. With the speed of a jackrabbit, she tore up the steps towards Maddie.

The arsonist was right behind her.

She wasn't leaving an innocent woman to burn in this building. She would not become the man she hated the most.

Maddie was making it out of here alive, damn it. If it was the last thing she did, if she died trying, that dog and Maddie were making it out of here alive.

Chapter 12

"TALK TO ME, MADDIE." A FAMILIAR VOICE AND A HAND shaking my shoulder. "God damn it, Maddie. I need you to talk to me."

Lights. Bright white lights shined in my eyes. My body swayed left and right, aching with every rock.

But then there were two big brown eyes. Two warm hands on my cheeks. "Bentley."

"Thank God." He exhaled with relief. "What happened? What hurts?"

Flashes.

Flashes of flame, flashes of smoke, flashes of heat, and flashes of pain. Pain all over. Pain in my knee, pain in my arms, pain in my legs, pain in my back. Most of all, pain in my head.

"I fell," I managed out, my throat dry and hoarse. "Everything."

"You can take a bullet and keep chasing after the guy, but you get this messed up falling." That, he said under his breath. "It's alright. You'll be alright. We're getting you to the hospital now. And don't you argue with me about it. Your oxygen was below ninety and you've got a hell of a cut on your forehead."

For the first time, I wasn't going to object to the hospital trip. Not because I thought I would die without it, but because I finally had health insurance. Thanks to Ox. But—

"Where's Tempest?" My eyes shot open, and I lunged upward in the bed, only then realizing that the rocking sensation was that of an ambulance. An ambulance that my dog was not inside of. "Is she okay? Is she hurt? Is—Oh, God, did she—"

"She's okay." Bentley eased my shoulders back onto the gurney. "Almost every cop in the area showed when they heard it was Maddie Castle laying outside a burning building. Kowalsky was one of them. He said he knew you, and he knew Tempest, so he has her in his cruiser. He's behind us. They're gonna meet us at the hospital, and he'll bring Tempest right up to you. Okay?"

Slowly, I nodded. The pain in my head stabbed. "Okay."

He pushed some sweaty, blood coated hair behind my ear. "Do you want me to call your dad? That way he can get some food for Tempest? She's probably hungry."

I nodded.

He reached for his phone in the pocket of his navy-blue paramedic uniform.

"But Bentley?"

He looked up.

"Don't let them give me anything."

Eyes softening, he gave a smile and squeezed my hand. "Promise."

A BROKEN WRIST, A SPRAINED ANKLE, A BROKEN RIB, A concussion, bruises on almost every surface of my body, and a few on my bones. I didn't know that bones could bruise, but I wasn't the expert, so I trusted the doctors.

My knee didn't hurt all that bad. Not compared to everything else, at least. That was a plus.

My oxygen level was back up by the time I got to the hospital. The doctor said I may have a bit of a cough from the smoke inhalation, but they weren't concerned about my lungs. Breathing hurt, though. Apparently that was common with a broken rib.

I was groggy and disoriented for the first couple hours, but by the time they took me to orthopedics for a cast on my wrist, the brain fog was lessening.

"They weren't trying to hurt me." Sitting up on the bed, I scratched behind Tempy's ears. She leaned closer into my thigh and cozied tight up against me. "If they had, they would have let me die in there."

"Stands to reason." Bentley sat on the scratchy hospital blanket beside Tempest. "But maybe you should worry about getting back on your feet before you dive down the rabbit hole."

I wrinkled my nose, eyes shifting around the white room. White walls, white countertops, white cabinets, white linoleum floors. "Nothing about this place inspires healing."

Furrowing his brows, he gave a halfhearted, teasing smile. "Is that why?"

"Is what why?"

"Why you count on me to stitch you up every time you get hurt instead of coming to an actual medical facility?" He gestured around. "You hate hospitals."

With a burning passion. "I don't *hate* them."

"You do." Smirking, he squinted at me. "You *hate* being here."

"Who likes them? There're dead people everywhere. It smells like a combination of bodily fluids and bleach." I pointed to a speck of red on the wall. "And I'm pretty sure that's blood. There is blood on that wall, and I'm supposed to like being here? The only people who like being in hospitals are psychopaths."

He laughed. "Eh, I don't know. I couldn't get that bleeding on your forehead to stop, so I was pretty happy when we got to a doctor who could."

I waved a dismissive hand at him and ran my fingers through Tempy's hair. "Where was she when you guys got there?"

"Jensen said her leash was tied around your wrist," Bentley said.

"But don't think you're getting out of this that easy. Why do you hate hospitals?"

Irrelevant. "So the arsonist didn't just get me out of the building. They made sure Tempest did, too. Then they made sure Tempest was safe with me." Biting my lip, I shook my head. "That's weird. Tempest likes them enough to let them hold her leash. It must have been a woman. She's usually aggressive with men she doesn't know."

"You're not going to answer my question, are you?"

Nope. "But I weigh over a hundred-fifty pounds. A woman would've had a hard time pulling me out. I think I was on the fourth floor when I fell." I paused. "But that could explain a lot of the bruises, right? She may have dragged me out of the building. I mean, hundred and fifty pounds of deadweight, even a man would've had to drag me. But it had to have been a woman or Tempest would've had blood on her."

Bentley frowned, apparently accepting he wasn't going to get an answer to the hospital question. "There was slobber on the back of your shirt. It's ripped, too. Like Tempest helped whoever it was pull you down the stairs and out of the building."

My heart swelled to a thousand times its size. I looked down at the fluff ball curled into the crook of my legs and found her face. Lifting her gaze to mine, happy tears gathered in my eyes. "Did you do that? Did you save my life?"

Her tail wagged.

Reaching past my legs, raising his voice to a baby-talk octave, Bentley scratched her belly. "I don't know why you're surprised. We all know Tempest is the best dog in the whole wide world."

"Yes, she is. She's a good girl." I talked in that baby voice as well at first, but then another question arose. "But I had just given her the command."

"What command?"

"To arrest the suspect. I told her to take 'em down easy, and Tempy knows what that means."

He huffed, patting Tempy's ribs. "Oh, I know she does."

Bentley had been my test dummy for that command. Some officers used German words for their commands, but I used English so that I could add modifiers. Modifiers that I would remember, at that. Tempest knew that "Take them down," meant to get the suspect on the ground at all costs. If that included violence, then that included violence.

But since she wasn't an official police canine anymore, she didn't have the same protections they did. Meaning that if she bit somebody, I could be forced to put her down. So I taught her, "Take them down easy," so that she would only get them on the ground and keep them there until I could get to her.

"I'm thinking she's more of a vigilante than a villain," Bentley said. "That would explain why she saved you."

"And why she hasn't hurt anyone." I glanced at my wrist, wrapped in a pink cast. "Not on purpose. Plus, the graffiti. She called him a murderer. She's not burning these buildings because of a shady business move. She's burning them because she blames him for someone's death." I rummaged through my backpack—which had somehow survived the fire and my fall—on the rolling side table and found my notebook. "Autumn said that when she was in high school Brandon had a mistress. The woman's barely older than Autumn now, so she must've been in her twenties then. But she got pregnant, and then she lost the baby in a freak accident. Hit-and-run."

Bentley arched a brow. "You think Brandon was the other driver?"

"Greta, the mistress, did." I had to look at my notes to remember her name. Maybe my head was a little bit foggier than I thought. "Or maybe hired someone to do it? Or maybe this is just a trend for him. Maybe when somebody gets in his way, he pays to get rid of them."

"Common theme with guys like that."

"I have to talk to her." After grabbing my phone from my bag as well, I jotted Greta's address into my navigation app. "It's only a three and a half hour drive. Did you get my text? About going to question her tomorrow?"

"I did. And I responded, but I guess you were knocked out by then." He found my fingers and placed them between his. "But yeah,

I'm in. I'm off this weekend, so as long as we're home by Sunday evening, I can make it work. And I'm sure as hell not letting you go alone with a concussion, broken wrist, broken rib, and a million bruised bones."

A smile crept up my cheeks. "You're the best."

He returned it. "I'm just glad you're not arguing with me about it."

"Hey, I take on what I can handle. But I can accept that, this time, I need a little more help than usual."

That was partially because of the therapy I'd started attending once a month, though. She was helping me learn that since I wasn't an able-bodied person, sometimes I needed accommodation. And that was okay.

Earlier, I had been angry that my knee was making my job more difficult. And what good had that done? I'd wound up in a hospital bed. So there was a little life lesson for me. I could be angry about my body being a pain in the ass, or I could accept it and keep moving.

"That's what I like to hear," Bentley said.

"But while we're there, since it's right outside Columbus anyway, I want to make a trip into the city. Where you used to live, I mean." Stretching my legs out, I rolled my ankle from one side to the other, desperate to feel it crack with relief. "I want to interview people about Daisy. Her drug dealers, her friends, the cops. Really, anybody who can give me any more insight."

The color emptied from his cheeks. "The cops, her coworkers, that's fine. But I don't want you messing with Kevin. Especially like this." He gestured over me. "Not when you can't defend yourself, Maddie."

I held up my left hand. "I can still hold a gun with this one."

"You're right-handed."

"I can pull a trigger with my left."

"No." His voice was firm, almost fatherly, like he was speaking to Grace. But his eyes were gentle. "It won't end well for anybody, Maddie. They're not going to tell you anything you don't already know. All that's gonna happen is a fight. Because when Kevin and I are in the same room, that's what we do. And no way in hell am I letting you go near him by yourself."

Letting me. As though I needed Bentley's permission. But I understood his worry. "I was a cop, Bentley. I can deal with a few tweakers."

"On a good day, yeah. But tomorrow's not gonna be a good day." He shook his head, wide eyes unblinking. "Please don't fight me on this. Please."

Frowning, I gave his hand a squeeze. If the roles were reversed, I would ask him the same thing. So I couldn't be angry. Wasn't sure if I even had the capability of being angry with the grogginess. "I understand where you're coming from, but I really do need to interview them, Bentley. They might be able to help me understand something I'm not seeing. Or they could just tell me something I didn't know, something *you* didn't know."

His frown only deepened.

"What about Simeon?"

His face screwed up. "What *about* Simeon?"

"They're in business together, aren't they? Simeon sells them products. They sell him products?" I asked. "What if I can get Simeon to come with us? That'll keep things civil."

"And then owe Simeon more than I already do." Glancing at the door, he lowered his voice. "I don't like that either."

"I'll settle his debt. I have money now." Again, thank you, Ox. "Simeon will do just about anything for money."

With a huff, Bentley straightened. "And you think *that's* what he would want from you? The guy has enough money, Maddie."

"He's helped me out before."

It was a scoff this time. A lighthearted one, but a scoff nonetheless. "And I wonder why."

"Oh, come on." Leaning in, I tucked some hair behind his ear. "You know I'm not into Simeon."

"Doesn't mean I have to like it." He cupped my cheek. "But I see your point. And I agree. Things would stay calm if Simeon came. If you can get him to tag-along, or meet us there, then fine. I'm in."

"It's a deal then." I leaned in for a kiss. Our lips had only touched for a heartbeat when a knock sounded at the door.

We pulled away as the door inched open. I expected it to be a nurse with my discharge papers, maybe a doctor with a test result.

But Brandon stood in the doorway instead. Harper was beside him, giving me a look that I couldn't quite describe, but I understood. It was as if her eyes said, *You want me to tell this guy to piss off?*

But her lips said, "How are you feeling, Mads?"

"Living the dream." I straightened up, facing them better as Bentley stood. "What's going on? Did you find anything?"

"Not much, but I do have some questions for you. Brandon wanted to speak with you first though, if you're feeling up to it."

Chapter 13

"I'd prefer to do this in private as well, Detective." Brandon stuck his hands in the pockets of his slacks. "If you don't mind."

Harper gave me that look again.

The look I sent her way assured her that was fine by me. One of the wonderful things about having known someone for a decade. We didn't even need to speak to communicate.

"Sure. I'll be right outside." Harper headed away from the room.

"I'll head back to the station and grab my car so I can drive you home, if that's okay," Bentley said.

I agreed, thanked him, then shared another quick kiss before he headed out. When the door shut behind him, Brandon took a few steps into the room. He looked different now than he had this afternoon, or the day before.

Rather than that poker straight spine, he slouched just the slightest bit. Like his shoulders and neck were tense. His color was off, too. Although he'd always been light skinned, there was a greenish hue to it now. Those styled salt-and-pepper waves were now tousled, messy, as if he'd been running his fingers through them and shooing them away from his face.

"You're feeling well, then?" was how he started the conversation.

"Been better, but hanging in there," I said. "Got to say though, you're not looking your best."

He huffed, leaning his hip against the end of my hospital bed. "Like you said. Been better but hanging in there."

"I bet. Considering the murder accusation and everything." My tone was matter of fact, watching every inch of his face for a reaction. He only clenched his jaw. "Think that was Greta? Or does someone else blame you for the death of their loved one?"

"Not to my knowledge." He said that quickly, abruptly. Like it was rehearsed. Like a lawyer had told him to answer everyone's questions with it. "Why were you there? At my building, after office hours."

No way in hell was this asshole about to accuse me of something. "I was at the coffee shop across the street researching. Stayed there all day after I met with you. I was getting ready to leave, stepped outside with my dog, and looked up at your building. That's when I saw the graffiti. And someone standing at the window. I figured if I got to them, I could catch them in the act."

But that wasn't the whole truth. I wouldn't have called the cops on the arsonist. I would've taken their story. And if it led to Brandon being the villain here? He was the one I would've turned in.

Couldn't say that out loud, though.

Breaths quickening, Brandon stepped closer. "Who were they? Did you recognize them?"

"I was looking up six stories. All I could make out was a silhouette," I said. "Why didn't the alarms go off?"

"They've been on the fritz for months. Kept going off when nothing was wrong, and the fire department was unimpressed with the repetitive alarms. Got them fixed a week ago, but then they did it again, so I ended my contract with the previous security company. Just hired a new one. They were supposed to come in next week to set up." He sighed. "No idea when we'll be able to have that done now."

"Anybody at the security company have good reason to hate you?" I asked. "Or maybe somebody who works in the building?"

Licking his teeth, Brandon gave me a heavy-weighted stare. I returned it. Silence ticked on. Eventually, he broke it. "We both know there are plenty of people who hate me, Miss Castle. Yes, I'm sure many of them are my employees. But I've never done anything that would lead one of them to call me a murderer."

Or maybe you've just done so many shady things to so many people that you can't keep track.

"You've never done anything," I said, "even inadvertently, that resulted in harm?"

"Not death—"

"Not even the death of your bastard?"

His jaw clenched harder. "Forgive me, but aren't you working for me? I'm not who you should be questioning, Miss Castle. I'm—"

"You're keeping something from me." I was aware he was the boss here. But I was a no bullshit type of person and that's all he had been feeding me since the get-go. "You're not giving me enough to do my job. You want me to find this arsonist, and you only gave me one person who might be responsible. And not because there's any real beef there, but because you were a shit dad. *She's* the one who tells me your barely out-of-high-school mistress blamed you for the death of her unborn baby. Which is a much bigger reason to hate you. To want to see you burn. And if you didn't tell me about her, who else aren't you telling me about, Brandon? What else have you done? How long is the damn list?"

Silence.

Silence that ticked on for what felt like a lifetime. We just stared at one another. His expression was blank. The guy could be a poker champion.

But in his eyes, I saw it. No remorse, no guilt, but the horrors.

There were too many. He had done so many awful things, he couldn't even organize them into a list. The only reason he'd mentioned Autumn was because that was the only case he'd felt guilt for. He knew he was a horrible father, that she'd had good reason for cutting off contact with him, and he wished that weren't so.

That was the only one of his failings he cared about.

The other things, all the other atrocities this man had committed behind closed doors, didn't matter. He had no empathy, no regret. He had blackmailed Emily Foster and saw nothing wrong with that. It was just business.

It was also a federal crime, but he didn't care.

If he didn't care about that, it was not a stretch to my imagination that he had done worse. That he had, in fact, caused that accident resulting in his mistress miscarrying her child. And that maybe he had killed or paid someone to kill for him.

Men like this—powerful, wealthy, successful—were the scariest villains of all.

I wasn't afraid of the arsonist. Her actions, no matter how morally inapt, were rebellious. Vengeance. I understood her.

Brandon acted solely in the pursuit of greed. Money. Status. Power.

That, I could never understand.

"Saturday morning, I'm heading out to meet Greta," I said. "Maybe you can compile a better list for me by then, starting with your employees and anyone else who has access to your building."

"While I appreciate the offer, I think it's best you take some time to heal." After reaching into his jacket pocket, he flipped open a checkbook. "I believe you've worked on my case for—What? Thirty hours so far? And you charge hundred an hour, so that comes to three thousand. But considering your injuries, and the ambulance ride, and the hospital stay, I'll provide you with a decent bonus."

Brandon ripped the check from the leather booklet and set it beside Tempest.

She growled when his hand got close.

He paid her no mind.

"Is that enough?"

I glanced at it, but I didn't pick it up. $15,000.

It was plenty. Far more than I needed. But if I was taking hush money and getting fired, I was going to need a hell of a lot more.

"I don't know. Nasty break." I held up my wrist. "I might need physical therapy. Not to mention the work I'll lose while I'm recovering."

A tightlipped smile. He retrieved the check off the bed, jammed it in his pocket, then scribbled out another. This one, he handed me. $25,000. "Is that sufficient?"

I returned the smile, but mine was a bit more condescending. "It'll do. Thanks. I hope you find whoever you're looking for. Assuming this is you bidding me adieu."

"Unfortunately." He started for the door. "Since you'll be out of commission and all. But I do hope you feel better soon and thank you for all the work you've done so far."

Such a kind sentence. The way he spoke it, though? It may as well have been a middle finger.

"You were such a joy to work with," I said.

The smile stayed across his lips, but his eyes were daggers. He didn't say another word as he walked out the door.

As soon as he was out of sight, Harper made it across the threshold. Shutting the door behind her, her eyes widened. "He's a treat."

"He's what the arsonist says he is."

"You think he's a murderer?" She sat beside Tempy on the bed and scratched behind her ears. "You got any proof?"

"Just the vibe so far." I held up the check to let her read it. "And the hush money severance."

Her eyes widened. "He fired you."

"Yep. When I said I wouldn't get to the bottom of this unless he told me the truth about the horrible things he's done."

"Oh, yeah. He's got something in his closet."

"I'm guessing there're a lot of somethings in there. And I'm gonna find them. Whose case's this?"

"I asked Anders for it when I found out you were working on it. He was getting tired of hearing Brandon's mouth, anyway. But when I called my lieutenant about it, he said to call a guy at Quantico. Apparently he's familiar with Brandon." She tucked herself against the footrest of the hospital bed, facing me with her feet beside Tempest. "So, if you need legal help on this case, just know you've got backup."

"FBI?"

"Yep. All they'd tell me was white collar crimes, but they said if I find anything—anything at all on this guy—call them ASAP."

"Shit." I wasn't sure if this was a good or bad thing. Not to say that I always agreed with the FBI, but it solidified my trust in my gut. "Wish I could say I'm surprised."

"Me too, judging from what Anders told me."

Flipping open my notebook, I stretched out my legs and stifled a yawn. "We need a list of his employees. First and last names, personal histories, etcetera."

"Already working on a warrant for it."

"He wasn't willing to turn it over voluntarily?"

"Nope." She dug around in her purse, came out with a bag of candy, and offered me one. "You want to hear my theory?"

I tore off the foil wrapping and popped it into my mouth. Between chews, I said, "Throw it at me."

"Each of these fires is a punishment. Someone sending him messages, telling him to admit to something. And when he doesn't, they set another fire."

Arching a brow, I swallowed. "That checks out. But she."

"She?"

"She." I nodded. "Tempest would've attacked a man who tried to drag my body out of a burning building. So it was either a woman, or a man she knows. And she doesn't know any man with close ties to Brandon Adams."

"Mmmm." Popping another candy at her mouth, she raised a shoulder. "Valid, but wouldn't stand in court."

"No, but it helps us," I said. "Look, I'm starting to think that Brandon deserves this."

"Probably. We all know guys like him."

"And if I find the person responsible..."

I made a certain face, and she knew exactly what I was thinking. I could tell because she stopped chewing and pressed her lips together.

"We on the same page?" I asked her.

"You get me an answer to the graffiti," Harper said, eyes speaking words that dare not leave her lips. "A reason to put the son of a bitch who deserves it behind bars? And yeah, we're on the same page."

That was one thing I loved about working with Harper. These days, anyway. She'd been more of a stickler a few years back. But a lot had changed.

It wasn't that Harper never saw the grays in law enforcement. She always had. But she used to be more concerned with covering her ass than doing what was right. Now, her priority was punishing those who caused the most harm. Not those who operated outside of the law, like yours truly.

That was one reason our friendship had rekindled over the last few months. When she'd slept with my fiancé, we'd fallen out. Then he'd died. And with him out of the picture, as messed up as it may have sounded, it was a hell of a lot easier to want her in my life again. Like the betrayal wasn't staring me dead in the face anymore.

None of that mattered now. With her in a high enough law enforcement position, with my willingness to work outside the government, we could do good things. I could say that was the best part of our friendship, but it wouldn't be the truth.

The truth was, I had missed her. I was happy to have her in my life again. I was grateful for the way she could help me with a case, but moments like this were better. Sitting together, eating candy, and simply talking.

"You're the best," I said, snatching another candy from the bag.

"I know." A shit-eating grin. "Oh, and I meant to tell you, I've been looking through the missing person's database too. Because of that poem Daisy wrote? But I haven't found anything yet." She popped another candy in her mouth. "Well, that's not true. I found a lot of girls who look like Daisy, fit her same demographic. Some disappeared in similar locations to her, but I'm looking for a needle in a haystack. Can you get another message to her? Some way to ask for more details?"

"Yeah, we did last night. Grace left her a comment on that poem. Asked why the new bird didn't have a name. Hopefully we'll hear back soon, but it was almost two months before she even posted another story."

"I don't think we're exactly in a race against the clock." Opening another candy, she frowned. "I'm sorry, that came out insensitive. I just mean—"

"No, it's okay. I know what you mean." A deep breath escaped my nostrils. "There just isn't much to go off of. We're waiting for her to trickle little details that we have to decipher with a microscope."

"Why do you think that is? Like, what the hell could he be holding over her head? He must be reading it, or at least have an eye on her while she's writing, but the only reason that makes sense is if he's got a gun to her head somehow. Why else would she have to give us hints so discreetly?"

"Or a gun to the head of somebody she loves." Shrugging, I shook my head. "It doesn't make sense to me either. But I'm going to Columbus on Saturday. That's where an old mistress of Brandon's lives. I was going to go tomorrow, but I think I could probably use a day to recoup beforehand. While I'm there, I'm going to meet with the local detectives and anyone who knew Daisy well. Hopefully they can tell me something about Mr. Deluca."

"I'm glad you mentioned that, because I was just thinking about it." She sat forward, leaning in. There was a certain excitement in her eyes. Like there always was when she got a lead. "In that book, *Sins and Silk Ties*, Lily met Mr. Deluca at the club where she worked. Maybe one of the other girls saw them together. Maybe we can get a description."

"I was thinking about that, too. Only problem is, the cops investigating should've thought about that a year ago. When the image was still fresh in the other girls' minds. When we could've searched through security cameras. Now? We'll be lucky if anybody remembers Daisy at all."

A sigh. "We can hope."

"Hope like hell."

Chapter 14

THEY RELEASED ME AROUND 4 A.M.

Bentley drove home, promising we'd get my car tomorrow. That was fine by me. As much as I liked being independent, I didn't like pain, and I had a lot of it at the moment. Being able to rest my leg up on the dashboard and recline in the passenger seat made the long drive easier.

Grace called while we were on our way, apparently worried. Bentley's sister Phoebe had picked her up when he'd realized he wouldn't be home at the end of his twelve-hour shift. By the time he'd finished and picked me up, Grace had still been awake, so we'd swung by Phoebe's to pick her up on our way.

She was far more vibrant than me, given my many ailments. But I gave her a brief synopsis of my day either way. I left out the parts about our plan to go to Columbus, unsure if Bentley wanted her to come along or not.

It was dawn by the time we pulled into Bentley's drive. He insisted on walking me to my door. I didn't fight him on it this time. I was pretty groggy. Grace suggested they stay at my place tonight so they could keep an eye on me. Although I appreciated the offer, I declined. I may not have been at my best, but I could make it around my house on my own. Especially when all I wanted to do was roll into bed.

Which was exactly what I did. After letting Tempest out to do her business and feeding her, I plopped onto my bed and fell into a dreamless sleep within moments. I woke to the sound of my phone ringing a few hours later.

Grumbling as I found it in the sheets, Sam's photo lit up the screen. I slid the green bar and held it to my ear. "This better be good. You woke me up."

"I think checking on you after you were trapped in a burning building is a pretty damn good reason to call," he said, his tone somewhere between playful and annoyed. "Bentley let me know this morning. Said he had to get on to work. I'm on my way, I've got food, and don't you argue with me about it."

Last night, Bentley had said he didn't have work until 3 o'clock today. I glanced at my watch. My eyes bulged. 4:45 p.m. "Shit, I didn't mean to sleep this late."

"After a near-death experience, I think you're entitled," Sam said. "How are you feeling?"

Sore. The killer headache had lessened. My wrist ached like a son of a bitch, but breathing wasn't too difficult until I yawned. Then it felt like a vice was wrapped around my chest. I guessed that my lungs expanding put pressure on that broken rib. "I'll live. What kind of food are you bringing?"

He chuckled. "Bacon, eggs, pancakes, waffles, and cookies. Lots and lots of cookies."

My stomach growled. "Yeah, I think I'll keep you around."

Another laugh, this one softer than the last. "You're not mad at me then?"

"About Dylan?"

"More so about keeping it from you." He paused. "I wasn't exactly *keeping* it from you. I just hadn't thought about sharing it, you know? We've just been getting to know each other, and—"

"I understand." And I did. It was just easier to cut him off before he could go on an hour-long ramble, like he often did when he was nervous. "I'm not mad. Not at you. At Mom, maybe."

Sam's sigh of relief reverberated through the speaker. "Good. That's good. I wouldn't blame you if you were, but—"

"But I'm not, so you don't need to get anxious about it." Stifling another yawn, I forced myself vertical in the bed. "I feel disgusting, though. I'm gonna let Tempest out and leave the door unlocked. I'll probably be in the shower when you get here. Let yourself in, all right?"

* * *

"It's amazing you survived a fall like that," Sam said after I explained what I remembered from last night. "You could've broken your skull open on that concrete."

"Thankfully, I didn't." I took a bite of my cookie, basking in the glorious taste on my tongue. Still chewing, I stood from my seat at the kitchen table and walked to the fridge. "Do you want some milk?"

"Let me." He stood, too. "You should rest."

"If I rest too much, my knee's going to get too tight, and I won't be able to walk tomorrow." It was a predicament, however. Sitting helped that throbbing in my head. Walking helped the tightness and the muscles around my knee. But walking made me lightheaded and sitting hurt my knee. Still, I gestured to the spread of food laid out on the table. "Thanks though. Thanks for bringing all this."

"Don't mention it." While he let me grab the milk, he got two glasses from the cupboard. "I'm just happy I can help."

And he did. Since he'd come back into my life, he'd helped me tremendously. If I needed something and I called, he came. I knew guilt was a component, and I tried not to exploit that. But it was nice to have a parent I could count on.

Aside from the things he did for me, I just enjoyed his company. He was kind and compassionate. Smart, too, despite what one may think of a convicted felon. On several occasions now, we had talked about more than just the day-to-day nothings of life. We'd discussed religion, politics, the prison system, and the justice system, and the faults in it all.

It wasn't that I just liked having him around because he was family. I liked who he was. The only thing I didn't like about having him around was the sense of emptiness when I thought about how much I'd missed. If he'd always been in my life, if he hadn't gone to prison, if he'd always been there for me like he was now, who would I have been? How much less would I have suffered?

That was something I was working through in therapy. My therapist suggested practicing mindfulness. So when I thought about that, how much I'd missed out on with him, I practiced focusing on the moment I was in instead. That at least he was here now.

But when I thought of that this time, that sense of emptiness stayed. Because he wasn't the only one I was missing out on.

"Do you think you could help me with something else?" I asked, settling back in at the dining table.

After grabbing a few napkins, he joined me in the adjacent chair. "Anything, kid. What is it?"

"Dylan." At that word, he tensed, averting his gaze from mine. "I'm sorry. I'm sure it's hard for you to talk about him, considering everything."

He shrugged a shoulder. "I made my bed. Now I have to lay in it. What do you want to know?"

"What he's like, maybe? What he does for a living. If we have anything in common. If it would be crazy for me to show up at his house."

"I'll remind you, you weren't exactly thrilled with me when I did that." Stretching across the table, Sam grabbed another cookie. "But he's a lot like you, from what Andrea told me. Headstrong."

I snorted. "So, an asshole?"

"We'll go with headstrong." He smiled. "I know he works with computers. He got in some trouble for it when he was in high school, if memory serves. Hacked into one of the teacher's computers, found out the bastard was taking pictures of his students. Teenage girls. I'm sure you can guess where this is going."

"Wait." I cocked my head to the side. "He's a hacker."

"Something like that. He gets paid for it now, according to his mom."

So that was why he lived such an extravagant lifestyle, even though he had just graduated college. "Huh."

Sam arched a brow. "Did I give you an idea there?"

"If he hacks for hire, I've got plenty of jobs for him." Scratching my head, I exhaled slowly. "I'd rather just meet him. Form a relationship, like the two of us have. But I reached out to him online, and he didn't respond. I don't know if he will. But maybe if I were to show up and ask him to help me track down the IP addresses where Daisy has posted stories, that might be my way in." I paused. "That sounds gross. Manipulative or something."

"Eh, I can't judge." Filling his glass with milk, Sam dipped his cookie inside. "I definitely started doing stuff around your house as an excuse to see you."

Laughing, I shook my head. "You don't have to do stuff around my house to see me, Sam."

"I know that now. But I do like doing stuff for you." He wiped some crumbs from the corner of his lip. "Point being, I get it. It could be a good way to make contact. It would be shitty if he set the boundary, outright telling you he didn't want you in his life like he did to me. But just offering him the job? And using it as a way to kindle a relationship? I don't see anything wrong with that."

For a few heartbeats, I nibbled my lip. Sam made a valid point.

Dylan hadn't set a boundary with me. It would be shitty if he had, considering that I had never done anything to him, but I would respect it if he did. For all I knew with the information I had, though, he may not have even seen my message. There was a very good chance that I had gotten lost in a sea of private messages from unfamiliar accounts.

So, what was the harm?

"My car's still in the city," I said. "Any way you could drive me?"

* * *

Sam didn't object to driving me to my car, but he was afraid for me to drive, given all my injuries. I then suggested he drive me to Dylan's. He wasn't a fan of that either, for good reason. Dylan had made it clear that he didn't want anything to do with Sam. As much as it pained him, Sam wanted to respect that.

I suggested, instead, he drop me off close to Dylan's house and I could walk the rest of the way. Still, Sam wasn't crazy about the idea, but he agreed.

Along the drive, we talked more about the relationship. He explained he didn't know Dylan well. He only knew the bits and pieces Andrea had told him.

Dylan was a "social loner." He mostly enjoyed being by himself, didn't enjoy drama or chaos, but had more friends than he knew what to do with. People liked him, even if he wasn't a huge fan of them.

Smart. Off the charts smart. Child prodigy smart. So smart that he graduated high school *and* college early. Not only did he have a high IQ, but he was an excellent musician. Which surprised me, since I hadn't seen any mention of music on his social media. But according to his mother, he could play just about any song in human history on a piano by the time he was ten.

And that was it. That was all Sam knew about him.

That only made all of this so much harder.

Meeting him, getting to know him, would be a thousand times easier if he and Sam had a relationship. But they were strangers. *We* were strangers, and I had just hopped out of Sam's truck with Tempest to show up at his door unannounced.

Even for me, someone who showed up at strangers' doors unannounced on a regular basis, this was weird. Inappropriate.

But how else was I supposed to do this?

"The worst thing he can tell me is to go screw myself," I said under my breath, starting up the long, wooded drive with Tempest beside me.

I walked for a few minutes before the house came into view. It sat atop a small hill, framed by woods all the way around. An old, remodeled Victorian. The walls were white, framed in black trim. The turret on the left stood high, maybe a couple feet higher than the A-line peak at the top. A beautiful porch started beside the turret and stretched to the right, wrapping all the way around. Some white wicker furniture sat outside, and a pretty porch swing drifted in the wind.

In the driveway was a new silver Toyota Prius. Sensible, sustainable. Not extravagant. The house wasn't either, really. It was just nice. Middle-class American, but not suburban middle-class. Unique, but quaint at the same time.

As soon as I started up the steps, the front door swung open. And there he was.

He looked just as he did in his photos. Taller than I had imagined, though, somewhere just over six feet. Then again, he was at the door, and I was at the bottom of the steps. Of course he looked bigger. But his expression didn't help. His forehead was creased, jaw tight. He paid Tempy no mind. Only studied me.

Probably should have waited until at least a few of my injuries healed for this introduction. "Hi there. I know this is weird, just showing up at your house, but I'm Maddie—"

"I know who you are." Another once over. His face was blank, posture stiff. He tapped his fingers on his thigh. That was his only movement. "What do you want?"

Why did it feel like I had just been kicked in the chest?

He knew. He knew about me, and he didn't seem to want me here.

My voice came out strained, quiet. "I, um, I just found out about you. The night before last, Sam told me about you. And I—"

I stopped myself because I wasn't sure where to go from there. I wasn't welcome here. The look on his face, the tone of his voice, said it all.

But he just kept staring at me. Waiting for me to say more. The door was still open. Granted, he was standing in front of it, but he hadn't slammed it in my face. So I went on.

"Look, I'm sorry. I know this is inappropriate. But I didn't know how else to get in touch with you, and I wanted to."

"Why?" Stated so simply.

I opened my mouth to respond, but honestly? I wasn't sure how. Why *did* I want to get to know him? Why *was* I here? How could I put it into words without making this already odd situation that much stranger?

"What do you want?" he asked. "I'm not giving you money. You can't stay here. If you need a kidney, you can't have that either, so why are you here?"

Another kick to the chest.

That was why he hadn't reached out. He knew I existed, had probably googled me, and discovered I was a certain type of person. Trailer trash. More than likely, not the type of company he wanted to keep.

"I don't want anything." I shook my head. "That's not true, actually. I don't have much family, and I saw an opportunity here. To form a relationship with you, maybe. Get coffee. Maybe dinner sometime. Maybe see each other at Christmas or some shit. And when I asked Sam about you, he said you were a hacker. I'm a private investigator." I swallowed, trying not to avert my eyes from his steely gaze. "I've been working this missing person's case for a while, and I can't get the cops to help me, but I know the girl posted something online. A few days ago, and a few months ago too. I wanted to ask if I could pay you to track down the IP address for me. Mostly because I want to find this girl, but also because that'd give me an excuse to start a conversation with you. And that's all that I want. Not your money. Not a kidney. Just to talk to you."

He eyed me up and down for a moment. His face stayed blank. Eventually, he said, "Security penetration tester."

"I'm sorry?"

"I'm a security penetration tester. That's my job title. Not hacker."

"Is hacker an offensive term or something?"

"No. But that's my title. I'm not just some kid with a computer. I have a career doing this. It means a lot to me. If you're going to use the word *hacker*, I would appreciate if you put ethical in front of it."

Now it was me eyeing him up and down. There was something in his inflection, paired with the way that he stood, and those tapping fingers on his thigh that made me cock my head to the side. While his voice was deep, there was almost a rhythm to the way he spoke. Singsong like.

While he was blunt and lacked a smile, he hadn't shut the door in my face. He wasn't kind, but I wouldn't call him mean or rude either. Although my experience in law enforcement wasn't associated with mental health, I knew some of these mannerisms from calls about someone having a meltdown. Usually, those people were neurodivergent, on the autism spectrum. I had to wonder if that was the case here.

"Okay," I said, nodding. "Ethical hacker. But you still prefer Security Penetration Tester?"

"Yes. Yes, I do." He was still tapping his fingers on his thigh, but a bit slower now. "Who is this girl? The missing one?"

"Her name's Daisy. Daisy Miller." I reached into my pocket for my phone. "I can send you the links to the websites where she posted, if you could use that?"

"Well, yes, I couldn't do much without the websites." He only tapped his thumb now, speaking his cell phone number aloud. "I charge by the hour. An IP address should be easy enough to track down. Shouldn't take me more than an hour. I'll text you my invoice. But expect it to be somewhere around five hundred."

Damn. Maybe I should've gone into Security Penetration Testing. "I'll send it right over."

"No, wait until I've done the job," he said. "Can you afford this? I thought you were poor."

Trouble understanding social cues. Like, you know, calling someone poor. "I do alright."

"Private investigators don't make much money. I checked."

"A friend of mine died earlier this year and he left me a lot of money. So really, I'm doing alright."

"Okay. I would've charged less if you couldn't have afforded it."

I chuckled. "I thought you were worried about me being after your money?"

"I'm not worried. I just want you to know that I won't give you any."

Another laugh. "I appreciate the honesty. But why would you charge less, then?"

"Because if the cops aren't looking for her, but you are, and you need help to find her, it's just decent to do so." He wasn't tapping his hand at all anymore. Instead, his eyes were on Tempest. "Does she bite?"

"Not unless she thinks you're a threat."

"Does she think I'm a threat?"

Tempest sat at my side, smiling and panting up at Dylan. Noting that, I shook my head. "No, I think she likes you. She probably smells you. Dogs can smell DNA, you know. She can tell we're related, so she trusts you."

"No. I didn't know that." He still looked down at her. "Can I pet her?"

"Yeah, just get down to her level first."

After walking closer, down the stairs so he was only a few feet away, he did just that. He squatted, reached out his hand to let her sniff him, then slowly petted from the top of her head down the back of her neck. That was the first time he smiled. "She's a German Shepherd, right?"

"She is."

"I had one once. He wasn't this well-behaved, though."

"She wasn't either when I first got her. But I'm a dog trainer. I got her under control after a while."

"I know. I read the articles." Still, he was petting Tempest, smiling at her. "I'm thinking about getting a dog. My therapist thinks it would be good for me. It's a process to get a well-trained service dog."

That sounded like confirmation of my theory. "What type of service would you need? Emotional support?"

"Sort of. The pressure tasks for emotional support, yes. Tactile stimulation, I believed my therapist called this part. Petting them." He hadn't stopped smiling or petting her for a moment. "As well as blood sugar and allergy alerts."

Pressure tasks were when a service dog would lay atop a person during a moment of stress. Much like a weighted blanket, the pressure could help to calm the nervous system, specifically in autistic people. "You're on the spectrum?"

"Yes."

"I trained some dogs on tasks like that. Have you started the process?"

"No, I've just been considering it. Why?"

"I don't train puppies much anymore, but I have connections to local trainers. I know one in Pittsburgh who works with breeders and does a good job of matching the dog with the right person. If you want, I might be able to help."

"That might be nice." After a moment, he straightened. "Thank you. She's very soft."

"It's the salmon oil. If you get a dog, make sure to put it on their food each morning."

"I'll remember that." He was tapping his hand on his thigh again. "I've got to get back to work. Text me that information. I'll get back to you with what I find soon."

Chapter 15

"Not what I was expecting." I shut the passenger door, turning my attention on Sam. "You didn't tell me he was on the spectrum."

He furrowed his brows. "He's autistic?"

Fastening my seatbelt, I nodded. "Yeah. He is."

For a few seconds, Sam only blinked. "I wonder why his mom didn't tell me."

I shrugged. "Maybe his diagnosis came after she died. He's relatively low needs. Doesn't seem like he has any developmental delays. But that could be part of why he hasn't wanted contact with you. People on the spectrum usually have rigid beliefs when it comes to right and wrong."

With a huff, Sam put the car in drive. As he accelerated down the wooded road, he scratched his head. "I guess that makes me feel better. I thought he just hated me. People like that though, they're just blunt, aren't they?"

"They are. And most of the time struggle with social cues and emotions," I said. "I doubt he was intending to hurt you when he shut the door in your face."

Another careful exhale. "I don't blame him. I deserve however he wants to treat me."

That wasn't true. While I understood Dylan setting the boundary, and I didn't blame him for it, I didn't believe Sam *deserved* to be hated. It was a complex issue, of course. Neurodivergence made it all the more intricate.

But Sam hadn't killed that man out of pure hatred. Sam had killed a crooked politician. I still wasn't sure about the details, but that much, I knew for certain. That had been why I was able to let him into my life. Maybe Dylan would've felt the same way if he knew all the details, rather than just what the police reports said.

* * *

IT WAS A LONG DRIVE HOME. THE SUN WAS SETTING BY THE TIME we pulled into my driveway. As soon as I made it into the house, my phone buzzed in my pocket. *Simeon* lit up the screen. His text read, *Are you busy? Can I call?*

On the way to Dylan's, I had texted him and asked if he could give me a call when he got a chance. Decent of him to ask to call me now.

Sam was still outside chatting with Bentley, who was working in his yard, so I headed to the bedroom with Tempest.

Once I settled in on my bed, I texted, *Yep*.

His call came through a moment later. "What do you want this time, Mad dog?"

"What makes you think I want something?" Stretching out my leg toward the foot of the bed, I stifled a yawn. "Old friends can't catch up once in a while?"

"I'm still struggling to remember the part where we were friends."

"You know we're friends."

A soft, raspy chuckle. "I don't have all night."

"You caught me. I do want something."

"That's been established."

"Kevin Lawson. That whole family. You know them?"

He snorted. "*You* know them?"

"Kinda. Sorta."

"Then I pity you," he grumbled. "Yeah, I know them. Why do you ask?"

"I need to interview them."

The noise he made was hard to describe. A laugh? A grunt? Somewhere in the middle. "How's Bentley feel about that?"

"See, that's where you come in." I explained the situation, followed by Bentley's conditions, ending with, "I need more to go on, man. This kid's missing, and the cops haven't done a damn thing."

"Like usual." A deep sigh. "Which I'm typically grateful for."

"But in this case?"

Another sigh. "How old is she?"

"Barely legal to drink."

A long pause stretched on. After another one of those odd sounds, that grunting harrumph, he said, "How do you do this to me?"

"How do I do what?"

"Make me feel like it's my damn job to save the world. You're the cop."

"I haven't been a cop for a long time."

"Yeah, well, I've never been one."

"But we both know you're a big softy. Somewhere, deep down."

It was definitely a chuckle this time. "This girl, she's Bentley's sister-in-law?"

"Technically." Stroking my fingers through Tempest's fur, I stifled another yawn. "But she was little when Bentley married her sister. Her mom was an addict. Dad wasn't around. Bentley was practically a parent to her."

Another moment of silence. "I'm always helping Bentley save his kids."

"So, is that a yes?"

"It's an, *I guess*."

I grinned. "You're the best Mafia lord I've ever met."

"Don't call me that."

"What should I call you then?"

"Simeon will do. And you owe me for this, Castle."

"Put it on my tab."

"Yeah, yeah." I was just about to pull the phone away and end the call when he said, "But watch your ass tomorrow. You're used to dealing with junkies. Tweakers are different."

"Like you said, I was a cop. I'm aware."

"These guys are different than me, Maddie." A certain warmth filled his voice now. Concern. "They're different than my guys. Don't threaten them. Don't accuse them. Use that bubbly charm of yours. Talk to them the way you talk to Bentley—the way you talk to me. Don't talk to them like you talk to your suspects. We don't need a fight. Just ask them your questions, and we'll get out of there."

I'd been doing this long enough now. I knew which persona worked with which suspect. "Duly noted."

"And wear something low-cut."

* * *

WHEN I FINISHED MY PHONE CALL, I WENT OUTSIDE WITH Tempest. Beneath the setting sun, Bentley sat in the grass before the mulch bed that faced my trailer. Sam sat a few feet away, swatting at mosquitoes as he trimmed the dying leaves off Bentley's rosebush. Their voices were indistinguishable, but the looks on their faces were clear when they glanced my way.

Deep purple circles lined the bottom of Bentley's eyes. He managed a smile for me, but it wasn't as genuine as I would've liked. Sam's expression wasn't much different.

Sam's pain, I understood. Dylan must've crossed his mind regularly, but having to face the state of their relationship couldn't have been an easy task.

But Bentley? I wasn't sure what the matter was. He always knew how to put a smile on my face, though, and I liked to think that I knew how to do the same for him.

With a childish grin, I sprinted across the yard to him. When he saw me coming, that smile grew more genuine. It turned into a laugh as I collapsed onto his lap. Greeting him with a kiss, I tossed my arms around his neck.

Chuckling, he kissed me back. "You're gonna hurt your knee."

"Nope." I gestured to my wrist, then the sewed-up gash on my forehead. "I should get hurt more often. Distracts from the pain in my knee."

"Isn't that strange?" Petting Tempest, he turned back to his flowers. "Even if there are parts all over your body that hurt, your brain's gonna focus on the one that hurts the most. That's how topical analgesics work, you know. *Biofreeze* and things like that? They don't actually stop your pain. They just make your brain focus on the icy sensation instead of the pain."

Could always count on Bentley for an anatomy lesson. "I think it's pretty neat, actually."

"I think so too." He glanced at Sam, then back at me. The kind of look that said, I'm going to tread lightly until you tell me to do otherwise. "Was that Simeon?"

"It was, and I owe him, apparently," I said. "But his answer was yes."

"Cool." Another glance at Sam, as if to make sure he wasn't paying too close attention. "I talked to Phoebe. She's gonna keep an eye on Grace while we're there."

"Where you guys going?" Sam asked.

Apparently, he was paying more attention than Bentley realized. Rather than put Bentley in an awkward position, I said, "Just a couple of interviews in Columbus tomorrow."

He set his garden shears down. "It's gonna be dangerous? That's why you can't bring Grace?"

"Not really," I said. "Some sketchy people, though. Not the best environment for someone her age."

"Is it just the weekend?" Squaring his shoulders, he lifted his chin. "Because I can come along if you need some muscle."

"No, that's—"

"That's actually not a bad idea, Mads."

My head whipped around to look at Bentley. Face screwing up, I shook my head. "It's not really necessary either."

"It might be," Bentley said. "They're friends with Simeon, but they *hate* me. I don't like the idea of doing this at all, but if we are going to go there, if you are going to interview them, I like the idea of someone like Sam being around."

"Simeon's going to be there. And Sam's only been released for a couple months. If something doesn't go right, he could end up back in jail."

"Shit, how dangerous is this?" Turning to face us, Sam's posture got firmer. Defensive, protective. "What's this about?"

"Nothing—"

"Those dealers I told you about." Still petting Tempest, Bentley turned his way. "The ones Daisy was selling for."

"You mean the meth cooking pimps?" With a huff, Sam shook his head. "Hell no. You're not going in there alone, Maddie. Especially not if your boyfriend has beef with them."

"I'm trying to remember the part where I became a damsel?" I looked between them. "I don't need help. Simeon's gonna be there just because he insisted he needs to be." I gestured to Bentley, then to Sam. "And you're still on probation. You can't leave the state without permission from your P.O. I can handle this, Dad."

Sam's breath stopped and tears all but welled in his eyes.

Shit.

Since he had reentered my life, I knew him as Sam. I didn't know why this time, I called him Dad. I never had before. Our relationship was progressing, and I considered him a father now. But I hadn't planned on that coming out. It certainly wasn't a manipulation tactic.

Didn't matter if it was, anyway. Because it only made him double down.

"My P.O. likes me. I'll give him a call." He stood. "I'm coming, and I don't want to hear another word about it. If this is as dangerous as

Bentley says it is, I would trust you to do it on your own any other day. But you have a head injury, a broken rib, a broken wrist, and a bazillion bruised bones. Just let me help you, kid."

I wanted to protest, but there was no use. He had already made his decision. So I turned my frustration on Bentley instead. Once Sam was out of sight, rounding the front of the trailer, I stared at him in disbelief.

He went back to his plants. "Don't look at me like that."

"Like what? Like you overstepped?" I searched for his gaze, but he kept it on the flowers. "That was uncalled for, Bentley."

"Tough."

Sputtering a laugh, I waited for the second part of that. The sarcastic smile. The playful tease. The apology he would usually give me.

None of those came.

"What the hell's the matter with you?" I asked. "This attitude isn't fair. I didn't do anything—"

"You almost died yesterday." He dropped his garden shears, turning to face me with wide, furious eyes. "You are reckless. You're reckless every day, Maddie, but when you're doing it to make your living, I won't interfere. I think about it. Every time you leave, every time you're working a high-profile case, I think about tracking you down and carrying you away to safety. But I don't, because I know you would hate me for it.

"You like your independence, even if you do some stupid shit with it. Your job is dangerous, and it means the world to you. I knew that when we got together. That's a part of being with you, a part of loving you, and I accept it. But this isn't about your job anymore. This is about my kid. And the last time you went out there trying to save my kid, someone died. Someone you cared about, and it screwed you up for months. So when it comes to this shit with Daisy, I'm gonna make sure you're safe, even if it pisses you off. You can be mad at me, and you can scold me, but I'm not gonna be in that position again. I'm not letting you run headfirst into my battle without a damn good shield."

He turned back to his flowers.

I just stared at him, processing that.

Did I see where he was coming from? Of course. In his position, I would feel the same way. Letting someone fight my battles was no easy task. Especially if there was risk involved.

It wasn't what he said that bothered me, but how he said it. His tone. His eyes. The frustration, the worry, and everything in between. I knew it came from a place of love, but this wasn't his way.

The light in Bentley, his omnipresent smile, had brought out mine. He was the reason I'd climbed out of the dark place I'd been stuck in. Out of the anger, and the hatred, and the addiction, into the woman I was proud to be now. Smart, goal oriented, and ever compassionate for the underdogs neglected by the messed up world we lived in.

I'd known he wasn't doing his best lately, but this was the first glimpse I'd seen of him reminding me too much of myself. Of that dark pit I'd been stuck in for months before he'd come along with a rope to haul me out of it. It hadn't been his job to lift me out of that hole, but he had.

In a perfect world, I'd drag him out of his. I just wasn't sure how.

After a silent moment, I said, "I get it."

His stiff posture softened. He still didn't turn to face me, fiddling with a flower whose wilted pedals were well-trimmed now, but he gave me a fraction of a glance.

"But I don't like being talked to like that." I kept my voice soft, doing my best to communicate in a healthy way. A way I'd learned from him. "That's not how we do this. We don't yell at each other."

Shutting his eyes, he lifted his hand to them. He rubbed them, then down the bridge of his nose. With a shake of his head, he let out a deep breath. "I'm sorry. I didn't mean to lash out at you."

"It's okay." I touched his chin, bringing his gaze to mine. "What's this really about?"

His expression was tough to describe. Eyes sunken, skin pale, lips pressed together. It took him a few moments, but eventually, he got off his knees, collapsed to his ass, and ran a hand through his hair. "I didn't get much sleep last night."

Because he was in the hospital with me. "I'm sorry. I could've gotten an Uber or something—"

"No." He found my hand and intertwined his fingers with mine. "No, I wanted to be there. I've just been working too much. Then all this with Daisy is piling up, and I'm just feeling like such a piece of shit. I should've been looking for her. I shouldn't have given up. I ran here to get away from it. Dealing with it was too hard, so I ran, and now she's there. Wherever *there* is. And I can't pretend like that's not partly my fault."

Frowning, I squeezed his hand. "It's not."

"But it is." Finally, his eyes met mine. There were tears in them. "She was my kid. Maybe not legally or biologically, but I was all she had left. And I gave up on her. I just accepted she was gone and moved on with my life and rekindled this relationship with you. I just acted like it didn't happen.

"Then there's whatever's going on with Grace. And I don't even know what it is. I don't know why she's so mad at me. Her therapist doesn't either. She talks about what happened with Eric, but she won't talk about me. I don't know how to fix it. But how can I fix it when I don't know what I'm doing wrong."

"She's a teenager. They go through shit, and they hate their parents for it, even if the parent is doing everything right." I wiped a tear from his cheek. "And you are."

He managed to smile at that, but it was weak. "I wish that were true. But if I was any good at this, Daisy would be with us right now."

"You gotta stop beating yourself up over that."

"How can I? I've read her stories, Maddie." Huffing, he grabbed a fistful of brown hair and held it away from his face. "I know how she saw me, how much she resented me. And I can't blame her. Maybe if I fought harder, I would've gotten custody. Maybe she wouldn't have ended up where she did. Maybe she would have never met Kevin, and she never would've started dancing, and..."

When he trailed off, all I could do was shake my head.

In Daisy's stories, it was clear she held some resentment for the character she based off of Bentley. But in the same way any kid resented a parental figure. He wasn't perfect, and she wished he were.

By no means was he her villain, though. She admired him, loved him, and she knew how much she mattered to him. While she was angry, it wasn't at him.

"She was angry at the life she was born into," I said. "You were the only constant, Bentley. She lashed out at you because there was no one else to take her pain out on. Just like Phoebe did to your mom when you were kids. She was angry at your dad, but she took it out on her because it was safer. Just like for me, it was safer to be angry at the world than it was to be angry at my mom."

He had a hard time holding my gaze again.

"But it doesn't matter, anyway." I squeezed his hand once more. "When we find her, you two can hash out all your shit."

I expected a laugh at that. Maybe a halfhearted smile.

Instead, I just got a teary-eyed, puppy dog look. "You think we will?"

Telling someone that I would find their missing loved one was like skating on a sheet of melting ice. There was no way of knowing how this would turn out. But my gut said we would.

Chapter 16

Normally, Bentley handled dinner. But given his brief meltdown, it was best for me to handle it tonight. I didn't cook, of course. We didn't need anyone ending up in the hospital with food poisoning. But I was a pro at ordering *DoorDash*.

After we ate, as usual, Grace and Sam started on dessert. A peanut butter cream cheesecake. Bentley and I were a few minutes into a friendly debate over the ending of *Game of Thrones* when Sam interrupted us from the island, saying, "Oh, my P.O. was okay with it. He said he might check with you, though, Maddie. If he does, make sure to let him know we're just going to visit some family."

I grunted, looking over the back of the couch to face him. "So, you want me to lie?"

"Stretch the truth." He shrugged. "It's not like I'm asking you to cover up a murder for me."

"Just waiting for that day," I said under my breath.

"Where you guys going?" Grace spoke over the stand mixer, untying her apron. "Can I come?"

"Maddie just needs to interview somebody in Ohio," Bentley said. "You're gonna stay at Phoebe's."

"Why can't I come?" Her forehead scrunched down. "Is it about Daisy?"

"No, it's not." He stood and collected our empty cups off the coffee table. "It's about the arsonist. I just don't want her going alone after what happened yesterday."

"But I thought you got kicked off that case."

Ugh.

If he thought it was best to lie to Grace, it wasn't my place to interfere. Putting me in the middle wasn't fair, though. I didn't like to lie, especially not to the people I cared about.

"Yeah, but, um... you know me." Standing as well, I stretched my leg out. "When I get started on a case, I don't stop until I solve it."

"The arsonist isn't that dangerous." Still, her face was screwed up in confusion. "She dragged you out of the building. That's what Dad said."

"But the person she's interviewing is." Avoiding eye contact, he snuck past her to get into the fridge. "You'll be alright with Aunt Phoebe."

She scoffed. Her eyes slid over me, then Sam. Neither of us were great at being put on the spot. Bentley was the worst of us all. He couldn't even look her in the eyes, which she surely noticed.

"You're lying," she said to Bentley, expression somewhere between annoyed and sad. "This is about Daisy."

"It's about the arsonist—"

"No, it's not. You got a lead, and you're following it to Daisy, and you don't want me to come because you think I'll get hurt, but—"

"I don't have a lead on Daisy, kid." I shook my head. "I wouldn't keep it from you if I did."

"But you *are* going to interview people about Daisy, aren't you?" she asked. "That's what you're going there for. I can tell. You're all shit liars."

"Watch your mouth, Grace," Bentley said, only then meeting her gaze.

She scoffed. "You can sit here and lie to my face, but God forbid I say 'shit.'"

"I'm not lying—"

"Yes, you are!" Yanking the apron away from her neck, she tossed it onto the counter. "I don't get it. If it's not dangerous, just tell me. Explain why and I'll shut up."

"We *are* going to interview a suspect in the arsonist case, Grace." I walked closer to the kitchen island, Tempest scurrying up from her seat on the floor behind me. "There's nothing to get upset about."

"Bullshit." I couldn't tell if she scoffed or laughed. "I can tell by the look on your face, too. Dad just lied to me, and you're not sure how to respond. So now you're trying to shut me up so this doesn't turn into a fight. But too late. I'm tired of being treated like a little kid. Something's going on, and you guys aren't telling me, and it's bullshit. I'm the one who helped decode Daisy's message. I can help."

"That's the problem." Bentley's voice was soft, gentle. Despite his outburst with me earlier, he was doing his best to remain a stable pillar for his daughter. "This isn't your responsibility, sweetheart. It's my responsibility to handle everything with Daisy, and this is Maddie's job. We can handle it, but you're too young. You don't need this pressure—"

"Go to hell." She spoke between gritted teeth, stomping toward her bedroom.

"I'm not trying to fight with you, Grace," Bentley said, trailing after her. "I just don't want you to have to stress about this—"

"You want me to be like *you*!" She spun to face him, only a foot or two away. Grace stood an inch or two shorter than me, and Bentley towered over her. Yet right now, she looked so big, and he looked so small. "You want me to block it out. You want me to pretend it isn't happening, just like you did for the last year. You want me to pretend everything's fine, but it's not. It's not fine. Some psychopath is holding my best friend captive, and you don't care!"

Even from my awkward view, only able to see Bentley's profile, there was no denying the pain in his eyes. "I care more than I can put into words."

"You didn't care when she disappeared!" Tears gathering in her eyes, she shoved Bentley's chest. "You were happy! You were happy you didn't have to deal with her anymore. When she disappeared, it was good for you. You got what you wanted, didn't you?" She gestured around the living room. "You got to leave her behind. You didn't have to look back, and you were grateful for it. Even if you won't admit it, I know you were."

There were tears in his eyes, too. He shook his head. "That's not true."

"Yes, *it is*!" With tears streaming down her face, she smacked him in the chest this time. "You let Ox die to save me, but you just acted like Daisy was never a part of our lives. She disappeared, and you pretended like she was never there!" A sob tore its way up her esophagus. "You didn't look for her! You didn't fight for her! You started dating a private investigator, and it took you six months to tell her! You knew Maddie could've started working on this from the beginning, but you didn't give a shit, Dad. And I hate you for it." Weeping, she shoved his chest again. "Mom wouldn't have stopped looking for her. I wish you were the one who died. Because you don't give a shit about anything but your perfect little suburban fantasy!"

Bentley didn't say a word.

His lips were swollen, trembling, but he pressed them together. Probably because if he tried to speak, he would cry too.

"Not gonna deny that, are you?" Wiping her eyes, Grace took a step back. She stared up at him for a moment, then let out one more little sob. "It's all bullshit. This whole family is bullshit."

She turned around, stomped the rest of the way to her bedroom, and slammed the door behind her.

We all winced at that sound.

At my feet, Tempest whimpered. I stretched my good hand down to scratch her head.

For a few heartbeats, I just stood there. Sam did too, giving me the same expression I was probably giving him. The kind that said, *What do we do?*

Bentley didn't move either. He didn't chase after her, didn't turn to look at me, didn't ask us to leave. Just stood there, staring at the spot where Grace had stood, with tears in his eyes.

I didn't know what to say, but I had to say something. "She didn't mean—"

"She did." Bentley's voice was almost too quiet to make out. After a throat clear, he headed toward the front door, not looking at anyone along the way. "I need some air."

* * *

I gave it to him. Needing space after an argument was only natural. What wasn't, however, was the sound of his pickup truck starting a few minutes after he walked outside. Typically, if he wanted me to keep an eye on Grace, he would ask me to. This time, he just assumed I would.

Obviously, I would.

She was old enough to be alone in the house by herself. From time to time, that was fine. After that blowout? I wasn't leaving her. Neither was Sam.

He dropped a plate of peanut butter cheesecake at her door. Over the blaring music, I doubted she heard him knock. A few minutes later when I went to the bathroom, however, the plate was gone.

After an hour, Bentley still hadn't returned. I texted him to ask if he was okay. He didn't respond. Another half an hour later, I checked his location. While it wasn't necessary for the average man to share his location with his girlfriend, I was a paranoid ex-cop. I wanted the location of everyone I'd ever cared for a few button clicks away.

He was at Barrel and Brew. A bar ten minutes down the road.

Did I like him drinking his troubles away? No. But in the many months we had been together, I hadn't seen him touch alcohol once. Right now, I didn't blame him for needing the relief that came at the bottom of a shot glass.

Almost two hours after he left, he texted to ask if Sam could come pick him up. That wasn't an indicator he was shitfaced drunk. He was a paramedic. Far too many times, he'd been the first to arrive at a scene which would have never existed if not for drunk driving. After even a sip of alcohol, he wouldn't get behind the wheel.

I asked Sam if that would be a trigger for him. "Not unless he's got a bag of dope and a needle on hand," he said before walking outside.

That gave me an opportunity to talk to Grace again. I had tried twice already, but she had only turned her music up.

This time, she opened the door.

Her face was red, blotchy, the corners of her eyes chafed from tears. She hadn't spoken a word yet, but the guilt was obvious. Especially when she said, "I know."

"You know what?"

"That was uncalled for." With sunken shoulders, she struggled around the clothes and junk all over her floor. Nearly tripping twice along the way, she eventually sat on the unmade bed. "I know, okay? I don't need a lecture."

"Have I ever lectured you?" Navigating the minefield she called a bedroom was no easy task with a bad knee. I relied on Tempest's support to get me to the bed. I sat beside Grace, and Tempy settled in on the floor at my feet. "Because I don't remember ever doing that."

"I don't remember ever talking to my dad like that." She kept her gaze on the floor. "First time for everything."

"Hopefully the last," I said.

Only Tempest's panting filled the silence.

For a moment, we just sat with it. The silence.

I wasn't even sure what I wanted to talk to her about. In every interaction with Grace, I tried my best not to overstep. She wasn't my kid, and I wouldn't pretend she was. It wasn't my place to parent her. One thing she had said in her rant was my area of expertise, however. That, I could comment on.

"I'm not gonna tell you what to do with your dad," I said. "I have some opinions about the way you talked to him, but I'll keep those to myself unless you ask for them." I paused. "There is something you said that bothered me, though. Something I think I have the right to discuss with you."

"That I wished he died?"

"That's one opinion that I'm not going to give unless you ask for." Getting comfy on the bed, I lifted my good knee under my lap and stretched out my bad leg. "About Ox."

She frowned. "I know. I shouldn't have said that."

"You shouldn't have. Mostly because you were wrong. Ox didn't die to save you." At the mention of his name, my heart swelled. Although I was improving, I was still working through his death. "He died because of me."

"He was coming to save us both," she said, voice weak.

"But you were already with your dad. I was the one chasing after that son of a bitch with a hunting rifle." I shrugged, biting the inside of my cheek. "If he had the choice, he would've died for you. There was nothing Ox liked more than being a hero. But he ran after Eric because *I* was running after Eric. That's my cross to bear. Don't put that on your dad."

"I shouldn't have put any of that on him." With teary eyes, she met my gaze. "I was mean. I know that. I know it was uncalled for, and I wish I wouldn't have said it. But it just came out. I've been holding it in for so long, and it just exploded."

Chewing my lip, my frown deepened. I could've corrected her. I could've told her all the reasons why what she said was wrong. Why her "feelings" were wrong.

Because they were.

The fact was, Bentley did the best he could in a thousand impossible situations. He'd done more for Daisy than he'd had to. She wasn't his responsibility. As much as he felt it was, and as much as Grace did, Bentley wasn't Daisy's parent. I didn't blame him for moving on when she'd vanished. Especially because she'd left no trail to follow.

But I wasn't a therapist, and I couldn't phrase that appropriately. I also wasn't a parent, and it wasn't my job to scold her right now. I did, however, consider myself her friend. And friends were honest with friends.

"Why do you think that is?" I asked.

She shot me a look. "Why do I think *what* is?"

"Why do you think you blew up?"

A quick glance. Shoulders coiling inward, hunching, she shrugged. "I don't know."

"I do. You've been holding it in. You waited until you were infuriated. You're like a pot of water that's been sitting on a hot plate for months. All it took was a little more heat, and you boiled over. Now there's a mess all over the stove, and you gotta clean it up. But if you would've just poured some water out a few weeks ago, or a couple months ago, there wouldn't be a mess right now."

One more quick glance. "I guess."

"That's as close to a lecture as I'll get." Standing, I nodded to the living room. "I'm going to hang out here until your dad gets back. If you want to talk more, you know where to find me."

She didn't respond to that, and I didn't force her to. I just struggled around the piles of laundry with Tempest. But as soon as we were out of Grace's room, she ran to the front door.

"You need to go outside, girl?" I asked.

Tail wagging with excitement, she howled.

I chuckled, grabbed her leash off the end table, and clicked it around her harness. As I stepped outside, my phone buzzed in my back pocket.

A text from an unknown number.

Of course, I opened it.

I'm sorry you got hurt. I never wanted that. This is about Brandon. He's not who he says he is.

The arsonist.

The arsonist just texted me.

Was this my in? Was this my opportunity to close the door on this case?

I texted back, *I know you didn't. And I'm not after you anymore. I'm after him. But I need something to go on. Can you help?*

I didn't expect an immediate response. But just as I slid it into my back pocket, the phone buzzed again.

My heart skipped with excitement.

But it wasn't the random number.

It was Dylan.

Chapter 17

She was right.

As he rode in the passenger seat of Sam's truck, watching the summer foliage drift by the window, breathing in the humid air, gazing at the setting sun surrounded by orange and purple clouds, that's all he thought. *She was right.*

Grace was right.

When he made it home, he pecked Maddie's cheek. She was talking on the phone, so she wasn't in a rush for a greeting. Still, all he thought when he walked to his daughter's bedroom was, *She was right.*

The door was open. She lay on the bed, facing the wall. Even from here, he could hear her headphones. Was that *My Chemical Romance* she was listening to? It sounded like it. Wasn't she too young for *My Chemical Romance*?

Pushing that thought away, he just looked at her there for a moment. This morning, when he'd walked past this bedroom, he had grunted a curse about all the clothes on the floor. Now? Now, he was grateful for them. At least she was here.

She was angry. Every teenager was angry, but Grace had more reasons than most. She could have been like Maddie at her age. Rather than scream at her mother, she'd done what Bentley just had. Found a place with a bottle of brown liquor, sat down, and drank.

Of course, teenaged Maddie would drink until the bottle was gone. Bentley had only had two.

Grace could've done that. Bentley knew there were people in this trailer park who would've given her a drink if she asked. Girls her own age, boys of the same demographic, and men who loved to give attention to little girls who wanted it.

Bentley didn't want to be that parent. He had been that parent with Daisy, and that was why she was where she was.

Wherever that may've been.

With a heavy heart and a hard swallow, Bentley struggled around Grace's mess of a bedroom and sat on the bed beside her. She undoubtedly felt the shift of his weight on the bed. But she didn't turn. Not until he tapped her shoulder.

Rolling over, she wiped the edge of her eye. For a moment, she looked like the baby she'd been almost fourteen years ago when he'd gone into her room in the middle of the night. She would cry and cry, but then she would see him, and she would just look at him. The same way she looked at him now.

Like he would save her from whatever hurt. Whether it was a hungry tummy, or a dirty diaper, or a burp stuck in her chest, she trusted him to fix it. She gave him that same look now, but Bentley had a hard time believing she still trusted him.

Tugging off her headphones, she pulled the purple blanket closer to her face. "Hey."

"Hey." His voice cracked. He cleared it away. "Can we talk?"

She nodded. Didn't say anything, though.

Fair enough. He was the one who wanted to talk.

"Maddie wants to interview Kevin," Bentley said. "She is going to Columbus to interview somebody about the arsonist case, but she figured while she was there, she could interview Kevin, too. I lied because I didn't want you to come. I don't want you around those people."

She gave him that look again. That was all she did for a while. Eventually, she said, "Why didn't you just say so?"

"I don't know." His voice cracked again. "I don't know, kid."

There it was again. That same expression. Waiting for Daddy to give her a bottle, or change her diaper, or burp her over his shoulder.

Only, that obviously wasn't what she wanted.

It had been easier when that had been what she'd wanted. Babies were so much easier than teenagers.

"But you were right." Those words tasted like vinegar on Bentley's tongue. "I wish you weren't, but you're right."

"About what?"

"That I ran away." He had to press his lips together to keep them from trembling. It took him a moment to continue. "You were wrong about me not caring. But you are right that I ran away. And that a part of me wanted to forget."

Her brows crunched down. "You wanted to forget Daisy. You're admitting that."

It wasn't that black and white. "I just wanted to stop hurting."

Tears gathered in his eyes. But apparently that didn't answer Grace's question, because she just kept waiting.

"I don't think you remember everything, Grace. You were so little when she first started using. You probably don't remember me fighting for custody with your mom, and then again by myself after your mom died. But I did. I fought like hell because I loved that little girl just as much as I love you."

"And if I disappeared, you'd want to forget about me, too?"

Shaking his head, Bentley swept the salty water from his cheek. "No. No, of course not. There's no part of me that's *happy* she disappeared. But I kept taking care of her and enabling her, because that's who I am. I care so much that it destroys me, kid.

"But I didn't give up. Even though it was killing me, I kept caring. I kept trying to help her, and she kept slapping me in the face." Grace was still giving him that scrunched-up face. He figured it was best he finally leveled with her. "Do you remember that time you woke up in the middle of the night? You said you had a bad dream about an explosion?"

Slowly, Grace nodded.

"It wasn't an explosion. It was a gunshot downstairs." Bentley swallowed the tears that ran down his throat. "Kevin's dad had shown up at the door. Daisy owed him money. He said if I didn't get it to them, there'd be hell to pay. Then he shot your school picture. And he wasn't messing around. Those guys don't."

Grace's expression softened.

"I wasn't happy she was gone, sweetheart." He blinked at the tears in his eyes. "But I grew up with a mom who was always walking on eggshells because of my dad. And it messed me up. It messed me up *bad*. And I saw it happening to you. As much as I tried to keep you away from everything that Daisy was doing, it kept pouring over. You were having nightmares, and panic attacks, and you were falling behind in school, and—And I didn't want you to grow up like that. Like I did. So when she disappeared, and I couldn't find her, and neither could the cops or anyone else, I thought the worst. I thought she was dead, and I'd never see her again. It was too late to fix it.

"I just wanted to make her better. That was what I wanted. I wanted to help her climb out of the shit she was in. But I couldn't. She wouldn't stop messing around with Kevin, and she wouldn't stop using, and she wouldn't stop selling herself, and I knew where that headed. I knew that put you in an early grave. And when she disappeared, that's what I thought happened. The natural reaction to the kind of life that Daisy led. But I was damned and determined to make sure you turned out different.

"So... Yeah. There was a part of me that was relieved when she was gone. I'm not happy she is wherever she is, that she's gone through whatever she's gone through. But when I couldn't find her? After I got past the panic, and the worry, and the grief, yeah. I was glad that I could finally do it right."

Bentley tucked some hair behind her ear. "I was glad that I could give you the life that you deserve. I was glad we could leave. That you don't have to grow up the way she did. That I could keep you safe."

That felt like confessing to murder. Worse, maybe.

The look on Grace's face didn't make it any easier. Neither did the words she spoke next. "And I'm supposed to be okay with that? You gave up on Daisy to protect me, and that's supposed to make me happy? Should I respect you for that, Dad?"

"It wasn't just for you." This wasn't easy for Bentley to admit aloud either, but the remnants of liquid courage were helping. "It was for me, too. Finding peace without her was for both of us. I do have a suburban fantasy. I want us to be normal and happy. And I know that sounds selfish. It is, I guess. But it was selfish for Daisy to do what she did, too, Grace."

She scoffed. "So now you're victim blaming? It's her fault that she is where she is?"

"That's not what I said." Bentley's tone remained level, and he did his best to regurgitate what his therapist had told him. "This asshole who took her, he's to blame. But she is also to blame for her addiction. I can recognize the trauma she went through and why she turned to drugs. I can understand why leaving that life wasn't easy. I can even understand why she ended up with Kevin. But understanding something doesn't justify it.

"The life she was leading was killing her slowly, and that was her choice. If she wanted to do that, wanted to throw her life away, so be it. But coming to me, crying for help, asking for money, getting us involved with drug dealers, putting us at risk... that was selfish. That was wrong. She was a grown woman by the time she disappeared, Grace. She wasn't a little kid anymore, and she still chose to put us at risk. And I am allowed to feel some relief for no longer having to deal with that."

That wasn't the whole truth. He did still have to deal with it. Working for Simeon meant still dealing with drug dealers. But Simeon was a different beast than Dale, Kevin's dad. A devil Bentley could bear selling his soul to.

The irony was that there was nothing selfish about his alliance with

Simeon. He had made that deal with the devil to save the little girl who sat before him. Much like he had bartered with demons for Daisy's safety.

But there was a nuance to it. Grace had been kidnapped by a serial killer, and Bentley had turned to Simeon to fight fire with fire. There was no feasible way to blame Grace for what had happened to her.

Daisy's relationship with Kevin? Those demons Bentley had bartered with when they'd threatened to kill her over the money she owed? Daisy was to blame for that.

This was what made it so difficult. Everything was gray. There was no black and white in Bentley's life.

Teenagers didn't understand nuances. Grace saw right, and she saw wrong. Because Bentley had saved her, Grace thought his failure to save Daisy was a lack of empathy. That he resented Daisy so much, he'd grown to hate her. That he no longer cared what happened to her.

That wasn't true.

It was just too complicated for someone Grace's age to understand, especially from the inside looking out. She couldn't see the full picture.

"And what do you think that does to me?" Grace had tears in her eyes now. "You gave up on my sister for me, Dad. You decided I mattered more than she did. Don't you see how guilty that makes *me* feel?"

"It wasn't that she mattered less than you, Grace." Frowning, Bentley shook his head and wiped that tear from her cheek. "But the ship was sinking, and she had already fallen overboard. I jumped in to get her back on the boat, but the waves took her. You were still right there, though. I couldn't protect her anymore because she was already gone. So I jumped back on that boat, and I carried you, and I rode us to shore, because there was no other option."

Those tears came down faster, harder. The eyebrows she had furrowed with anger now pinched in the middle, softer. After all he had said, nothing resonated. This was the only bit that seemed to make an impact.

"Do you see my point now? I had to keep rowing the boat, because if I didn't, the waves were gonna take us too." Bentley wiped some snot from his nose on the back of his sleeve. "And I just had to save the kid closest to me."

Silently crying, bundling that blanket before her chest as if it were a teddy bear, she nodded. "I get it."

Then, much to Bentley's shock, she sat forward, tossed her arms around his neck, and hugged him. And she looked at him with such trust. Just like she had when he held her and comforted her as a baby.

In his ear, between quiet sobs, Grace said, "I didn't mean that. About wishing you were dead instead of mom."

Bentley hoped that was true. He wouldn't blame her if it weren't, but he hoped. "It's okay."

"I just miss her." She sniffled. "I miss them both, and I wish they were here."

With a hard swallow, blinking at tears, Bentley kissed Grace on her forehead. "Me too, kid. Me too."

Chapter 18

"Yes, I found the IP address." Dylan's voice was short, matter of fact. "I texted you the address. But, of course, I was curious, so I googled it as well."

"You a detective now, too?" I asked, releasing Tempest's lead. With only the dim glow of the porch light and the stars shining overhead, her black fur vanished into the yard. Unfortunate.

I liked to keep an eye on where she was out here. While I didn't mind if my yard became a minefield of dog shit from time to time, I didn't want Bentley to have to deal with it. He took way more pride in his yard than I did mine.

"No, I was curious," Dylan replied. "I already said that."

"I was kidding." What Sam had said about Dylan being a loner, but people liking him, was starting to make sense. He may not have been what other people considered a good conversationalist, but I found him entertaining. "But that's great. Thank you. Where did the IP addresses take you?"

"The first was a public library in Essex, Maryland, and the second was a public library in eastern Pennsylvania. Near the Lancaster area, to be more precise. Like I said, I sent you the exact addresses." Keyboard clacking filled the background. "What interests me is that to use public libraries these days, you're typically required to have a library card. If this girl is missing, but she's posting her stories from public libraries, it would stand to reason that she has a public library card with these facilities. Maybe you could call them. Usually, you're required to share your home address with the public library. They won't give you a card without one. I believe you have to reside in the county to get the card. So maybe that will tell you where she is. But then again, that doesn't make much sense. She couldn't have an address in both Lancaster and Essex."

It was a hell of a start. Dylan had the right idea, but I doubted it was that simple. "Either she's using a fake address with a fake library card, or she went to the library and asked somebody if she could hop onto their computer while they were still logged in."

"That would make more sense." More keyboard clicking sounded. "Either way, I think this information is valuable."

"It absolutely is. Thank you very much." Tempy pulled on the leash, and I gave it a bit more slack. "How much do I owe you?"

"Five hundred dollars. I just need your email so I can send you the invoice."

"Sure, let me text it to you right quick." Still holding Tempest's leash with my good hand, I did my best to type it out with the bad one. After I clicked send, I held the phone to my ear again. "Did it come through?"

"It did, yes. I'm sending the invoice now."

"Great, I really appreciate this. While I still have you though, is this something that you do regularly? Little hacking jobs?"

"So long as it's ethical, from time to time, yes. I wouldn't hack into somebody's bank account or something like that, but I have done things like this for friends. Why do you ask?"

The light of Sam's high beams shined up the driveway, gravel crackling under his tires. "Because I run into issues like this occasionally. Sometimes it's deleted texts off a victim's phone, or trying to get into their social media, or accessing cleared browser history. It can get complicated since I'm not a cop anymore. Getting warrants for these sorts of things isn't easy either, and then it takes time for the data to come back from the social media company. It would be nice to know that I can reach out when I run into problems."

"Yes, you can reach out." The clicking in the background ceased. "I like doing these sorts of things. I enjoy programming as a hobby, but it's nice to do it for a good cause."

"Then I've got another job for you." As Bentley walked past, I waved. He gave me a halfhearted smile and a peck on the cheek before continuing inside. "It's different from the last one, though."

"Please elaborate."

"I'm working on another case." I gave a brief synopsis of the arsonist, including last night's fire. "But then I got this text. It said what I already suspected. The arsonist wasn't trying to hurt anyone with the fires. That's why she pulled me out. But I'm thinking she messaged me from a burner phone. You wouldn't have a way of tracing that, would you?"

"Burner phones exist to be anonymous. You believe Brandon is aware of who's doing this to him, though, correct?"

"I don't think he knows who it is, but my friend tossed out the idea that he's being blackmailed, if that's what you mean."

"It is, yes. It would stand to reason, then, if the arsonist already had a burner phone, and they were blackmailing him, that at least part of it would've been done online. In theory, I would be able to look through his personal accounts to find messages from the arsonist. This will be much more tedious, however, and will cost more. I won't charge you by the hour because this will take much more time, and if this Brandon is who you believe he is, I would like to see him punished. But it will take time out of my day, and I value my time. So I will still have to charge you at least two thousand dollars."

At least the guy knew his worth.

"That's no problem. What do you need from me to get started?"

"If you could send me a file with his email, phone number, social media, and anything else you gathered on his person, I'll begin after I cook dinner."

"Sounds like a plan. Thank you so much."

"You're welcome. Before we get off this call, I wanted to ask about that trainer you know. Could you connect us? I'd like to meet with them and discuss getting a service dog."

"Yeah, no problem. I'll send that over too."

"Great. I appreciate it. Also, if you would like to get together to have a meal, or a coffee, I would like to do that too. I work until five, and it takes me roughly an hour to settle in thereafter. I do have a two-hour lunch during the day, but I use that for myself. On the weekend, though, I am usually free. Maybe next weekend, we could meet up."

Chest warming, a smile inched its way up my cheeks. "Next weekend works for me."

"Perfect. I'll send you a text with more details later."

Sam came out a few moments later, said he needed to pack a bag, gave me a hug, and told me he would be back in the morning. That reminded me, I also needed to pack a bag. Bentley was still talking to Grace anyway, so I shot him a text saying I was walking next door to get my things ready, but I had a lead on Daisy.

Once I was home, I gave Tempest a lick mat from the freezer to keep her occupied while I got my things together. It wasn't like I lived on the road, but I needed an overnight bag often enough. Most of my essentials were already together—toiletries, extra phone chargers, laptop bag, etc.—but I needed a few outfits. As Simeon had suggested, I ditched my usual hoodies and sweatpants for some jeans and tight shirts.

It was almost 11 by then. We were planning on leaving around 7 a.m. to get to Columbus by noon, but I could get by on four hours of sleep if necessary. It gave me enough time to check into the libraries Dylan mentioned.

Given the time, I couldn't call the facility to ask for details. The one in Lancaster was closed on weekends as well, but I could call the other one tomorrow while we were on the road.

Otherwise, all I could find was the roundabout idea of the towns. Which would be valuable once I arrived but wasn't much for the moment. They were normal. There was nothing spectacular or notable about either library. But they were both in small towns, which had me scratching my head.

Mr. Deluca—who I assumed was holding her captive from what Daisy had written—was an intelligent man. It made sense that if he would allow Daisy to leave his sight, he would do so in places like these. Public, free, and practically untraceable.

But why a small town? Why even *bring* a hostage to a small town? Everyone talked there. If they were driving and at any point were pulled over, small town cops would remember every detail about Daisy and Mr. Deluca.

If I were holding someone captive but wanted to give them the opportunity to go in public, I would do so in a heavily populated area. One where the person behind the reception desk wouldn't remember me.

Then again, in a major city, Daisy would've had far more opportunity to sneak away from him.

Which brought me back to square one. What was he holding over her? Why couldn't she walk up to someone at the library and ask for help? If not for the poetry, I may have suspected Stockholm syndrome. But clearly, Daisy knew he was the villain.

Something just didn't make sense. I had to be missing something.

A knock thudded at the door, pulling my attention from the laptop screen on my thighs.

Tempest didn't bark, so I knew who it was.

"Come in," I called.

Bentley walked in, plate of cheesecake in hand. He wore a strained smile. "Sorry about earlier. But I brought food."

Flipping my laptop shut, I returned the smile. "I already ate cheesecake. Now, if you walked in with brownies, maybe I would accept your bribe for forgiveness."

"Well, lucky for me,"—he dug in his jacket pocket and held up a few chocolate bars—"somebody was selling these for their kid's school fundraiser at the bar, and I thought of you. Is this an acceptable bribe?"

Grinning, I held out my open palm. "Acceptable indeed."

With a laugh, he handed me one and joined me on the sofa. Settling in as I tore open one of the chocolates, he did his best to remain positive with his expression and tone. But I knew him well enough to know he was not his best tonight. "I really am sorry. You were right. We don't talk to each other the way I talked to you tonight."

"I appreciate that, but it really is okay." I popped a piece of chocolate into my mouth and took his hand. Once I finished chewing, I said, "We all have bad days. Even the perfect Bentley Roycroft."

"I don't know what world you're living in where I'm perfect, but I'd like to take a trip there sometime." He navigated around my legs, situated them on his lap, and started massaging my knee. "Thank you for being so understanding, though."

"Thank you for staying up at the hospital with me all night." Squeezing his hand, I nodded next-door. "How'd things go with Grace?"

"Okay." A shrug and a deep breath. "I don't know. She's not a little kid anymore. She's got her own opinions, expectations for the people around her, and I don't think I'll ever live up to them. But she apologized, and we talked, and I think it's as good as it's gonna get. We watched a movie together, and she's in bed now, so I guess things are better than they were."

I frowned. "You surpass those expectations. She's just going through a lot right now."

For a while, he didn't respond to that. Eventually, he cleared his throat. "You said you had a lead on Daisy?"

"The most concrete that we have so far." I explained how I had commissioned Dylan—touched briefly on how I'd spoken with him today

—and what he had gathered, ending with, "It could be a dead end. But someone at these libraries had to have seen them together. If I show the employees a picture of Daisy, we could get something. The make and model of a vehicle, maybe security camera footage of them together. Hell, maybe she talked to somebody who was sitting beside her at the computer, and they know something. Either way, this is an actual, solid lead."

As I was talking, Bentley seemed to just soak it in. And for the life of me, I couldn't figure out what he was thinking. The long lull of silence didn't help, either.

On an average day, before the chaos of the last few months, Bentley had been a ray of sunshine. So positive, so emotionally secure, that I had seen him as the perfect man. I doubted that description was a fa□ade. He hadn't pretended to be someone he wasn't. He, like Grace, was just going through some shit.

The problem was, in our relationship, he was the emotional one. He was the one with big feelings and massive displays of affection, the life vest when I felt like I was lost in the ocean.

I had never needed to be that for him. I didn't know how to be now.

Eventually, he broke the silence with, "So she's okay?"

That depended on how he defined okay. "She's alive. I don't have any doubt about that."

"Well, yeah. But I mean physically." His eyes met mine, and I understood the feeling behind them. It was the same look he'd given me when I'd told him Grace had gone missing. "Mentally, I know he's hurting her." Tears pearled in the corners of his eyes, and he blinked them away. "But if he were beating her every day, or torturing her, that would be obvious. He wouldn't let her go out in public if she were covered with marks, right? I know that doesn't mean he's not hurting her physically at all, but it's got to be infrequent enough that he can take her out in public from time to time. The other day, when she posted that poem, she must've been safe. At least for those few minutes."

It was a nice fantasy. But in my experience, including my current broken rib that made breathing a chore, not to mention my knee, covering an injury with clothing didn't make it hurt any less.

Outside of that, psychological pain still hurt a whole hell of a lot. I wouldn't say that it hurt more than physical pain. But the wound of that pain, the one buried deep in the victim's heart, did hurt at least as much as the physical pain.

When my mom used to beat me, the physical pain had been less severe than my current chronic pain. What had hurt so deeply was knowing she could do it again. Knowing she *would* do it again. My life had been in her hands, and I couldn't trust her with it. In her presence, I'd feared for my life.

That fear *was* just as bad as the violence.

But I wouldn't tell him that. He needed hope right now.

"Yeah, that makes sense." Pressing his lips together, he nodded.

"Do you want to talk about it?" I squeezed his hand again. "Everything going on with Daisy, I mean. How you're feeling about it all?"

"I just want to bring her home." Blinking hard at the tears, he shook his head. "Can we talk about it another time?"

Although I struggled at the angle since my legs were spread out over his lap, and he was facing the coffee table, I managed to lean in and give him a soft kiss. "We can. What do you want to talk about right now?"

"How about your brother?" This smile was natural, not forced at all. "We haven't been able to talk about him at all yet."

Something I was also excited to talk about. "We're having lunch next weekend. And I have him working on the arsonist case, which is kinda cool. *He* is kinda cool."

"Yeah?"

"Yeah." I tucked a throw pillow behind my back so I could get comfy against the arm of the sofa. "He's really passionate about cooking."

"Guess that gene skipped you."

I stuck my tongue out at him, and he laughed.

"Also seems really into hiking. Oh, and he's getting a service dog, so maybe we can have puppy play dates." I paused. "That sounded weird, but you know what I mean."

Bentley laughed a little harder. "I do know what you mean."

"And he's very serious about calling himself an 'ethical hacker.'" I held up air quotes. "Really makes me wonder what an unethical hacker is."

"I don't know. Maybe the serial killer who watched you through your security cameras?"

"Valid point." After breaking the chocolate bar apart, I tossed another chunk to my lips. "But I think it's deeper than that with him. Like he uses hacking as some type of social justice."

"That gene, you did *not* miss."

"Really makes you wonder why Sam killed that guy, doesn't it?"

With a harrumph, he shrugged. "You're a family of vigilantes."

Chapter 19

"Hell, no." Simeon crossed his arms, glaring at my Subaru. "I'm not riding in that."

"What's wrong with it?" I dropped my backpack into the trunk and propped my hands on my hips. "It's all-wheel drive. Only got a few dozen thousand miles, and it's great on gas."

"And it's covered in flowers and butterflies." Simeon shook his head. "Absolutely not."

"Aw, is someone afraid of getting called a girl?" I pinched his cheek.

He pawed my hand away. "Do that again, Castle. I dare you."

Laughing, I walked around him to the rear door and opened it for Tempy. She jumped inside. As I shut it, I said, "Look, if this is about protecting your image, drive yours." I gestured to his Range Rover in the driveway beside Bentley's pickup. "But you already said you don't want Tempest screwing up your leather."

He cursed under his breath. "I won't forget this. You still owe me."

"We need to go back to the tally board. I'm pretty sure this makes us even for something."

"It wouldn't kill you to do it out of the kindness of your heart," Bentley said, walking past him with a suitcase. He loaded it into my trunk. "We *are* doing this to find a missing twenty-year-old girl."

This time, it was a grunt under his breath. "What heart?"

"Yeah, yeah," I said, circling around to the passenger side. "Keep playing the heartless criminal. We all know you're a big softy in there."

He shot me the bird. As I laughed, he turned to Bentley. "You sure you don't want to ride with me?"

"I'm good, man." Yawning, Bentley stretched his arms overhead. "My masculinity is not threatened by riding in a flowery car."

"My masculinity isn't either, but my image is." Simeon pulled off his jacket, revealing a band T-shirt underneath. "Which, yes, is important when we're going to meet these assholes."

"I'm not worried about my masculinity," Sam said, walking out my front door and checking the lock behind him. "But I don't know how I feel about being jammed in that tiny backseat with a hundred-pound German Shepherd. You mind if I ride with you, kid?"

Simeon looked his way, brow arched with confusion. "Who are you?"

Sam had gone inside to use the bathroom while Bentley and I loaded up the car. Simeon had only just arrived, so we had yet to make the introductions.

"My dad," I said, gesturing between them. "Sam, this is Simeon Gunn. Simeon, this is Sam."

Sam's head cocked to the side. "Any relation to Eric Gunn?"

"My dad." Simeon held out his hand. "And you're Sam Castle. Pretty sure my dad died bitching about the debt you owed him."

Face turning red, Sam chuckled and shook his hand. "You didn't inherit that debt, did you?"

"We'll call it square." After finishing the handshake, Simeon dropped his hand to his side. "You can ride with me, if you want."

"I think I'll take you up on that," Sam said.

"I'll lead the way," Bentley said, opening the driver's side door to my car. "Because if you do, Simeon, you're gonna beat us there by an hour."

* * *

"My name is Maddie Castle," I said into the phone at my ear, watching the Ohio countryside whizz by the passenger window. "This is going to sound weird, but I'm wondering if you might be able to help me. I'm a private investigator and someone I'm looking for was in your library a few months ago."

"Oh, my," the librarian said. She was older, I had to assume, by the sound of her voice. But compared to many librarians I'd chatted with over the years, friendly so far. "Can I ask what it's about?"

"A young girl went missing late last year," I said, sifting through my notes on my lap. "Her name is Daisy Miller, but I don't think she would've introduced herself as that. The case is very complicated, and how it traces back to your library isn't any simpler."

"Wow, never would've thought our little town would be involved in a great big scandal like this." She paused. "What is the scandal, exactly?"

Ah. That was why she was giving me her time. Not because she cared about the case, but because she cared about the drama. In fairness, I'd probably go stir crazy in a small town like hers too.

"I don't know if I'd call it a scandal. I believe Daisy's boyfriend is holding her against her will."

She gasped. "Goodness."

Rubbing the bridge of my nose, I rolled my eyes. "Yeah, it's not a great story. But I'm hoping to find a happy ending for it."

"Sure. So what do you need from me?"

"Anything would help. Does your library have security cameras?"

"We don't, but there are a few in the parking lot across the street. That's where most of the patrons park. If the girl was here all the way back in May, though, I'm not sure if we'll still have the footage. Technically, it isn't *ours*. It's the businesses' across the street. But I can talk to them. They probably would be willing to help. Do you know the exact date and time she was here?"

"I do, yes. I also have a picture of her I can send you. Could you give me your email?"

She gave it to me, ending with, "My name is Carol, by the way.

That way, if you need to call me back or something, you know who to ask for."

"Perfect. Thanks, Carol." Putting the phone on speaker, I clicked over to my email. "I'll send that file over right away."

"Great. I'll print this picture out and hang it up on our bulletin board. I'm gonna tell all my other librarians to give you a call if anybody recognizes her."

"No, don't do that." I spoke quickly, a wary tinge in my voice. "The man holding her captive doesn't know we have this lead. If he sees a missing person's flyer of her in your library, things could end very badly for Daisy."

"Of course. Right. What do you want us to do if we see her, then?"

"Call me or the police. Don't approach her. Don't act suspicious."

"Wow, okay. Sure." Carol's voice was somewhere between shocked and worried. "Is there anything else I can do to help?"

"Would you be able to check your computer histories for the date and time I sent you? I'm assuming people can't get onto the computers without logging in with a library card. She either used a fake one or somebody else's account. Either could help me find her."

"I'm not sure if I can do *that*. It goes against policy to share other people's information, you know. But here's what I can do." She lowered her voice. "I'll call whoever was using our computers on that date at that time and tell them they have an overdue book. That they need to come in and pay for it. Then, when they do, I'll see if it's her. If it is, I'll call you. If it isn't, I'll ask them to call you. Then they can give you whatever information they have."

I rolled my eyes and pulled the phone away from my face so she didn't hear my dramatic sigh.

For an older woman who watched lots of mysteries on TV, I was sure that sounded like an excellent plan. Because in fiction, everything just worked out. Even if it didn't make much sense, it just did.

In reality, the average person could give a shit less if they got a call from the library telling them they needed to come in and pay for an overdue book. If I got a call from my local library right now telling me to come in to pay for an overdue book, I'd spout some profanities and hang up. Most people would. Especially if they knew it wasn't true.

Dylan was going to rob me blind, because now I had another job for him.

"You know, that's a great idea, but I'm not sure it'll work," I said. "How about you just ask your staff to take a look at Daisy's picture, see if anyone recognizes her, keep an eye out for her yourself, and let me know if anything comes up?"

"Are you sure? I don't mind helping. It sounds fun, actually." She giggled. "And bringing that girl home, that would be lovely."

The order in which she mentioned that chain of events wasn't lost on me. "I'm sure. But I appreciate your help. Please keep me posted if you see her."

Suffice it to say that I was ready to get off that call. With a grunt of annoyance, I laid the phone on my lap.

"No luck?" Bentley asked.

"Just a bored old lady looking for some drama."

After finding my texts with Dylan, I typed out another one.

Hey, any chance you can find the names of everyone logged into the library computers in the time the stories were posted on that website?

"You don't think she can help?" Bentley asked.

"Probably not. I'm not that concerned with that library in Essex anyway. The most recent one we know Daisy was at is in Lancaster. First thing Monday morning, I want to be there. Talking to people over the phone is just about useless. She was there, between those four walls, not even a week ago. I'm gonna find something there. I know it."

"Yeah?" There was a certain melancholy edge to Bentley's tone.

Even if that had been normal lately, I still turned to face him better. "Yeah."

Still looking at the road, he laid his hand over mine. He nodded, twined our fingers together, then nodded again. As if trying to convince himself.

"You don't want to get your hopes up," I said. "I get that. It's probably best you don't. But my gut's usually right, Bentley. My gut says I'm gonna find her. And I'm going to find her because of that library."

"I believe that you believe that." He spared me a glance but turned right back to the road. "I want to believe it, too. I'm hoping like hell you're right."

"But?"

"*But* I'm not gonna hold it against you if you're wrong." Slowing for the stop sign we were approaching, he finally looked at me. There was still that dismal look in his eyes, but his hand got tighter, and there was something there that words couldn't describe. "I know how you are with a case. I know you're not gonna stop. I know you're going to keep looking, and I know you're never going to lose faith. Not until you have a good reason to."

"I don't think I see where you're going with this."

"I'm just saying that if it *is* a dead-end, like most of the leads we've gotten, I'm not gonna hold that against you." He lifted our hands with fingers curled together to his lips. After a gentle kiss on them, he said, "I haven't been doing that great lately, mentally. And I've already taken it out on you. Which is bullshit, because you're the only one who cares. You're doing more than anyone has to help me find her. But if you can't, I'm not gonna blame you.

Frowning, I shook my head. "I'm not mad about last night."

"I know. But I am. At myself, anyway." Behind us, someone honked. He shot them a look in the rearview, turned back to the road, and accelerated again. "I'm not gonna let it happen again. I won't raise my voice at you, and I won't take this shit out on you, because you don't deserve that. But also because it's just wrong. And the fact is, no matter how much I love Daisy, my life was hell for a long time because of her. I want to help her, I want to bring her home, but I'm not going to let her put wedges between me and the people I love again. If that pisses Grace off, then it pisses her off.

"But I've done a lot of emotional work to not be the guy I was last night. And it'll just get worse. That was a glimpse of who I am when I am putting someone else's bullshit above my own. Maybe I'm being selfish, but I just can't do it again. I finally have something good here. I've got a good job, a great kid, and an amazing girlfriend, and I'm not going to let all this shit ruin it. If we don't find her, we don't find her. I'm not going to let that ruin everything I've built."

I hadn't seen that coming.

Clearly, it had been preying on his mind, and I understood. I'd been in the same shoes before. No matter how much I'd loved my mom, I'd had to acknowledge that I couldn't let her life ruin mine.

"It's not selfish," I said, sweeping a loose brown curl behind his ear. "It's responsible."

A deep breath blew from his nostrils. "That's what my therapist says, too."

"You've got yourself a good one."

"Not according to Grace."

"Grace is a teenager who thinks she knows everything. Just like we all were at that age. One day, she'll get it."

"I sure as hell hope so." He kept his eyes on the road as we continued. We'd gotten off the highway a few minutes ago, and now the speed limit was only twenty-five. The ever-cautious Bentley had barely topped twenty. Simeon was probably there already. "I just don't get it. When I was her age, I understood. I sympathized with what my mom was going through, not my dad and his 'demon of addiction.'" He lifted a hand to air quote. "I had a *little* bit of empathy for him, but I felt a hell of a lot worse for everyone he screwed over."

The situation was different. But even if it weren't... "Daisy never did to Grace what your dad did to you."

"No, because I protected her from it. No one was there to protect me from all the shit my dad did. And yet, for finally giving my kid a better life, I'm the bad guy. It's not like I didn't want to give Daisy a good life, too. I fought like hell to. But I couldn't. I did everything I possibly could, and it wasn't enough. I couldn't save her. No matter how hard I tried, there was no saving someone who didn't want to be saved."

Apparently, I was serving as a therapist today. "You're right."

"And I don't understand how that makes me the villain."

"Because it's easier for Grace to be mad at you than it is to be mad at Daisy." It was the same reason I'd been in constant fistfights as a teenager. The person I'd wanted to hit, I couldn't. "Right now, she just wants someone to take the anger out on. You're the closest outlet."

He cursed under his breath, then gestured to a home ahead on the left. "Should've brought her along so she could take it out on them."

So this was it.

It looked exactly as I imagined it would. Drug dealers' homes usually looked the same. Of course, mine didn't look much different than theirs, so it wasn't a statement of judgment, but a simple fact.

A tiny ranch with rusted white siding. Rusted in the places that hadn't fallen off entirely, at least. Of the few windows on each wall, at least half were covered in plywood. Whether from a fight gone wrong or lack of maintenance after a storm, I didn't know.

No flowers grew outside, no trimmed bushes, and no pretty mulched beds. Knee-high grass, a shitty old car—also covered in rust—and a few broken lawn chairs. That was all that decorated the place.

"Yeah, well," I said, reaching around to unbuckle my seatbelt, "you're not just the closest outlet. You're the safest one."

"You think she wouldn't throw a few punches at these guys?"

"I know she would." Adjusting my shirt so that it met Simeon's dress code, I raised a shoulder. "But isn't it better she punches someone who isn't going to punch back?"

"I guess." Bentley grunted his annoyance, then huffed when he saw me adjusting my clothes. "You stay close in there, all right?"

To ease his mind, I squeezed his hand and planted a kiss on his cheek. "I promise."

But that was just to stroke his ego. I had a loaded gun on my hip and a hundred-pound German Shepherd trained in arrests in the backseat. No matter how noble, I didn't need Bentley's protection.

Chapter 20

"This wasn't what I pictured when you said you wanted to chill, Gunn," Kevin said.

Assuming he was Kevin. Judging by Bentley's clenched jaw and unusually dark eyes, I had to assume I was correct.

Although I hadn't seen a picture of Kevin yet, this guy matched the image in my mind. He wore a pair of loose blue jeans low enough to expose almost all of his navy blue plaid boxers. And that was all he wore. No shirt. No abs, and no beer belly, either. Also to be expected from someone addicted to methamphetamines. He was so thin, I could see his ribs beneath his skin. There were no muscles through his arms, far less than even I had.

His face was no different. Because of how skinny he was, his cheekbones were much more prominent. They made his pale blue eyes, and the dark circles beneath them, that much more off-putting. Unmaintained, patchy facial hair lined his sharp jaw. Thin, greasy blonde hair dangled against it.

If I squinted hard enough, I could almost imagine a time when he didn't look like this. Before the drugs had caused such malnutrition. Before his teeth had decayed and some had even fallen out.

Bentley had told me he was in his twenties, but I would've put him at forty. That was what drugs did. Some more than others. Meth, while not as immediately dangerous as opioids, was a slow killer. Not because of the drug itself, but because of the lack of sleep, malnutrition, and dehydration spread out over the length of the addict's use.

If I squinted, though, I could see what Daisy had. Maybe, before he'd gotten in too deep, there'd been some warmth in those blue eyes. Maybe that long hair had reminded Daisy of a young blonde Fabio at one point.

Simeon replied. "I told you I was bringing a friend."

"You didn't say it was *him*." He jammed a finger in Bentley's direction. "That asshole's not welcome in my—"

"He's not gonna say a word," I said, stepping between them. Not enough for Bentley to notice and push me aside, but just enough to lessen the tension. "Bentley is just here because he doesn't want me here alone. Which I think is ridiculous, because you want the same thing I do."

Snorting, he crossed his arms against his chest. "Yeah? And what's that?"

"To find Daisy," I said. "I'm a PI."

A scoff. "You brought a cop to my door, dude?"

"She's not a cop," Simeon said. "She used to be, but now she's a PI. They're not required to report anything they learn. She already knows who you are and what you do, and she doesn't give a shit."

"I have no idea where Daisy is." He started to shut the door.

I pushed my foot against it. "I know. You have nothing to do with her disappearance. But I think you might know something I don't. That's why I'm here."

"I don't know shit—"

"When was the last time you saw her?" Bentley asked. His voice was way softer than I expected.

"You said he wasn't gonna talk—"

"I'll shut up in a second," Bentley snapped. "But that day, when you showed up at my house searching for her, you said you'd seen her.

You didn't say where, and then you stormed off. I just need to know when the last time you saw her was."

"Watch the way you talk to me."

"Watch the way you talk to *him*," Simeon said, stepping forward. His expression was flat, voice no different. Emotionless, but firm. "I don't want this to turn into something, man. A girl you claim to care about vanished. We just have a couple of questions, and we'll be out of here."

Tracing his tongue along his teeth, Kevin released the door. He didn't step aside to invite us in, which I was grateful for. The smell wafting outside from in there was atrocious. A combination of burned plastic—aka meth—weed, and cat piss. Every trap house I'd ever been in smelled like some combination of weed and cat piss, and I had never understood it.

"I don't love that whore," Kevin said. "Haven't for a long time."

"You've got a lot of balls to call her that when you were the reason she became one," Bentley said.

Simeon shot him a look. One that said, *Shut your God damned mouth, dude.*

"Turning tricks is different than what she did." Kevin leaned against the doorframe. "It's one thing to spread your legs for money."

I fought the urge to snap back like Bentley had. Instead, I said, "Did she cheat on you?"

"Yeah, some rich asshole," Kevin said. "When I saw them together, I thought he was one of the Johns. Looked a lot like this guy we worked with every Tuesday night. Even drove the same car. But it wasn't Tuesday, and she was with him."

"When was this?" I asked.

"A week before she went missing or something?" He shrugged. "I don't know. Dude was a dick. I just tried talking to her, and he pulled a gun on me."

"Did you catch what kind?" I asked.

"A Glock, I think."

"And you're sure that he wasn't the john she took care of on Tuesdays?" I asked.

"Yeah, it just looked like it from a distance. When we were up close, it was obvious he was someone else. Just had a similar vibe."

I clicked my pen and jotted all of this in my notes as quickly as possible. "What do you mean by vibe? The way he held himself?"

"That, too, I guess," Kevin said. "But it was more to do with the way he dressed. Most of the guys we take care of are either like us or suburban dads. This guy dressed real nice. He had a beard, but a nice one. Like he went to the barber a few times a week to take care of it or some shit."

"By dressed nice, do you mean polos and slacks?"

"More like suits and ties."

Information I already knew. "But you said you recognized the car. Do you remember the make and model?"

"Real nice caddy. SUV though, not a sedan. I don't know what year, but it was all black."

This was the sort of intel I could've used months ago. Make and model of vehicle, physical description. They weren't much. Certainly not a name. But it was a start.

"And this was the last time you saw Daisy?" I asked. "When the guy she was with—"

"The guy she was *cheating on me* with."

Bentley scoffed.

"What?" Kevin asked, narrowing his gaze at him. "She was. We were together, and—"

"Don't I know."

"What? We weren't together? Is that what you're saying?"

"No, I know you were together. But you don't get to put a scarlet letter on her when you were forcing her to sell herself for your benefit."

I shot him a look. "Bentley."

"I didn't force her to do anything." Kevin's eyes darkened. "Everything that we did, we did together. We were a team, whether you like that or not."

"Bullshit," Bentley said. "You beat the shit out of her if she didn't do what you told her to. You—"

Kevin's laugh cut him off. "Oh, yeah. Like she was some helpless little princess. She hit just as hard as I did, and—"

"And that's supposed to make it okay?" Bentley stepped forward.

Sam yanked him backward.

Bentley jerked around to meet Sam's gaze. Bentley opened his mouth to speak, but Sam beat him to it. "We're gonna go wait in the car."

"No," Bentley replied.

"I think that's a good idea," Simeon said. He tossed Sam his keys. "Roll the windows down. Wouldn't want the animal to overheat."

Bentley glared.

"We'll be over in a few minutes," I said, then spoke in a quieter voice to Bentley. "Just go calm down."

Bentley's eyes were a little bit softer when they met mine, but he still gritted his teeth and shook his head. He spun around and headed toward the car. Sam had to jog to keep up with him.

I knew what Bentley was thinking. I knew what he was feeling. He wanted to defend his kid. I loved him for that, but he was a damned idiot.

If the circumstances had been different, if we had just run into Kevin somewhere, I'd look the other way. Hell, I'd even join the fight. But that wasn't the case here. This raging asshole, who everybody else here hated, who we all *knew* was a raging asshole, was an asshole with information. Information we needed. Information we had come here for.

Picking a fight with him wouldn't help anyone. Even if he deserved a good fight. Even if he deserved to have his ass handed to him. Even if he deserved to rot six feet under.

No matter what he deserved, this information could help us. There was a possibility of bringing Daisy home.

"Sorry about him." I wasn't. But unlike Bentley, I had experience interrogating people. Good cop, bad cop rarely worked. What often did in a situation like this, was getting down to their level. "He's pissed she's gone. You guys obviously didn't work out, and he was never the biggest fan of you, but I think now, he's kinda wishing he had encouraged your relationship more. Maybe then, she'd still be here."

Shoulders broadening, Kevin stood taller. "Yeah. Maybe she would be."

"I mean, I've read some of her old journals, and I know how much you meant to her," I said. "All those guys on the streets you protected her from. You were like her knight in shining armor. I'm sure if she could rewrite the story, she'd be standing beside you right now."

Kevin nodded, pushing out his chest.

Stroking his ego may have sounded like a bad idea, but men like this were simple. Especially because he was stupid. Getting Mr. Deluca to cooperate—when and if I ever found him—wouldn't be so easy. Should anything ever happen between me and Simeon, and I needed to manipulate him, I doubted I could. He was too smart for that.

But Kevin? Kevin was a trashy drug dealer, likely with an incredibly low IQ. All I had to do was make him feel a little bit better about himself and he would open up like the pages of a book.

"Anyway," I said, "I don't want to take up all your time. Just a few more questions though, if you don't mind?"

"Sure." Relaxing against the doorframe, he gave me a long, slow once over. "I've got all day."

"Great." I gave a soft, sweet smile. One I hoped looked genuine. Judging by Simeon's eye roll and smirk, it did the job. "So, this was the last time you saw Daisy? When she was with this man?"

"No, that was a few days before. The last time I saw her, I think it was two days before she was officially reported missing."

"And where was this?"

"Outside the clinic on the west side of the city. Ask Bentley, he knows the place." Kevin nodded toward Simeon's SUV behind us. "I always took her to her appointments. I don't know what she was there for. I tried talking to her outside, but she pulled out her mace. I dipped, but I saw her go inside. And that was the last time I saw her."

"Is this just a general health clinic?"

"Nah, it's one of those places for women, if you know what I mean."

I arched a brow at that. Was he suggesting she'd had an abortion? A rape kit, maybe?

"Right," I murmured. "You don't happen to have a picture of the guy, do you?"

"The guy who held a gun to my head?" he asked. I nodded. "No, it happened too fast. I was trying to talk to her after work, and I saw that she was walking with him. By the time I caught up, he already had the gun in his hand. I only saw him for a second before it was over."

Dammit. "Would you be willing to sit with a sketch artist?"

Kevin laughed. "I'm not working with the pigs."

"Of course not," I said. "But the cops aren't even investigating this. Just me and a friend of mine at the Pittsburgh PD, but we wouldn't have to get any cops involved. I can pay a sketch artist to meet you somewhere, and you sit with them for a couple of hours, and they draw while you describe the guy."

"I don't know." He glanced at Simeon, then shrugged. "Maybe I could do that. I'm not making promises. I'm pretty busy, but I might be able to swing it."

"Great," I said. "I think that's just about everything, but I really appreciate you helping me. If you think of anything else, give me a call." I extended my card his way. "I'm gonna get in touch with that sketch artist though, and maybe I can text you one day with details? Time, date, and place?"

"You can text me anytime." Again, his eyes flicked over me. This time, a smile twitched at the corners of his lips. "Give her my number, would you, Simeon?"

With a smile that said, *Oh, you sweet child*, Simeon said, "Sure, man."

As we spun around and descended the creaky steps, Simeon lowered his voice to a whisper. "Alright, I guess I see it."

"You guess you see what?"

"Why you're good at this," he said, voice still low. "It's a little weird, though. If I didn't know better, I'd swear that you were a psychopath."

Chapter 21

BENTLEY APOLOGIZED REPEATEDLY ON OUR WAY TO THE CLINIC. "I know I could've screwed this whole thing up fighting with him, but I was just so pissed."

I told him it was fine, and that I understood. Out of anyone on this earth, I'm the person who would understand. Then we'd go silent for a few moments, letting the music on the radio keep it filled. Sam would make a comment about a pretty bird out the window, or a coffee shop that looked cool, and we'd talk about that for a few heartbeats. Then silence would return. A few minutes later, Bentley's apology would repeat again, just in a different format. Each time, I responded in the same way. Even as we walked up the stairs to the clinic entrance, he apologized again.

Finally exhausted by the conversation, I spun to face him, took his face in my hands, and—probably too aggressively—said, "It's okay. I'm not mad at you. But talking about the same thing over and over again is driving me insane, Bentley. I got the information I needed, and hopefully it can help."

With a hard swallow, he nodded. "I'm s—"

I jabbed a finger in between us. "If you say you're sorry one more time—"

A half laugh escaped him. "I'm done. I promise."

And so we carried on inside.

It was a weekend, so I wasn't even sure if the place would be open. Much to my dismay, not only was it open, but it was also packed. What seemed like thousands of snot-covered, germ-ridden children took up all but one seat in the waiting room. Bentley offered the seat to me. Given the creamy mystery liquid on the black armrest, I declined.

Plus, my knee was killing me. Sitting only helped if I could lift my foot up and keep my leg straight. Obviously, not an option. My head was doing better though, and my rib wasn't hurting too badly today either.

The wrist was a whole other story. So long as I kept my forearm flush with my rib cage, it was fine. As soon as I lowered it to my side, all the blood seemed to rush there, making the swelling and resulting pain that much more intense.

But I wasn't ready to retire to the hotel for the night. So I padded across the linoleum floors, observing both the brochures on the walls as well as the demographics of the patients. The people here looked a lot like my neighbors. No one dressed particularly well. Only one woman wore any makeup. Everyone else looked like me. Baggy sweatshirts, stained jeans or sweatpants, and messy hair swept up into even messier buns.

The sad part about it was that, as Kevin had said, this was a gynecologist's office. It was all about women's health. But every seat was taken, primarily by children. There were at least twenty of them in here, and only six or seven women.

How tragic it was that we lived in a world where mothers couldn't spend an hour on their own health without caring for a sick child.

Most of the brochures discussed birth control options. There were a few on vaccinations, sexually transmitted diseases, and other general healthcare. Of course, termination was also on that list.

With that running through my mind, a few guesses formed about why we were here.

More importantly, why *Daisy* had been here.

"They're going to be a few minutes getting me the documents." Bentley sat quietly at my side again. "I had to sign off on a bunch of shit. Daisy did give me authorization to all her medical information, though, so they're allowed to share everything with me."

"Might be a lot to print off." Shutting the pamphlet about STD testing, I turned to face him. "She was probably in here often."

"That's what the receptionist said." He ran a hand down his beard. I realized how much longer it was than usual. "I guess that's a good thing, right?"

"Better she was in here than suffering when she didn't have to." I managed a smile for him. "I know this whole situation is horrible, but this place isn't the worst."

"Yeah, I know. She could've told the doctor something important. It might be in her notes somewhere."

True. But not the point I was making. "I meant that even though it's horrible, like a lot of Daisy's story is, she was here taking care of her health. That tells me something."

Bentley leaned against the wall on his left. Then his face screwed up. He yanked his arm away, saw a mystery glob of fluid, and grumbled under his breath. After grabbing a tissue from an end table and dabbing it away, he said, "What does it tell you?"

"That even though she was walking through hell, she still had some hope for herself."

He arched a brow, waiting for me to go on.

"The other times she came here, it was because Kevin made her." I kept my voice low. "It's not uncommon with pimps. It's a sort of quality assurance for their customers."

A greenish color crept into Bentley's cheeks.

"But this last time, she came by herself. Something was going on with her body, and she chose to see a doctor."

"Uh-huh," Bentley said.

"She came here to take care of herself, and that tells me that she doesn't want to give up. She's a fighter."

His eyes softened at that. With a deep breath, he looked at the wall before he slouched against it. "She's one of the strongest people I've ever met."

Dodging the snot on the wall, I leaned against it too. "It's okay to say that and still be angry."

A huff. He avoided my gaze.

"I'm just saying," I said.

"Is it though?"

I wasn't sure what he meant.

His eyes finally met mine. "Is it really okay to be so damned angry at her and still love her? Because I know she's a great person. She always was. But she's made some horrible decisions and I just want to shake her and scream in her face."

"I think that is a completely normal response," I said. "It really is okay to be angry at her and still love her. Being angry at someone is better than not caring for them at all."

"The thing is, I know *this* isn't her fault." Crossing his arms, he bit his lip and stared off into the distance. "This part. Her disappearance, her abduction. She didn't choose that. It's not her fault at all. It can't be." He huffed out a breath. "But you said that in the book, she met him at the club. I didn't want her to work there. She knew it was dangerous. And it's not her fault that it was dangerous. That's just the nature of that kind of work, you know?"

"Especially for someone so young."

"But that part, I do blame her for. Kind of, anyway." He rubbed his eyes with his thumb and forefinger. "She didn't have many options, I know that. She had a record. That made getting a job hard. But she was a pretty, young girl, of course she could get a job stripping. It was an easy option to make good money. Money she needed to pay her piece of shit boyfriend back."

He stood in the same moral grayness that I did.

In part, her actions had led her to where she was. But some of those actions hadn't been under her control. Statistically, she'd been doomed from the start. I didn't know who she was now, or who she would be if we got her back, but on the road she'd been headed on when she vanished, the outcome she was in was most probable.

And that was so screwed up. Even though she'd accumulated her own record, why did that happen? Because the system we lived in was broken.

Daisy's mom was an addict. She should have been removed from her custody before her death. Daisy had a sister and brother-in-law who desperately wanted her, who fought for her in court, who—yes—would've struggled financially to raise her but could have given her a decent life.

But biological parents had far too many legal protections. Child protective services always kept the children with the mother. If you asked a social worker, they'd say, "We remove the children when there's no other option," disregarding the fact that Daisy's mother had caused her far more harm than good.

At one point, she still could've lived a normal life. She would've had an estranged, drug addicted mother, but she also would've had chorus concerts, summer camps, and a bedtime. Her new parents would've been very young, and they may have struggled financially, but neither of them would have offered her a meth pipe at the ripe age of fourteen.

Bentley may not have seen it, but that's why he was angry. He was angry at the system, as he had every right to be. All it did was create broken, damaged people. Like me, and him, and Daisy.

Some of us were able to escape the worst of it, like he and I had, but we were the anomaly. Daisy was the rule.

"You know what I think?" I asked, voice soft.

"I bet you're going to tell me," Bentley said.

"That you and Grace have something in common."

"Aside from our charming smiles and sweet brown eyes?"

I chuckled. "Those too."

"What else?" A fraction of a smile tilted the corner of his lips.

"The way you feel," I said. "Your anger. Grace takes it out on you, because that's safest. And you take it out on Daisy, because she's not here, and you're not really hurting anyone with it."

There went his smile. Another deep sigh. "That therapy thing, it's really working for you, huh?"

"It ought to be for forty bucks a week."

A dry, humorless laugh. He pushed some hair from his face, grabbing a fistful at the back. "If we get her back—"

"When we get her back."

He frowned but continued. "*When* we get her back, I won't take it out on her. I'll try to encourage her, if she'll let me, but I won't tell her everything I think. I did, when she was younger, and I don't think that ever helped anything."

"I wasn't there, so I can't say," I said. "But that's as much as you really can do. You can lead the horse and all that."

"Never could get her to drink, though."

"As long as you show her the water, the rest is up to her."

"But how do I accept that?" Squinting, he raised and dropped his shoulders in defeat. "I think this is what Grace doesn't understand. No matter how much I did for Daisy, it was never enough. I was compensating for what she wouldn't do herself. And I have sympathy for what she went through and everything, but if we get her back, and it's the same old shit, what am I supposed to do?"

"Start with not enabling her," I said. "It was one thing when she was a kid. She had no one else. She was making bad choices, but you couldn't change it. It's not like you had custody of her. The most you did to enable her then was let her sleep on your couch when she ran away from a horrible foster home."

"Enabled her a lot more than that when she was out of the foster system," he said under his breath.

"So don't do that again," I said. "You're doing as much as you can to help Daisy now. You're here. You've got a PI. You're trying to get her out of the cage she's stuck in, and that's because this isn't her fault. You would do this for anyone because there's right and there's wrong, and someone is wronging her."

Biting his lip again, he nodded slowly.

"But once she's out, don't let her drag you back into her shit," I said. "Don't let her bring her shady boyfriends come around. If she uses and has no intention of getting clean, don't give her money. Don't do favors for people like Kevin to clear her debt. Stop giving all of yourself to somebody who's taking advantage of it."

Exhaling again, his lips vibrated in a trill. "You make it sound so easy."

"I think it will be," I said. "Because if anything is a wake-up call, it's what Daisy has gone through for the last few months. When she gets out, when she's home, I think she'll be more grateful than ever for you. But if she's not, even if it pisses Grace off, you're the parent. You have to do what's best for your kid. Even if that means cutting her off from someone who is wrecking her life."

"You're right," he murmured. "My therapist says the same thing. But it feels like picking one or the other, doesn't it?"

"It feels like you have two horses at a river, and one of them's drinking, and the other's laying down and dying. You need to get back on the road, but you can't wait forever. So you leave the one who's dying. You hope eventually they'll drink and catch up, but if they don't, that's their choice. You have to save the one who doesn't want to lay down and die."

His eyes flicked between mine for a moment. Then he nodded again. Like if he did so enough times, he would convince himself that it was something he could do.

But I believed she would wake up. No matter who she'd been when she vanished, what she'd been through there was transformative. I was sure when this was over, all she would want was a sense of normalcy. Safety.

"Bentley Roycroft," the receptionist called from the other side of the room.

"Think I should hang back?" I asked.

"Pretty sure whatever I do with that paperwork once I have it is up to me." He started that way and gestured for me to follow him.

When we made it to the desk, the woman on the other side extended a stack of paperwork at least three inches thick. "The information from her latest visit is on top. This is just from 2022 and 2021. We have more, but you were most concerned with her recent appointments, right?"

"Yes, ma'am," Bentley said, accepting the papers. "Would you be able to email me the rest?"

"Yeah, but probably not until next week. I'm about to take a vacation, and nobody else is gonna want to sift through all of this."

"Can't say I blame them," I said. "But we really appreciate this."

"No problem." She eyed the stack of paperwork for a moment. "You might want to go sit down somewhere before you read through all that."

Encouraging.

* * *

Bentley had handed me the paperwork. I waited until we were in the car to look at it. For all I knew, we were about to find out she had HIV. That wouldn't be easy news to accept.

"Is that everything?" Sam asked, roughing up Tempest's scruff in the backseat.

"It's what we need," I said. Turning to Bentley, I softened my voice. "You want me to read it first?"

Breathing a bit unevenly, unable to hold my gaze. He only nodded in answer.

With a deep breath of my own, I scanned over the first page. Basic intake information. Normal heart rate, normal temperature, normal blood pressure.

I flipped to the next page.

And my stomach spun.

Patient's last menstrual cycle began 8/1/21. Pregnancy test ordered. Urinalysis positive.

"Now it makes sense," I murmured. I leafed through the rest of the page, but it was the information any doctor would give a patient who they just confirmed was pregnant. Follow-up in two weeks, get blood work to confirm HCG levels, start prenatals.

"What makes sense?" Bentley asked.

Holding up the document, a smile curved the edges of my lips. "This is what he's using against her. This is why he lets her out in public. This is why it took him *so long* to let her out in public. This is why the first story was only uploaded in May."

"And what is *this*, exactly?" Sam asked.

"She was pregnant when she disappeared," I said, passing the document to Bentley. "When he leaves her at libraries to post her stories, he takes the baby. That's his collateral. That's why she doesn't ask anyone for help."

Chapter 22

We checked in at a Holiday Inn. There were a few restaurants nearby, and we were only staying for the night, so it was plenty accommodating. On the way there, Bentley hadn't spoken a word.

I wasn't sure I understood why. Why did this news leave him speechless when other news hadn't? In Daisy's line of work, pregnancy was just a job hazard. I was surprised it hadn't happened sooner.

On top of that, it was good news. In my book, anyway.

When I was a cop, I'd seen a lot of young girls on the streets. Some of them didn't change when they became mothers, but many did. Assuming that Daisy was forced to remain sober over the last year while in captivity—which made sense, considering Mr. Deluca was the least supportive of her habit—I had hope. The fact that she was alive, that she was now a mother, and that she was sober, upped the stakes.

In captivity on her own for so long, she may have given up hope. But instincts were unavoidable. When she looked at that child, regardless of everything else she was going through, her will to keep the baby alive would be strong. She couldn't depend on the other adult around to care for it. That meant she had to care for it herself.

It was possible this child was the only reason she was alive. More so, he likely used the baby as collateral. That was the reason she was able to get us messages.

But I supposed all of this was sensitive for Bentley. However he handled it was okay with me.

Still, I had come here for a job. We'd attended to half of it, to the best of my ability, and now it was time to tackle the other half. Greta Jenkins.

I left the guys at the hotel, loaded Tempest into my car, and set the GPS. She lived in a suburb outside of the city, so it was only a twenty-five minute drive.

A drive my leg appreciated. Because Ohio was so flat compared to mountainous Pennsylvania, there was far less accelerating and braking.

Until I got into Greta's neighborhood, at least. Much to my dismay, she lived atop a hill in a lower-end suburb. The kind where the houses probably sold for $150,000 to $200,000 versus $300,000 to $500,000.

Although many homes were similar, they weren't quite as cookie-cutter as the suburb Emily lived in. They were smaller, but the yards were a bit bigger, giving the occupants room to have interesting gardens and pools. Rather than the monochromatic look of higher end suburbs, this was the kind of suburb where there was no HOA dictating what color you could paint your fence.

Greta's house was cute and quaint. Little window boxes lined each window, peonies and marigolds erupting from them all. Navy blue shutters and trim lined the white siding. The front yard, bordered by a small driveway to the garage in the back, wasn't expertly landscaped, but was coated in water guns, a few kites, and a slip and slide.

Maybe not as fancy as Emily's place, but just as well-loved.

After parking at the curb, I walked up the winding cement path to the door with Tempest at my side. Even from out here, the hustle and bustle of family life sounded on the other side. Children played inside and sang along to Disney songs floating from the TV speakers.

I hated to interrupt on a Sunday, but I needed to wrap up this case so that I could focus on Daisy's.

I knocked, and a woman called, "Quiet down, guys!" Her footsteps followed. Then the door swung open.

She looked just as she did in her social media photos. Her salt-and-pepper hair was pulled into a messy bun on top of her head. The green of her eyes was as warm and joyful as the toys in her front yard and the happy baby on her hip.

"Can I help you?" she asked, looking behind me and then at the dog at my feet.

"I hope." Smiling, I extended my hand. "Are you Greta Jenkins?"

"I am." She shook the hand I offered. "And who are you?"

"You don't know me, if you're looking for a clue." Lowering my hand to my side, I searched for the right way to phrase this. "My name's Maddie Castle. I'm a private investigator. And you're not in any trouble, but you came up in a case I'm working, and I was just hoping you could lend me some insight."

Confusion pinched her forehead. "What's the case about?"

"Brandon Adams." The warmth in her eyes and the pink in her cheeks disintegrated. I half expected her to close the door in my face, but she stood there frozen. "He doesn't know I'm here, so you aren't in any danger. I'm sure this is a shock, but I just think that you have information I need. I really hate to be a bother, and I can even pay you for your time, but—"

"Are you working for him?" Her voice was low, so that no one else in the house could overhear. "Or are you trying to take him down?"

"The latter."

She held the baby a bit tighter, then nodded. "There's a park two streets over. Meet me there in half an hour?"

* * *

A BASEBALL FIELD WITH A CEMENT TRAIL AROUND IT, A JUNGLE gym, a parking lot, a pavilion, and some trees surrounding the edges of it all. Typical neighborhood park. One that Tempest really appreciated walking around. She had been in the car a lot today, and I knew she was missing her exercise. So was I.

By the time Greta pulled up with her minivan full of children, who all darted for the jungle gym, I was finally getting some relief in my knee. Which meant it was time to sit back down again at one of the tables in the pavilion.

After offering me a juice box, which I happily accepted, Greta wasted no time. "Where do you want me to start?"

"The beginning, I guess." I took a sip from my juice box. Apple. Damn, I couldn't remember the last time I drank apple juice. Made a mental note to buy some when I got home. "I know you were his mistress, but I don't know how that started."

"How do rich men always find their mistresses? I was his intern. Unpaid. Lucky me." Laughing dryly, she dabbed some spit up from the cheek of the baby boy in her lap. "I was young and impressionable. I thought it could help me get started in my career. My dad used to say that unpaid internships were modern slavery, and I agree with that now, but what can you do, you know?"

"Sure," I said. "What kind of business were you hoping to go into?"

"Real estate. I did eventually get my license, and it's what I do now." A prideful smile. "But I was still in community college back then. Barely eighteen when I started working for him. Not even nineteen when the affair began. I'm sure you know the story. Man insists he's going to leave his wife for you. You're everything to him. He buys you nice things, takes you to nice places. They're just going through a lot right now, and he'll leave her soon. Then you'll have your happily ever after."

"Obviously not how it panned out," I murmured.

"Obviously." Sighing, she stared out at her kids playing on the jungle gym. "I was twenty when he got me pregnant. And I was so excited." She laughed, but there was no humor in it. Perhaps a bit of contempt. "He'd been telling me he was gonna leave her for so long, I was sure this would be it. This would be why. It was finally enough."

Greta sipped a juice box as well. When she got to the bottom, and it made a slurping sound, she set it back down.

I did my best to give her a sympathetic expression.

"Anyway, there was this guy working for him. He wasn't on his books. Not any of the legal ledgers, anyway. I'd just seen him around. When we went on dates, sometimes Brandon would stop at an ATM, and then we would drive into some shady alley, and he'd get out, and he'd give the guy money, and then we would go on our date. Once, he showed up at the office. I was the intern, so I spoke with him, and that's where I learned his name. Devon Abbott. That's why I recognized him when he crashed into my car."

Devon Abbott. I jotted that down. "Did you just see him as he hit you?"

"No, he got out to check on me." Still gazing at her children, her voice got quieter. "I was barely conscious. But I remember him checking my pulse, and I swear I heard him crying when he said he was sorry. He probably didn't realize I was awake, but he said something like, 'I didn't have a choice.'"

"You think Brandon blackmailed him into doing it?"

"I wouldn't put it past him. Especially with the type of person Devon was." She shrugged, still staring off into the distance. "I googled him. This was years ago, so I don't know what he's up to now, but back then, he had a lot of drug charges. I wouldn't be surprised if he had done something worse. Brandon found out about it and dangled it over his head so he could make him his devious little henchman."

"From what I've gathered about Brandon, I wouldn't be surprised either."

"Real piece of work." After digging around in her picnic bag on the ground, she held out a bag of potato chips. "You want some?"

"Don't mind if I do. Thanks." I accepted and tore the bag open. "What kind of dirty work did Brandon do?"

"I never knew the details. That's probably why the cops didn't do much when I accused him of orchestrating the accident." Greta popped a chip into her mouth. When she was done chewing, she said, "But shady people—not unlike Devon—would stop by the office sometimes. Once, a guy came in with a baseball bat and destroyed everything in Brandon's office. I overheard him talking with accountants. There was a room in the back of the building that no one had a key to except for Brandon. It wasn't his office. It was a windowless, dark room. But sometimes, if he and I were there late, people would come in through the back door, and they'd move boxes in and out of that room. Still no idea what it all was. Stopped asking questions after the accident. I figured it was time for me to move on with my life, but I have no doubt. That man has always been dirty."

Interesting. None of it was surprising, and it explained why the FBI was already watching him, as Harper had told me. But it still wasn't pointing me anywhere.

"What is this case, exactly?" Greta asked. "If you just want to put Brandon away, let me know if any charges are filed, and I will testify against the bastard. But if you're still in the process of building a case, everything I have is hearsay. Unless you point me in a certain direction."

"Someone has been burning his properties," I said. "That is, he's lost millions of his investment dollars. The last fire was his building in Pittsburgh. Whoever it was, they spray-painted 'murderer' all over his office."

"Wasn't me, just to clarify." She smirked around the straw of her juice box. "But that does ring a bell. Not long before I got pregnant, there was something to do with a fire? I don't remember all the details, but I remember the location. It was somewhere in Fayette County. Brandon really wanted this piece of land. He had already bought up most of the street in this town, and he wanted to build a shopping center. But there was a woman who wouldn't sell. A few months go by, and suddenly, that land is available."

A knot balled up in my chest. "After a mysterious fire burned it?"

"Yep." She tossed another chip into her mouth. "The owner of the land, the one who wouldn't sell? She died inside."

Chapter 23

When I got back to the hotel, a new manager was on duty. He gave me a hard time about Tempest at first. Even though I wasn't legally obligated to disclose my disability with anyone, it often came to a point where I had to. Like I did today. Rolled up my pant leg, showed him the massive scar on my knee, the consequential swelling, and he shut up pretty quick.

Just as I opened the door to the room, the scent of garlic and pasta sauce, paired with just the slightest bit of chlorine, floated to my nose. The place was nothing special. Just two queen beds, a small bathroom, red and orange checkered carpet, boring white walls with cheap photos of flowers, and a TV on the wall facing the beds.

On one of them, Bentley lay on his side, scrolling on his phone. On the other, Sam lay with his feet at the head, a pizza box strewn out before him, all atop a white beach towel. Wearing a pair of swim trunks, he chomped into his slice and watched some sport or another playing on the TV.

"Hey, kid," Sam said. "Did you get any leads?"

"A few things, yeah." I collapsed beside Bentley. As I pulled off my shoes, he stretched over to kiss my cheek. "Did you enjoy the pool?"

"He did a back flip into it and almost busted his head open," Bentley said.

"Almost only counts in horseshoes and hand grenades," Sam said. "It was a blast. I haven't been swimming in twenty something years."

"It's been a while for me, too." I stretched toward Sam's bed for a piece of pizza. "But I want to leave here first thing tomorrow morning, so I don't think I'll have time to check it out while we're here."

"Aw, you should for a little while." Sam gave me a sad face. I wanted to say it was parental, but it was almost childish. "You're young. Enjoy your youth while you still have it."

"When I'm done with these cases, I'll take a nice break." Tempest trotted past me and jumped up on the bed between me and Bentley. "Tonight I need to do research. Also need to relay everything I found to Harper, then try to spend some time looking through missing persons again. And I should revisit that poem. There's gotta be a message in it. It doesn't match the same code Daisy used last time, though. And that's what I don't understand. Why change it? Did he figure it out? But what difference would that make? Why would he still let her go out in public?"

"Good questions," Bentley said, scratching up and down Tempest's back. "But maybe focus on the things you do know first. Like this research you need to do."

"This is why I keep you around." I wagged my finger in his direction, speaking between bites of pizza. "You keep my head on straight."

A chuckle. "Did you learn anything today? With the mistress you interviewed, I mean."

"Apparently, twenty years ago or so, a building that Brandon was trying to buy mysteriously burned down," I said. "The woman who refused to sell it to him was inside. She died."

"That would explain the whole murderer thing," Sam said.

"My thought exactly."

* * *

Laptop in one hand, pizza in the other, I started down the rabbit hole.

First, I googled, "House fire, Fayette County, 2006." Of course, there were about a thousand house fires in Fayette County during that year.

Okay, not a thousand. Twenty-eight. That was still a lot to sift through.

There was a fat chance I would get a hit, but I searched each of those documents for the name Brandon Adams, Brandon, Adams, or Prime Point Realty, the name of his development firm. No luck there either.

Then, I searched for "2006, Brandon Adams."

Not to my surprise, there were dozens of articles. In each of them, I looked for the county. Some in Allegheny, some in Westmoreland, some in Somerset, and only a handful referencing Fayette County.

Eventually, I got a hit.

Town Council Approves Shopping Center

On 6/15/05, real estate developer Brandon Adams requested permission to break ground on Prime Point Plaza, a shopping center in Jefferson Township.

It went on to discuss why the town council had argued over approval, something to do with traffic from the highway entering their small town, which was all irrelevant to me. What *was* relevant was the address. Now that I had the name of the shopping center, Prime Point Plaza, I could search the history of the place.

I plugged the address into Google, and within moments, I had my answer.

Fire Takes Shop Owner's Life

Last night, a gas fire started in Curiosity Cabinet. Witnesses say the owner Michelle Nelson, 55, lived in an apartment over the store. A neighbor called 911 around 4 AM, but the fire department believes the fire began over an hour before.

Michelle passed in her sleep due to smoke inhalation.

THAT NAME SOUNDED FAMILIAR. NELSON. I COULDN'T PLACE where I knew it from, but I had heard it before. Heard it, or seen it, or something.

Had someone with that last name come up in my research? No, Autumn's wife's last name was Harris. Emily's family was Foster and Scott. There was no Nelson associated with Greta either.

Where did I know this name from? Searching only "Nelson" on Google would amount to thousands of results. How could I narrow it down? Maybe Google wasn't the solution here. Maybe I needed to go back to my notes. I always jotted down last names.

Leafing through them, I thought back on everyone I had interacted with during this case. The woman who'd died in the fire was in her fifties, meaning she would be approaching eighty by now. It stood to reason that whoever wanted vengeance for her death would've been younger. No one in their eighties could've carried me out of that building.

I'd already discovered it was a woman. Then again, I hadn't interacted with many men on this case. The first one to come up was Devon, who I only learned about today. It was possible he knew about the fire, or maybe that he had set it, and he was out for vengeance against Brandon, but that still didn't explain where I knew the name Nelson from.

While I was thinking about him, it didn't hurt to do some digging on him too. I popped "Devon Abbott" into Google. The last name was common enough, but dozens of results still flashed across my screen. Probably wasn't the Devon Abbott who died two years ago in Erie, PA. Doubtful it was an eighteen-year-old, valedictorian from Pike county either.

After enough digging, I found a short article.

Allegheny County Man Arrested for Drug Trafficking

Sounded like my guy.

In 2013, Devon was arrested for moving over three-hundred pounds of cannabis across the New York, Pennsylvania border. Currently serving a several decades-long sentence that would amount to a life sentence. No way would he outlive the years he was given.

Valuable piece of information. Anyone on a sentence like that was easily swayed into a testimonial for a shortened sentence.

My phone buzzed in my pocket. Dylan's name flashed across the screen.

His text read, *Here's the list of library patrons who were logged in within a two-hour timeframe of when the girl posted that story. You should be able to find their home addresses on your own.*

As far as this Brandon goes, I couldn't find anything. If anyone is blackmailing him, they're doing so physically, not virtually. I was able to get into his home security cameras, though. Two weeks ago, a letter was left near his property. She must've walked, or taken an Uber or something, because I only have a glimpse of her walking up to his gate. There's nothing distinguishable about the image, but maybe you'll see something I don't. I'm attaching it here.

I'll send another invoice but considering how much work you've given me in the last few days, I am offering a small discount. No need to thank me. But you're welcome.

There was no stopping my laugh. I texted back, *You're the best. Thanks a million.*

I scrolled further down and waited for the multimedia message to load. When it did, I squinted at the image. It was zoomed in, so I couldn't make out much of the street or Brandon's home, but one thing was obvious. A figure wearing a black hoodie and black sweatpants was bending down to set something in front of Brandon's high-end, wrought-iron gate. They were small, petite in stature, which led me to believe they were a woman, as I suspected.

Like Dylan said, there was nothing distinguishable about this image. Nothing obvious, anyway.

But when I zoomed in, when I looked closer at her clothing, I noticed something that had my brow arching of its own accord. She was in all black, but there were little strands of white all over her.

I looked down at myself in the dim glow of the TV. My baggy sweatshirt and sweatpants were also covered in little strands of white. Dog fur. Just like almost every other dog owner always had on their clothes. I made regular jokes about the fact that I carried Tempest with me everywhere I went because I was eternally covered in her hair.

Who had come up while I was working this case who also had a dog?

Now I knew where I'd seen that name.

In Brandon's office. On his receptionist's name plaque.

Olivia Nelson.

Dog hair was hardly cause for a warrant. But it was enough for me to deep dive.

I hopped back over to Google, "Olivia Nelson."

Graduated top of her class from Penn State for business management. So advanced, in fact, that she made the Dean's list. Penn State may not have been Ivy League, but it was a damn good school. And even though the job market was horrible right now, with credentials like that, why was she working for Brandon as a receptionist? Especially when he was a real estate developer, and a degree in business management suggested she wanted to run her own?

That was about as much as I could find on Google. Obvious next stop was social media.

She was an older Gen Z, having just graduated last year, so I wasn't surprised that she wasn't on Facebook. She was, however, on Instagram. And no, her account was not private.

She didn't have a whole lot of followers, only a couple thousand, which was about average. Significantly less, and I would worry this was a fake account. Significantly more, and we would be in an entirely different ball game. She would have garnered enough attention online to destroy Brandon without ever needing to face him directly.

Olivia's photos were typical for a woman her age. Dinners out with friends, pictures in clubs and at concerts, and many of her dog. A very cute, very drooly, St. Bernard. Whose hair surely lived on her lounge clothes twenty-four hours a day, seven days a week.

Photos like those went on for roughly a year. I could have stopped scrolling, but I didn't. Not until I made it to the end of someone's social media. Only then could I cross them off my list.

And Olivia was not someone I could cross off the list.

Eleven months ago, she posted a photo of a polaroid from the late 90s or early 2000s. An older woman, who I recognized from the article I had read about the fire, holding a baby. The next slide was of the same older woman with a toddler—Olivia, I had to assume. They stood outside before a field of flowers. The child was perched on the woman's hip.

The next slide was the woman's tombstone.

Michelle Nelson

1952-2006

The caption read,

Words will never be enough to describe how much I miss you, Gran. I think about you every day. Your life was cut off too soon, and it's not fair. You were all I had left, then you were gone in the blink of an eye. It's not fair that someone so good, so pure, so kind, was taken from this world too soon. You took me in when Mom died, and I will be forever grateful for the years we spent together. They weren't many, but I remember you like I remember the back of my hand. I'll never forget you. I'll never forget that you deserved so much better than you got.

Was it an admission of guilt? No. Was it enough for a warrant? Also, no, but I didn't want either of those, anyway.

I only wanted answers.

Reaching over, I flicked on the bedside lamp. "I hope you guys got enough sleep because we gotta get home."

Chapter 24

NEITHER BENTLEY, SAM, NOR TEMPEST WERE PLEASED WITH MY rushed check out. It was 2 a.m., so I couldn't blame them. The alternative was that I left them here without a vehicle since Simeon had left the day before. They weren't fans of that idea either.

"Why can't you just wait and talk to her in the morning?" Bentley had asked.

"Yeah, what's the rush?" Sam had asked.

When I had a lead, I followed it. I didn't wait until it was a convenient time for me. There was no precise timeline I needed to have this done by, but I wouldn't have been able to sleep if I tried. I needed to get to Olivia, get her side of the story, and see if she had anything concrete I could use against Brandon.

They still weren't pleased with my reasoning, but they loaded up into the car. While they napped, I called Harper. Who also wasn't pleased with being woken at 2 a.m.

"Why?" was how she answered the phone. "Why can't you just be a normal person and call during normal waking hours, Maddie?"

"Because I know who the arsonist is," I said. "And, no, I'm not going to tell you who. Because technically, I don't know. I think. It's a theory.

It's a good theory, and it makes complete sense, but that's not the point."

An exasperated, annoyed whine. "Then why are you calling me at two in the morning?"

"Because I think I know how we can get Brandon." Clicking on my cruise control, I fished around for my drink in the center console. "I met with Greta."

She yawned. "Who's Greta?"

"Brandon's old mistress. Well, not old, but the affair is old. It's the one that ended when she got pregnant, lost the baby in a mysterious hit-and-run accident, and Brandon's wife mysteriously killed herself."

"It's too early for this shit."

"She said there was this guy. Devon Abbott. He did weird shit for Brandon. Brandon would also pick up money from ATMs and hand it to him in dark alleys."

"Okay?"

"But ten years ago, Devon went to jail for drug trafficking," I said. "Just a little weed. Okay, a lot of weed. Like, several hundred pounds a lot. But still, not the end of the world."

"Are you going to get to the point anytime soon, Maddie?"

"He's in there for life. Technically sixty years without the possibility of parole, but he was arrested when he was forty. So if he makes it out, he'll be a hundred by then. Meaning, basically, life sentence."

Harper yawned. "And?"

"And he might know about a murder, *the* murder, that led to the fires," I said. "Plus, whatever else Brandon was doing. I mean, the FBI doesn't have a case open against him for nothing, right?"

"Right." She still sounded half-asleep, so I wasn't sure if she was following me. "Wait, who did he kill?"

"A woman. A woman in Fayette County in 2006. He was trying to buy her land. She refused to sell, and then she died in a mysterious house fire. He wanted the land to build a shopping center, worth millions, but she wouldn't budge, and then she just dies?"

"I love you, Maddie, I really do, but I really wish you'd get your head on straight before you call me in the middle of the night."

Which was fair enough. I was a little erratic. And sleep deprived. But excited. Excited because this was a weird case, but I was almost a hundred percent certain it was solved. "I'm sorry. I know it's a lot. I should've called you earlier, but I didn't put it all together until just now."

"Just start over."

"Two decades ago, Brandon wanted to build a shopping center. This was in a small town, where there were a lot of old shop owners, and most of them were willing to sell for the right price. But Michelle Nelson didn't want to sell. She kept refusing. With her refusal, he couldn't build the shopping center."

"Okay. And then she died?"

"In a mysterious fire, yeah," I said. "He either set the fire himself or hired someone to do it. When the woman died, the land went up for sheriff's sale. He then bought the land and built the shopping center."

"I would definitely call that motive," Harper said, sounding more alive now. "But you know what a judge is going to say. None of this is enough. You have no evidence. Just a theory."

"Unless we have a witness, and I believe we do. A witness who I'm sure will talk to get out of life in prison."

"This is where the Devon guy comes in."

"Right," I said.

The whistle of tea brewing sounded in the background. "What makes you think he witnessed it?"

"Greta," I said. "After their affair, when she told Brandon she was pregnant, Devon hit her with a stolen car. She lost the baby, and she was in and out of consciousness throughout the accident, but she remembers Devon checking on her. He apologized and said he didn't have a choice."

"Brandon was blackmailing him."

"That's what I'm thinking. Which means he'll need some type of immunity deal for whatever he testifies about. But if the FBI is involved, the DA will probably sign off on it."

"Especially if he hit a woman and killed her unborn child."

Yeah, I supposed that compromised our witness. "True, but that's not part of the murder. Not the one with an actual body. Miscarriage doesn't count."

"Not in PA," she said. "What makes you think he set the fire?"

"Devon was his henchman," I said. "If Devon didn't do it, he knows who did."

"And even if he doesn't, he'll testify to just about anything to get out of life in prison."

"So, what do you need from me?" Harper asked, taking a slurp of her tea. "Deal with the DA, dependent on what Devon can tell us? And a meeting with Devon, obviously."

"That should cover it."

"Want to relay the information you gathered on Daisy's case now though?"

"I can, but I figured you'll be kinda busy calling the DA and the FBI and all that."

"Unlike you, I don't make those sorts of phone calls in the middle of the night," she said. "But in case I need help from any higher ups on either of these cases, it's better I have all the information now."

I took a deep breath and began.

* * *

Harper and I talked for another hour or so while Bentley slept in the passenger seat and Sam slept in the back with Tempest. We discussed my theories about Daisy, all of which she agreed with. It made sense, but we didn't have any proof. Just like I didn't have any proof of what Brandon had done.

That was so often the trouble with police work. We all knew what was really going on, but we had no evidence to convict the perpetrator.

Even when we did have the evidence, it often wasn't enough. Maybe for an arrest, but not for conviction.

Talking kept my mind occupied on the dark, winding highway. Certainly kept me awake, although I doubted I would sleep regardless. About halfway through my trip, Harper decided it was close enough to a decent hour. She said she would try to contact the DA and the agents in Quantico working on Brandon's case. As soon as she heard back, she would call me.

I'd already crossed the PA state line by then, so the rest of the trip was relatively easy. It was a little before 7 when we pulled into the trailer park. Bentley kissed me goodbye, Sam loaded into his truck, I let Tempest do her business in the yard, fed her a quick bowl of kibble, and got right back in the car.

Much to my relief, my knee wasn't bothering me. Maybe that was why I liked this job. When the adrenaline hit, it was like I was able-bodied again.

The drive to Olivia's was shorter than the one I'd taken from Columbus, but at least I knew these roads well. She was in Allegheny County, only a few roads over from where I used to live with Ox. Our condo—now my condo—was a bit nicer than Olivia's place. Still, it wasn't half bad.

Like her grandmother, Olivia didn't live in an apartment complex. Instead, her apartment was above a small bakery named Sugar and Spice. Although freshly painted, probably remodeled inside, it was an old building, judging by the intricate molding at the top and around the windows. Three gargoyles even sat on the roof, overlooking the street below.

The name *Nelson* stamped on the mailbox off to the right of the building assured me I was in the right place. A flight of stairs took me to her apartment entrance, which had surely been a pain when moving in, but from the outside, was eclectic. Iron was molded into decorative spindles with a bar on top that lined the steps. They were almost a ninety-degree angle. Not easy to climb, but Tempest was a reliable partner. She supported every step I took and, with the help of the handrail, I made it to the top.

At the old red metal door, I exhaled slowly. Everyone knew I wasn't the best at handling sensitive subjects. This obviously was one. Under my breath, I rehearsed what I was going to say several times in hopes that she wouldn't shut the door in my face as soon as she realized I knew.

With butterflies in my tummy, I knocked.

Dog barks erupted on the other end.

Olivia's voice followed, telling him to quiet down. A few moments passed. I waited.

The brass peephole flipped open from the other side, and her eyes met mine. "Miss Castle?"

"Maddie, please."

Speaking over the barking dog, she said, "What are you doing here?"

"Hoping to talk to you." I rolled onto my tiptoes, hoping to see the dog inside, but the peephole was too small. "Could we come in?"

A halfhearted, nervous laugh. "I know Tempest is a good girl, but Buddy isn't."

"Hey, if we can chat for a while, I'll give you a free training lesson."

She arched a brow. "Really?"

"Really really." I smiled, hoping it looked friendly. "Dogs tend to have aggression around the door, though, so might not be a bad idea to put him in another room."

Another awkward, uncomfortable laugh. "It's early. Maybe we could meet somewhere later. I really don't think Brandon would be happy with me talking to you, though, so maybe you could just text me?"

"Because he's not who he says he is, is he?" I quoted the text she had sent me from that burner phone.

Her breath hitched. Ever so slightly, her eyes widened. "I—I don't know what you're talking about. But I really need to get some more sleep, so—"

She started to shut the peephole, and my window was running out. "I don't want to go to the cops. But I do want to ruin Brandon. Just like you do. But if you don't talk to me, even if you keep pretending you're not the one who dragged me out of that building, it's gonna come out eventually. I want to protect you from the fallout, but I can't if you don't talk to me."

Peephole mostly shut, she only stared at me with wide eyes for a few heartbeats. I waited for her to speak. She didn't.

So I continued. "Look, there isn't much proof. Nobody is looking at you except for me right now. But they will. You know the repercussions of what you've done. You know you can end up in jail. That's why I want to sit down with you, discuss what you know, and come up with a plan. A plan to take him down, and to keep you safe from the fire."

She swallowed hard, still struggling to maintain the big dog at her feet. "Are you recording this?"

After fishing around in my hoodie pocket, I held up my phone so she could see it. I held the power button down and turned it off. Then I lifted up my shirt, exposing my sports bra, and spun in a circle.

A certain sense of solidarity crept into her expression. We just stared at one another for a few bird chirps. A sense of knowing radiated from both of us. My eyes into hers, and hers into mine, spoke a thousand words.

I didn't know the whole story. One piece of this, I knew for certain: The pain of growing up without a parent. Mine had been taken away by the system, another by drugs, which may have been a common ground.

Aside from that, though, we both saw what so much of the world didn't. That there was right, and there was wrong, and nobody else was doing a damn thing to fix it.

We waited for the flap of a hero's cape that never came. We waited for the sirens that should have meant help, but so often meant nothing. We waited for the day we had the power those rich men who'd exploited us had, and once we had it, her education, my money from

Ox, we were damned and determined to right the wrongs we could with these resources the rich men took for granted.

They may have called us vigilantes. But in a broken world, heroes were often the villains. No one was coming to save us, so we had to save ourselves. Even if that meant fighting fire with fire.

"Let me lock him in my bedroom," Olivia said. "Then we'll talk."

Chapter 25

I LIKED OLIVIA'S APARTMENT. IT WAS SMALL WITH ONLY ONE bedroom, but it felt open. There were no walls to separate the kitchen and living space. There wasn't enough room for a fancy dining table, but just enough for a small, eat-in kitchen. White wallpaper splashed with pink flowers covered all four walls. Except for the coffee maker, all her appliances were vintage pink. Cedar hardwoods creaked underfoot with each step I took to the kitchen table.

This apartment was a time capsule to the 1950s, and there was something intrinsic about that. The 50s were horrible times in most ways, but one thing I appreciated was the use of color then. These days, everything was boring beige. Color was refreshing.

Coffee spilled over the edge of the mug in Olivia's shaking hands as she walked across the room. "Cream and sugar, right?"

"Yes, thanks," I said, snapping my fingers toward the floor. At that signal, Tempest sat beside me.

"No, don't be silly." Olivia spoke quickly, avoiding my gaze when she set the coffee in front of me. She went back to the Formica countertop. "Do you like maple rolls? I—I just made some last night, and I know they're not really a nutritious breakfast, but I need my sugar in the mornings. It's brain food, you know. People say so many bad things about sugar, but it's vital to brain health. It helps us focus, and it makes us happy, and I don't care if I should have raisin bran. I like a maple roll for breakfast."

Nervous. Of course, she was nervous. I knew she had committed felony arson at least three times now. She was worried I was going to put her away.

I had no intention of doing any such thing.

"Hey, I won't eat a waffle unless it's drenched in syrup," I said. "I'd love a maple roll."

She reached into the microwave and came out with a plate covered in cling wrap. Still, she wouldn't look me in the eyes. "Do you want it warm? I like mine cold, but I know some people like cinnamon rolls and maple rolls warm, so I figured I'd offer, because—"

"Olivia?" I asked, making sure my voice came out gentle and calm.

Finally, she turned and looked at me. Her expression was difficult to describe. Usually, when I caught a criminal, they were angry. Sometimes sad. Olivia, however, was petrified. There was hardly any color in her usually blushing cheeks. Even from here, I could see her blood pounding in the vein at her neck. Sweat dribbled down her brow. No matter how hard she tried, her eyes were still wide. "Yes?"

"I appreciate the coffee and everything, but you don't need to be so nervous. Nobody knows it's you. I'm going to do everything in my power to make sure no one does."

Swallowing hard, tears bubbled in her eyes. "Thank you."

"I do this job because I love a good story." I reached over and patted the seat across from me. "So please, just tell it."

She returned to the table with the whole plate of maple rolls. At first, she still had a hard time meeting my gaze. "What do you know so far?"

"That your grandmother didn't want to sell her building," I said. "No matter how much Brandon offered, she refused. But he needed that land. Eventually, she died in a mysterious fire, which freed up the land. I didn't do much digging on who the property was given to after that, but I'm assuming they were willing to sell since he built that shopping center. I also know your grandmother meant a great deal to you. From what I read on your Instagram, I'm assuming she had custody of you. So when she was killed, you essentially lost another mom."

"That's one way to phrase it." Pulling apart the maple roll, she kept her voice low. "I know he did it. I know it wasn't an accident."

"I believe you. I'm just looking for proof." I waited for her to respond, but she just picked apart the maple roll and chewed on a few pieces of it. All the while avoiding my gaze. Which meant it was time to take this off of the illegal activities and onto something that would be easier for her to talk about. Herself. "How did you end up with your grandmother?"

"My mom overdosed when I was a baby," she said. "She was an only child, and I was an only child, so my gran took me in. I was so little when Mom died, I don't even remember her."

In essence then, yes, Brandon had killed her mother. "I'm sorry. Both of my parents were addicts, too."

"Did you lose them?"

"One of them." After grabbing one of the rolls, I held it to my nose and inhaled for a moment. My mouth watered at the scent of sugar, maple, and yeast. "My dad was in jail for most of my life. He and I have started to rebuild a relationship. My mom died, but only a few years ago. Between the foster homes when I was a kid, though, I don't know what was worse. Being with her or being with them."

Her eyes lifted to mine. "The foster homes were hell, weren't they?"

Good. We were connecting. "Sometimes. A few of them were nice, but they usually wanted the little kids. The babies. The ones who would take in someone older usually didn't have good reasons."

There it was again. Common ground. A certain synchronicity of the past, from her eyes to mine. "Gran died when I was eight. I found my forever family at twelve. Those four years were the worst of my life though."

"I chose the evil I knew and stopped telling anyone about what my mom did to me." Biting into the baked good, I sighed through my nose. "Anyway. At least you had your gran for a while."

"I should've had her a lot longer," she said under her breath.

"You should've," I said. "Where were you the night the building burned?"

"I was there. Inside. It was two stories." At the memory, her expression grew solemn. "We were getting ready for bed. She had just braided my hair. Gran had gone downstairs because she heard something. Then I heard yelling, and she told me to run." A big bite of maple roll. She chewed and swallowed before continuing. "I ran down the fire escape, and I saw him. He was in his car around the back of the building."

"Brandon," I said. She nodded. "You knew him?"

"Just as the fancy guy who was always wearing a suit when he came to talk to Gran," Olivia said. "She was always upset when he left. She cussed him out a few times. I knew she didn't like him, but I didn't know who he was yet. Even that night, I didn't really know who he was."

"But he was in the car while your grandma was yelling at someone downstairs," I said. "So he was working with a partner."

"I think so, yeah. When I got down into the alley, I ran behind a dumpster. I didn't know why my grandma told me to run, and I still don't know exactly what happened that night. But there was some more yelling inside. I couldn't make out what they were saying, but while I was hiding behind that dumpster, Brandon got out of his car and walked inside. Walked right past me, actually. He didn't see me, though."

"You didn't go to a neighbor's?"

"Not at first. We didn't have many neighbors left. Everyone on the street had sold to Brandon."

I nodded in understanding. "So he goes inside and then what happened?"

"More yelling. At first, Gran was yelling at them. Then she screamed—" Her voice cracked. Tears gathered in her eyes, and she quickly blinked them away. She took a minute to regain her composure, clearing her throat and sniffling, before continuing. "After Gran screamed, the men started yelling at each other. I remember Brandon's voice, but it was the other guy who said, 'what the hell did you do that for?'"

That was the moment Brandon had killed her. The fire was his way of disposing of the body. If he'd brutally murdered her, though, physical wounds would have shown up during the autopsy. Not unless her body was too damaged for them to find the wound.

Those were questions for Devon.

"I'm guessing the fire started a few minutes later?" I asked.

Another nod. "It was a big boom. That's when I ran. I thought they were gonna see me, because they ran out right after I did. I'd just made it around the back of the building when they came out the side. That's when I saw the other guy. He was really tall, taller than Brandon, and younger. Brandon looked like a dad, and the other guy was young enough to be his son."

If there was a boom, there had been some type of accelerant. Accelerant would have been found by the fire marshal. The article I'd read said it'd been a gas leak. A good enough fire marshal still should've been able to tell it was arson, but I could see it being overlooked.

More importantly, though, she saw the partner. "If I showed you a picture of the younger guy, do you think you'd recognize him?"

"Absolutely."

I reached for my phone in the center of the table. "Mind if I turn that on?"

Her face screwed up. "You know who he is?"

"Maybe. The one I'm thinking of was doing other illegal things for Brandon during this same time."

"And you have a picture of him?"

"I do."

Nervous excitement tinged her voice when she said, "Show it to me."

I grabbed the phone and turned it on. We waited in silence while it loaded. Once it started up, I pulled up Devon's mugshot. "He's a few years older here but—"

"That's him." Pointing to the phone, she lifted her hand over her mouth. "That tattoo. The one on his arm. I remember it. I even told the cops about it later. That's definitely him."

A smile teased the edges of my lips. I had to force it down. "Perfect. We're close to a complete case against Brandon then."

"Really?" With wide eyes, she leaned in. "How so? What else do you have?"

"We'll get to that." I shut the phone off and returned it to the table. "I need more information first. But go on. You were around the back of the building?"

"Right," she murmured, blinking a few times to bring her back to the story. "Eventually, I made it to a neighbor a few streets over."

"Surely the neighbors called the cops," I said.

"They did. Someone else must have called sooner though, because the sirens had already started."

"Did you tell the cops what you'd seen? Or heard?"

Trembling fingers picking at the dessert before her, she grew silent. For a few heartbeats, neither of us spoke. Then she said, "I know that I hyperventilated and passed out on the neighbor's couch. The cops did ask me questions, but I just kept crying for my grandma."

So she hadn't said anything. Was that why it was all so quickly swept under the rug?

"I didn't talk for a while after it happened. Not after I realized Gran was gone. When they did eventually get me into a foster home, I had nightmares about the bad man in the suit." A half-laugh escaped her. "I did tell my social worker about it, but you know how things like that go. They're so overworked and understaffed, they're just worried about immediate threats to the children. They didn't do anything about it. Not even when the mandated therapist asked my foster parents who the bad man in the suit was. Nobody would really listen, so I shut up. But I thought about it all the time. Every day. The first person who really listened to me was my mom. My adopted mom, I mean.

"She did try to report it to the cops, but it was a several-year-old housefire by then. They didn't care. Even if there was a case, they weren't interested in investigating it. When I was older, and I got to college, I tried again. I went down to the police department a few times, but nobody listened."

All the pieces were gradually falling together. "So you started making a plan."

"Not until right after I graduated." A slow, shaking sigh. "I was online looking for jobs. Something entry-level to just get some work experience, you know? And that's when I saw it. Full-time secretary position for Brandon Adams. I recognized his face. It was around this time last year, close to the anniversary of Gran's death, and it just all hit home.

"I wanted to see who he was now. But the fact that he still had his business said plenty. I still stalked him. Learned everything I could before I submitted my application. I ended up on some forums, and people were talking shit on him. Old secretaries, interns, and even maids and janitors who said not to work for him because he's a pig. He was this rich, privileged murderer, and he was just getting away with it. He walked all over everything and everyone. Somebody needed to knock him down a peg. And I knew I could do that. I'm not bad looking. I have the degree he wanted for a staff member in his office. Sure enough, he hired me on the spot in my interview, and then..."

"You started gathering the information you needed to blackmail him," I said.

"I started, and I haven't stopped," she said. "All anonymously, obviously. Throwing him curveballs that don't trace back to me. He's done so many illegal things over the years. Money laundering, drug trade, sexual harassment, probably sexual assault, not to mention what happened to his ex-wife, how he treated his daughter, and the fact that he killed my grandmother in cold blood." Her voice cracked at that last line. She cleared her throat and grabbed another roll. "I told him that if he didn't turn himself in for this, or for that, I was gonna start destroying his life. I never wanted money. But I know he's got damn good lawyers, and even though I have what *I* consider evidence, a good friend of mine is in law school and says nothing I've found is enough. Not to get him sent away. It's all circumstantial, and a confession is the only way to get him where he belongs."

"When he refused to give in, you started burning his buildings."

Slowly, she nodded. "I know it's not right. But neither is getting away with everything he has. It was the only way I could make him suffer. Even if he's not in prison, he's still miserable."

I respected a woman on a path of vengeance.

"But you said you're going to take him down," she said. "How? Because I have so much evidence, but like I said it's all circumstantial. It won't put him behind bars."

"The guy with the tattoo," I said. "I know he was involved now, and if you're willing to testify to that, we've got a strong case."

A hard swallow. "But what about the arson? If I testify, Brandon's gonna put two and two together."

"You were careful with all the blackmail and fires, weren't you?"

"Of course. I don't even know how you figured it out."

"Luck, mostly." I leaned back in my seat. "And because I spoke with another one of Brandon's victims. She told me about your gran's fire. But all that gives us is motive and means. With no tangible evidence, it won't stick."

"It could. Brandon has lawyers—"

"And I've got a better one—who'll take the case pro-bono, should it come to that—just because she hates men like Brandon." Shaking my head, I frowned. "You won't go down for this. Right now, our priority is building a concrete case for the DA. So. What else do you know?"

Chapter 26

Olivia asked me a few more questions, and I did the same. What evidence did she have? Was it anything that I could use?

It wasn't. Several times, Olivia had witnessed him allowing sketchy people into the building. They were usually dropping off boxes in a room that only Brandon was allowed in. Once, he had told Olivia to open the door for some of these men before they opened for the day. She did. The boxes they were carrying reeked of marijuana. "If only Tempest had been with me that day," she said. "Only a few of the boxes smelled like weed, but I have no doubt there were other drugs in there too."

I didn't doubt that either. But like she said, not enough to use in court.

Olivia had spoken personally with one of Brandon's staffers who'd quit because of sexual harassment. Another had claimed that Brandon had put something in her drink while on a business trip together. She'd woken up in his hotel room with no memory of the night before.

Unless there was definitive proof, sexual assault cases went just about nowhere in court. Her word against his. Even if they did have proof, like DNA from a rape kit, if it was someone they knew, it was an argument of, "She wanted it. She said yes," versus, "I told him to stop, and he didn't."

Nothing would come of that either.

How did she know he was laundering money? Because, in Olivia's words, he owned too many businesses where there was no actual business going on. The only business he was really doing was property development. Yet, he owned a bakery a few cities over. A bakery that never had many customers, but grossed over six figures, according to Brandon's books. The same applied to a couple of gas stations, restaurants, and other small businesses that dealt mostly in cash.

I agreed. It sounded like money laundering. But she had no proof. All she had were the clean books. She didn't have his cooked books.

The one thing we did have, though, was Devon. Olivia recognized him. That tied him and Brandon to the scene of Michelle Nelson's death. The third-party witness would, in theory, be enough to get a conviction for Michelle's murder. Considering Brandon was in his sixties now, the few decent years he had remaining would be spent in prison. So long as Devon testified.

As I left Olivia's apartment and headed to my car, that was all I could think about. I must've checked my phone a thousand times for Harper's call. That said, it wasn't all that serendipitous when her name flashed across my screen just as I sat in my car.

"Good timing," I said, pulling the door shut. "Did you hear back from the DA? Or the agents at Quantico?"

"Sure did," she said. "Both of them. Man, they want Brandon *bad*."

Not as bad as Olivia does.

"We're all on the same page then."

"That we are," she said. "Also, got us a meeting at the state penitentiary with Devon later today. It's in Smithfield, so a long drive, but I know you wanted in on it. Are you still in? Or are you crashing from staying up all night?"

"I am *in*." Starting my car with one hand, I stretched behind me to scratch Tempest's head with the other. "I'm already in the city, actually. I had to meet with someone. You want to take my car? Or yours?"

"I don't care which car we take as long as I drive. I'm guessing you've been up over twenty-four hours now, and no way in hell am I getting in a car with you behind the wheel."

"Pshh, I'm fine," I said. "But I would not be opposed to a nap in your passenger seat."

"It's all yours," she said. "Who was this someone you had to meet with? Our arsonist?"

"The less you know, the better."

She huffed. "Touché."

"Should I meet you at your place, then?"

"Sounds like a plan."

"See you in twenty."

* * *

BEFORE SHE LET TEMPEST IN HER CAR, HARPER MADE SURE TO cover her back seat with a blanket. Not only did she cover it, but she tucked it into the edges carefully. Her seats were leather and under warranty, but the last time she allowed Tempest in her car, she couldn't get the hair out for months. Had to spend two hundred dollars to get it detailed. As if that was the end of the world.

She always had been a bit more materialistic than me. I didn't hold it against her. These days, there wasn't much of anything I held against her.

No matter how much I missed Ox, his death had allowed me to finally let her back in. I felt guilty about it for a while. It eventually came up in therapy, and I expressed my guilt. She said, "But didn't Ox want you to be friends again? Didn't he say so in his letter?"

He had. Maybe that had more to do with why I felt better about our friendship now. Maybe it wasn't because he died, but because his desire for us to make amends was practically his dying wish.

Either way, this sleep deprived, miniature road trip reminded me how much I'd missed her. The way she mocked my singing, our dozens of inside jokes, and the laughter that billowed from both of us as we cruised down the highway. We had been laughing for the last hour and a half, and I wasn't even sure what about.

Gasping for breath between laughs, Harper shook her head. "God, I missed you."

I swiveled in the passenger seat to face her better. Out the window behind her, the Pennsylvania countryside of farms and trees floated in a blur. "I am taken, you know."

"Like that would stop me."

My mouth dropped, but I couldn't stop a smile at the edges. "Harper."

"Too soon?" She shot me a smirk. "Sorry. I just had to."

"Nah, not too soon." In the backseat, Tempy whined. As soon as I looked her way, she pointed at my bottle of water with her nose. Eternally impressed by my dog's intelligence, I stretched to the floorboards for her travel bowl. Pouring her some, I said, "It really doesn't bother me anymore. Which is crazy, because it really felt like my life was ending when it all went down."

"It kind of was," she said. "Which makes me that much more horrible, but I digress. I just can't believe we've made it back here, you know? Hanging out together, joking like we used to, even joking about what happened."

I held the bowl of water toward Tempest. It wasn't easy in the passenger seat of a moving vehicle, but I did my best to bow dramatically. "We have my graciousness to thank for that."

She snorted. "Maddie Castle and graciousness don't belong in the same sentence."

"You say that, but our therapist disagrees." Because, yes, we had the same therapist. Harper had given me her number. "She believes me to be far more gracious than I thought."

"You're one of those people who lies to their therapist to make yourself look better, aren't you?" Sarcasm tinged her voice. "That's a waste of money, Maddie. Nobody can help you if you don't want to be helped."

I flipped her off.

She laughed.

"I'm becoming more self-aware throughout the therapeutic process," I said, dumping some more water into the bowl for Tempest. "And throughout the journey, I discovered that I'm really not that mean. I always thought that I was such a bitch, but I'm just very blunt. I don't like to sugarcoat things. And I don't think that's a bad thing. I think I could have remained friendly with you after everything that happened with Ox, but I would have hated you secretly. We could've never had the relationship we have now. We never would've been genuinely laughing beside each other on a road trip."

"No, I would've been too worried you'd hold a gun to my head, make me drive down an old country road, then blow my brains out and dump me in a creek."

"Exactly. Because I am straightforward. If I were nice just for the sake of being nice, even when the people around me didn't deserve my kindness, I wouldn't be doing either of us any favors."

"Agreed," Harper said, decelerating to take the fast-approaching exit off the turnpike. "The last year or two have been rough without you, but I'm happy you took the time. Even if you hated me and did fantasize about blowing my brains out a few times, without that, we never really would have worked through it. And I'm glad we did."

"Not gonna lie, though." I took a slurp from my energy drink in the center console. "We probably wouldn't have if you hadn't covered up a murder for me."

Harper grimaced. "Don't say it like that."

"Say it like what?"

"Like I let you get away with killing some random guy," she said. "Which I wouldn't have done, by the way. So don't get any ideas."

"It's not like I just go around killing people for fun."

"As far as I'm concerned, you most certainly don't."

"You don't actually think I killed anyone else, do you?"

"If you have, I don't want to know about it."

"I'm hurt by that." I pressed a hand over my heart. "Eric Oakley is the only person I've killed. Well, excluding that guy in the traffic stop we did together."

"If you're forgetting about anyone else,"—she turned my way, eyes wide and focused—"seriously, don't tell me about it."

"Of course I'm not forgetting about anyone else." Except for Jackson. But that didn't count, because I didn't technically kill him. I just let somebody else kill him.

"I hope not," she said, slowing more as we descended into a small roundabout. "Just like I hope there is no concrete evidence Brandon's lawyers can use against your arsonist."

"What arsonist? I don't know any arsonist. I got kicked off that case, remember?"

She laughed. "Exactly."

"What is the deal you landed with the DA, by the way?" I asked.

"Right now, Devon'll be in there 'til he dies," Harper said. As we approached a stop sign on a back road overgrown with summer vegetation, she looked left and right. "If he tells us what happened at that fire in 2006, and it's enough to get Brandon for murder, we'll knock it down to early release on parole in two years. They told me to offer that, though. If that's not a sweet enough deal, we can get him out by the end of the month since he's not in there for a violent crime."

"Hell of a deal."

"Fingers crossed he takes it."

Chapter 27

It was the same procedure at almost every prison. Discuss with the guards why you were here if it was outside of visiting hours, show your identification, remove all personal belongings aside from your clothing, and place them in a locker. All we were allowed to take in was the key to said locker and Harper's briefcase, which they searched.

This time was a bit different. Although it was Sunday, and they had visiting hours on Sunday, we were here to make a deal. Not only was I no longer a cop, but even when I had been, I'd never had the clearance for something like this. Harper had to sweet talk the guard for quite a while before they let us through the metal double doors with Tempest.

Usually, people met with inmates in a visiting room. Most prisons and jails had a long galley or U-shaped room with glass windows separating the inmates from the visitors. Since you couldn't hear one another through glass, there was a phone on each end. Not once had I been able to hear out of those damn things clearly.

This time, probably because the FBI was involved, we were led into a small room. Didn't look much different than an interrogation room at the PD. Four off-white walls, a dingy drop ceiling, a metal table in the middle, and a few chairs around it. Although there was a camera in the corner of the room, there was no two-way mirror.

I wondered if that camera recorded sound. These days, most of them did. Which meant I had to tread lightly. I had no intention of threatening Devon. I doubted we would have to. I just didn't want to say something that could screw Olivia.

Harper and I talked about nothing and everything while we waited for the correctional officers to bring Devon into the room. Eventually, the door creaked open, and there he was.

Gray scrubs hung loosely off his large frame. Bentley was over six feet tall, and Devon was at least an inch or two taller. Although he was a bit scrawny in his mug shot, he'd clearly dedicated himself to fitness while in prison. His upper arm was as big in circumference as my head.

His face, however, was friendly. Albeit confused. Two big, innocent blue eyes found mine. Wrinkled with age or not, Devon had round baby-faced cheeks. Like the rest of his features, his nose was just a hair too dainty for his big, strong body.

"Devon Abbott?" Harper stood and extended a hand over the table.

He gestured to his cuffs.

"We won't need those, officer." Harper waited for the guard to unbuckle his wrists. Once they were free, she stretched out her hand again. After rubbing his wrists for a few heartbeats, he shook it. "My name is Detective Ashley Harper. This is my colleague, Maddie Castle, and her service dog, Tempest."

He looked at Tempest for a minute, then at me. His forehead scrunched up. "I don't got nothing, ma'am. It's just about impossible to get a hold of drugs in here, but I swear I don't got nothing."

"We know," I said, extending my hand as well. His grip was soft when he shook mine. "Tempy's trained in narcotics, but that's not why we're here."

His eyes turned down to her again, and a smile came to his lips. "Is she friendly?"

"Unless I tell her not to be. Do you like dogs?"

Smile widening, he nodded. "More than anything. I had lots of 'em growing up. I had one when they brought me in, too. Molly. My sister took her, but she died a few years back."

"I'm sorry to hear that. Do you wanna pet her?" I asked.

His eyes grew as big and inviting as the sun. "Can I?"

"Sure. Say hi, Tempy."

He kneeled in front of her, grinning ear to ear when she approached him. His touch was gentle on her ear, then her scruff. He whispered sweet nothings to her for a moment.

Considering the way he spoke, I had to wonder why they had put him away for as long as they had. It could've come down to a lack of education, but if I had to guess, his IQ wasn't very high. Supposed that made him easy for Brandon to manipulate, but any decent attorney could've used that to get him a lesser sentence.

"I bet you'd like to have a dog again," Harper said.

Devon kept smiling, but a certain sadness crept into his eyes. "I'm hoping I live long enough to. Even if I can't have one, because I'll be so old and everything, maybe I can work at a shelter or something. Just volunteer. Love on 'em a little bit, take 'em for walks or something."

"What if I told you that you could have your own again?" Harper asked.

Slowly, Devon's eyes met hers. "But I'm here for another fifty years."

"Maybe not." She sat and gestured to the chair across from her.

He kept petting Tempest with one hand but used the other to steady himself as he sat. "I know they wanted me to testify against Martinez, but that ain't happening. He's got guys in here. Plus, everybody he's got on the outside. I don't have a death wish, Miss Harper."

"We don't know anything about Martinez." Harper reached into her briefcase and came out with a picture of Brandon. She laid it on the table. "This is the guy I need information on."

Devon looked at the photo, then snorted. "Mr. Adams?"

"So you knew him," I said.

Still petting Tempest, he nodded. "He's kind of nobody, though."

"Not according to the FBI, who really wants to put him away." I snapped my fingers for Tempest to join my side. She did. "We think you can help with that."

The look in his eyes changed. At the mention of snitching, he laughed. He was joyful to see my dog. But now, without my dog, and after realizing we weren't after someone I assumed was incredibly powerful, his face was blank. There was a bit of question in his eyes. He kept his mouth shut, likely hoping that he wouldn't let the wrong thing slip.

"Do you remember a fire in Fayette County, 2006?" I asked. Beside me, Harper pulled out a photo of Michelle's shop and apartment. "Because I think you do."

He swallowed hard and shook his head. "I don't know what you're talking about."

"I've got a witness who can place you at the scene the night you and Mr. Adams burned that building," I said.

The weight of Harper's stare on me told me she was tying together how the arsonist fit into all this. But I kept my eyes on Devon, who was a few more words away from a panic attack.

"I didn't do nothing," he said.

"I know you didn't kill her, if that's what you mean," I said. Harper set a photo of Michelle on the table. I pointed to the photo of Brandon. "But he did, didn't he?"

He opened his mouth to speak, but no words came out.

"Here's what I think happened." Folding my arms, I laid them on the table between us. "Somehow, your path crossed Brandon's. I don't know the details there. Feel free to fill me in when I get to the end. But one way or another, he had dirt on you. He held that over your head, whatever it was. He made you do things for him. Like steal a car and crash into his pregnant mistress."

He pressed his lips together, and tears gathered in his eyes.

"Or, in this case"—I pointed to the picture of Michelle's shop—"he said to go and shake her up. Give her a reason to move. Harass her. Scare her into leaving so that she would sell the property to Brandon. Then he could build his shopping center.

"So that's what you did. You went to her shop late at night. You break in, you threaten her. You were just there to freak her out. But then there's yelling. She's telling you to get out, and you're yelling back, and then Brandon comes in. And he kills her."

Devon's eyes fell to the tabletop as he threaded his fingers into his hair.

Good. He had a heart, and I was yanking its strings.

"You're upset. This wasn't the plan. You say so. 'What the hell did you do that for?' My witness remembers you saying that. But you don't realize there is a witness. Now, you're not an idiot. This is murder. You've already got a couple priors. They're minor, but nobody is going to believe you over Brandon.

"So, Brandon says you guys should burn the place down. Maybe stage her body first. Then it won't look like a murder. It'll look like a house fire. She just left the stove on when she was done cooking. That was all.

"But you know the truth. You know that woman is dead, and her family never got justice for it. You played a part in her death, even if you didn't want to kill her, and that guilt eats you alive."

He was still staring at the table, a quiet sob escaping his lips.

"Around this time, you cut ties with Brandon, right? You thought you were basically a bodyguard for him. You did stuff for him, but none of it was ever that bad. You never thought there would be murder. That's for damn sure. And then you get caught up in another crowd, and you start moving drugs for people. You get caught. It's just weed. A good enough lawyer would've gotten you a much shorter sentence, but every day, you think about that poor woman. That little old lady *you let die.*"

He wouldn't look up, and he wouldn't stop shaking his head. He just used the inside of his scrubs to wipe his snot away.

"So you accept your sentence. It's long, but you know that old lady left family behind, a family who misses her every day, and you hate yourself for having anything to do with what happened. That makes it only fair. You sit here, alone in prison, for the rest of your life, because that family will never get any closure. They will never know what really happened to Michelle that day."

He still wouldn't look up.

It told me everything I needed to know. That my theory was entirely correct. I just needed him to admit it.

I reached across the table for his hand. He jolted at first, then relaxed. My touch soft, I pulled it away from his face. "But that's just it, Devon. Michelle's granddaughter, her only living relative, doesn't want you in prison for this. She wants Brandon behind bars. And you're the only one who can help us put him there. We know he deserves to be here way more than you do."

Inch by inch, he sat up. Swatting his tears away, those big, boyish blue eyes met mine. "You ain't lying?"

"We are not." Harper laid another document on the table. "If you agree to testify, you'll be out of here in two years on parole. All you have to do is tell us what happened that day."

He looked from her to me. "Two years?"

"Plus immunity from whatever you did do that day," I said. "You paid your debt. You've been in here long enough, Devon. Help us put the real criminal where he belongs. Help this young woman get justice for her grandmother's death."

For a long moment, he was silent. His eyes fell on Tempest. He watched every pant she pulled in and let out. Before long, a few more tears escaped down his cheeks.

"If you're afraid of him, we can protect you," Harper said. "The FBI suspects Brandon of high white-collar crimes. Putting him away is a huge deal. They'll get you in witness protection."

"I ain't scared of Brandon." He wiped his tears away. "He's a big checkbook, but he ain't got any high connections. Too cocky for that. The other guys I worked for, they were scary. But Brandon's just got his head really far up his ass. He'd get killed before he made any solid connections."

Sounded about right.

"But you will testify against him?" I asked.

"Will I be protected from everything I did when I worked for him?" Devon asked. "I guess my sentence can't get much worse, but if this is about making a deal, it would be nice if I could have a dog again."

"Will your testimony include any murders?" Harper asked. "Outside of Michelle's, anyway."

"No, I never did nothing like that."

"Then yes. Whatever you confess to, you will remain safe from prosecution," Harper said.

"You're not the villain here, Devon," I told him.

Another hard swallow. He eyed Tempest up and down a moment longer. Silence stretched on. He broke it with, "I detailed his car and stole his Rolex out of it."

I arched a brow.

"That's how we met." His voice was quiet, but his eyes were sincere. "That's what Brandon was using against me. I was on probation for possession. If he turned me in, I would've gone to jail. *Real* jail. Here jail." He gestured around. "Before this, I'd gone to County a few times, but not prison. Stealing something like that while on probation... It would've landed me there. That's why I was working for him. To pay off that debt."

"Adding blackmail to Brandon's list of charges then," Harper said, jotting in her notes. "Go on. Tell us more."

Chapter 28

"Where should I start?" Devon asked.

"How did Brandon kill Michelle?" I asked.

Exhaling a deep breath, he rubbed a hand down his face. "Me and her were arguing. He walked in a few minutes later, and he started screaming in her face. He was saying something about how he'd give her however much money she wanted. Just take the damn deal. She told him to go screw himself. That she was gonna call the cops. We were breaking and entering.

"As soon as she turned around to walk to the phone, he ran up behind her. It happened so quick..." A swallow bobbed his Adam's apple. "She was walking to the phone. He came up behind her, and he grabbed this little stone statue off the end table. It was one of those angel ones. The ones all old ladies have laying around the house. He hit her in the head with it."

"That blow killed her?" I asked.

He shut his eyes. He shook his head. "No. She fell. He got down on top of her, and he grabbed her by her hair, and he slammed her head off the floor again."

Holy shit.

"What were you doing when this happened?" Harper asked.

"I don't know, man." Devon rubbed his eyes with his thumb and forefinger. "I–I couldn't believe it at first. When he hit her, I mean. And when he got on top of her, that's when I sort of came to, I guess? I ran over and pulled him off. I kind of shoved him across the room, and I got down on my knees to check for her pulse, but I couldn't find one." Avoiding Harper's gaze, his eyes fell on something in the corner of the room. Maybe he figured that if he was looking away, we couldn't see the tears in his eyes. "That's when we started arguing."

"What did he say to you?" I asked.

"To shut up. That I was being too loud. Someone was going to hear us, even though his voice was ten times louder than mine." Still, he couldn't look me in the eye. "I started to go for the phone too, and he pulled a gun on me. Said that if I told anyone about this, he'd kill me. I didn't carry a gun. I'm bigger than him and everything, but he was the one with the gun, you know?"

All that made sense. "It's a scary thing when a gun's aimed at you."

He didn't say anything for a few seconds. Eventually, he cleared his throat. "That's when he said what you did. That I was nobody. A dumb burnout no one would believe. If I told the cops he did it, they'd still arrest me for it. Maybe he was right, maybe he wasn't, but—" A sharp inhale. "Anyway. The phone was right by the stairs. So we dragged her body over there. He turned on the gas stove. He lit a candle in the front of the shop. We went out the side door together. Then we got in the car and waited a few minutes. When the fire started, that's when we left."

"What happened to the angel statue?" Harper asked.

"He had me bury it. Said no murder weapon and no body meant no murder."

"Where'd you bury it?" I asked.

"A state park. Shawnee, I think," he said.

"Do you remember where in Shawnee State Park?" Harper asked.

Squeezing his thumb and forefinger down the bridge of his nose, he shook his head. "Shit, man, I don't know."

The story didn't sound impossible, but some pieces still didn't connect.

Grabbing Harper's notepad off the table, I clicked the pen. Quickly, I scribbled, *Shouldn't the coroner have done an autopsy? They would've known that injury wasn't from falling down the steps.*

She took the notepad from my hands. *Unless the body was too badly burned. We're still gonna need the murder weapon.*

"You don't believe me, huh?" Devon asked, teary eyes finally meeting mine.

"It's not that," I said. "But there's no evidence here to back any of this up."

Biting his lip, he propped his elbows on the table and rested his chin in his hands. He thought long and hard for a few heartbeats. Then he jarred forward with wide eyes. "The news. The news lied. They said that no one called the cops until an hour or so later, but that wasn't true. The cops were there in minutes. They were driving past us when we were leaving. And I remember asking Brandon about that when he closed on the deal for that land, and he said he took care of it. That one journalist was really enjoying her new Mercedes."

That would leave a paper trail.

"Did he mention anything about the fire marshal?" Harper asked. "Or the coroner?"

"That's the cop that looks at dead bodies, right?"

"They work with the cops, yeah," I said.

He nodded quickly. "We went there, the day after it happened. The morgue, I mean. It was a long ass drive though. I had to sign the visitor log. I know my name is in that book. Brandon's should be too. I followed him everywhere he went. I was like his bodyguard or some shit. I don't know what was said inside that room, but I know he talked to a person in a white coat. Older guy. White, balding, skinny."

"Do you remember where the long ass drive took you to?" Harper asked. "Because the coroner in Allegheny County should have been on this."

"It was further up north. I don't remember the name of the city, but I could probably show you on a map. I remember having to look at it. I was driving." He looked between us quickly, hope shining in his eyes. "Would that help?"

Maybe. But proving anyone who worked for law enforcement was crooked was difficult. The journalist was another story. If we could track down their name, prove that Brandon gifted them a new car, we had evidence of a bribe.

"It might do something," Harper said, standing as she slid a paper across the table. "We're going to go do some more digging. In the meantime, I want you to write down everything you just told me. Don't leave out any details, alright?"

"Yes, ma'am." Anxiety riddled his voice as he looked between us. "But I got more. Not just this, but other stuff. Like Miss Greta. He said that if I didn't do that, he was gonna tell the cops I was the one who killed Miss Nelson. Miss Greta, I know she saw me that day, and—and that's evidence, isn't it? Plus, he always has drugs in his building. Always. He keeps a few illegal guns in his safe at home. And he's got a gas station in Washington County. The basement, at least when I was working for them, they used it to store drugs, too.

"A-and the statue. I do remember where I buried it. I mean, I don't know how to describe it, but if I walked that trail again, I know I would. I could show you. If you take me out there, even in cuffs with a bunch of cops, I know I could find it. I know it was near a creek with a little bridge over it. I don't know how many miles out or nothing, but I know I'd know it if I saw it."

Harper and I exchanged a look. The kind that said it all. I nodded.

She started for the door.

"Wait, wait, wait," Devon said, spinning around to face her. "Please. I can help. I will. I'll help you get this guy. I swear I—"

"We know that, Devon," I said.

"I'm going to call my lieutenant," Harper said. "We're gonna find that damn statue."

"And you're gonna write down everything you just told us, and the rest." I tapped the paper before him. "Let me know if you need more."

* * *

He'd needed twenty-five more.

Over the next six hours, Devon and I sat in that room while he recorded everything he remembered about Brandon Adams. Which came to twenty-six pages of info—front and back—so far. Only pieces of it would be enough for the FBI. A lot of it was conjecture without proof. So far, most of it wouldn't amount to a conviction in court. It would, however, amount to a warrant.

Especially if we found that statue.

Throughout the day, Harper was in and out of the interrogation room, giving me updates. Also brought us lunch and dinner. Devon was beyond grateful for that.

Harper's lieutenant couldn't sign off on pulling Devon from the prison. That was above even his pay grade. But there were some strings dangling. He pulled a few, and he managed a video conference.

It was almost 9 o'clock at night when the warden came into the interrogation room with the laptop. He sat it in front of Devon and told us to make sure he didn't break it. To my knowledge, Devon had no violent history. Aside from what he'd done to Greta. In prison, though, he'd been well behaved. Probably because he was not an aggressive man by nature. Only by necessity.

"So here's the plan, Devon." Sitting beside him, I clicked around on the screen until the image loaded. When the video booted, opening to a screen of rich vegetation and chirping birds, I turned it toward him. "You recognize this place?"

Squinting, he nodded slowly. "That's Shawnee State Park."

"Sure is," Harper said. "This is a virtual tour. It walks all the hikes, big and small, of the entire State Park. Were you on a trail when you buried the angel?"

Another nod. "It was a small one off the main one. There were markers on it and everything."

"Good. We'll find it then." Harper pressed play. "We are going to sit here and hike this virtual trail together, and you're gonna tell me when you find where you buried the angel. We will then have an agent dig out that spot, and we will use that little angel as evidence. We'll get a warrant and arrest Brandon Adams. We'll make sure he's not in the same prison as you, and we've already informed the guards here that if any of your fellow inmates ask, you were in the shoe today. That way, no one knows you're a snitch."

"You still have two years in here," I said. "We don't want you to end up dead before then."

"But should someone figure out that you are, in fact, a snitch, we'll move you out of this prison if we have to," Harper said. "But we'll cross that bridge when we get to it. For now, drink your milkshake and find the angel."

Leaning back in the middle chair, he propped his feet onto the table and crossed his ankles. He slurped from his paper cup. "Yes, ma'am."

* * *

A FEW HOURS PASSED. MY KNEE WAS KILLING ME. MY BACK HURT from this god-awful metal chair. But eventually, Devon gasped and said, "Right there! That's it, right there! A few feet to the left, right beside that big pine tree. I remember that pine tree. I buried it somewhere right there."

Thank God, because I was beyond ready to go home.

Tempy was also ready for a bathroom break. While Harper made her phone calls, instructing the officers of where to search for the statue, I stepped outside with Tempest. It was a cool summer evening. The sun had just set, but the foliage in the distance insulated the heat and humidity well through the night in Pennsylvania.

The parking lot was roughly the size of a small shopping center. Grass rimmed all the edges. It was enough space for Tempy to do her business, for me to stretch my leg, and with just enough cell phone service for me to turn it back on.

As soon as the home screen lit up, so did dozens of notifications.

Texts from Bentley. Texts from Grace. Calls from both.

Heart hammering, I called Bentley first. His phone went straight to voicemail. I dialed Grace. On the third ring, she answered, "Finally! I've only been trying to get a hold of you all day."

"Are you okay?" I asked, panic riddling my voice. "Is your dad okay? What's the matter? Why didn't he answer?"

"We're fine. He's in the shower."

I clasped my hand over my heart. Now that I could pull in a deep breath, I did. "My God, Grace. You scared the shit out of me."

"*You* scared the shit out of *me*," she said. "You didn't tell us you'd have your phone off."

"Yeah, well, I wasn't planning on spending my entire day in a prison." Stretching my leg out, I slowed mine and Tempest's pace. "But that's not the point. You called for something. What's up?"

"I think I found the message in Daisy's story," she said. "I mean, I'm not sure. But we weren't sure last time either. And I have no idea what it means, but I think that there are two messages in the story. Actually, I take that back. I do know what one of them means. I even checked. Just like you would have. I went to the missing persons database, and I did some crosschecking, and I think I figured it out."

The girl spoke all of that in one breath.

Sleep deprivation finally catching up with me, I rubbed my temples. "What'd you figure out, kid?"

"Okay. The poem goes like this. *I've got a new friend. A pretty bird, just like me. With blue eyes of ice, and raven black hair. She doesn't talk much, and she won't be here long. Just like the last 3S. She's tall. As beautiful as the Atlantic. But she'll be gone soon. I'm sure she is by now. If I can't save her, I'll at least avenge her.*"

"Yeah, I'm familiar with it."

"Raven. Atlantic. Don't you get it?"

Eyes heavy, limbs no different, I had to lean against a lamppost to stay vertical. "I'm going on thirty-two hours without sleep. So no, I don't get it."

"Baltimore Ravens. Atlantic Ocean. Baltimore, Maddie. His other victim, the other bird, she was from Baltimore." Excitement tinged her voice. "And if I'm right, I think I know who she is. Jane Martin. Twenty-one years old, disappeared a month and a half ago, and looks a hell of a lot like Daisy."

I arched a brow. "Damn. Good catch."

"I'd like to think so too. I don't really know how it will help us, but that's more recent than Daisy's disappearance. So, in theory, we should be able to find some more recent evidence, right? Most cameras save data for sixty days, so if we get to Baltimore next week, maybe we can find something. Maybe we can find something concrete against this guy, right?"

"Always wanted to go to Baltimore." I stifled a yawn. "Yeah, I'm in. I'll do more digging tomorrow after I get some sleep."

"Awesome." The tone in her voice assured me that she meant it.

"You said you found a second code, though, right?"

"Not a code." Grace laughed. "A message. I think, anyway. At first I thought maybe it was a typo, but then I read it over again, and it looks intentional. She used capitalization last time too. This is just a little different."

I rubbed my eyes hard, trying desperately to keep them open. "What's different?"

"She says, 'just like the last 3S.' It could've been her finger slipping. I'm sure she's trying to work fast, but it's an S. In the next sentence, she capitalizes the word 'tall.' Not just one letter, but the whole word. In the rest of the document, there are no capitalizations. Just 3-S-T-A-L-L."

Cocking my head to the side, I spoke that aloud a few times. Until I landed on, "Third stall."

"Exactly." Pride rang through Grace's voice. "Third stall. Maybe I'm reading into things too deeply, but if she was at the library, there's probably a bathroom, right? When I hear stall, that's what I think. Bathroom stall. And she knows she's talking to me. I'm the one she's communicated with in the comment section. So maybe that's what she's trying to tell me. She left something in the third stall of the bathroom."

"It's a definite possibility," I murmured. "We can't get in there until tomorrow. I've got a couple hour drive home, depending on when I get out of here, and I think your dad has work tomorrow."

"He already called off. Kinda lied, actually. Said you got hurt at work and you needed someone to help you around the house."

I chuckled, rubbing my eyes. "It's a plan. Tomorrow, we make the trip to Lancaster. But I've got to get some sleep tonight first. So we might not get there until the afternoon."

"They're open 'til five on Mondays, so we're good to go as long as we get there by four," she said.

"We'll try and get out of the house around noon then, all right?"

"All right. Thanks so much, Maddie. And thanks for finding out that I'm an aunt."

"Anytime." Yawning again, unable to stop the smile that tilted the edge of my lips, I rubbed my eyes some more. "Tell your dad that if I don't answer, it's because I'm going back into this prison. I'll call him back as soon as I can, okay?"

"Okey dokey." She paused. "But, Maddie?"

"Yeah?"

"Are you driving yourself home?" she asked. "Because you sound really tired. And you're recovering from a concussion."

"I'm with Harper. She's driving back to her house, and then I'm driving from there."

"But how about you don't? Sam's been here all day, and he and dad could ride together. One of them can drive your car home. If you've gone that long without sleep, after back-to-back road trips, and we have another one tomorrow, I just don't think you should be behind the wheel."

Another chuckle. "Do they know you're offering up their services?"

"You're on speaker. Sam's in the kitchen. He suggested it."

"So we're snooping now, old man?"

"I'm not snooping," Sam called. "Just a concerned parent."

As tired as I was, this was one of the few times I was willing to accept the help. "If you're so concerned, I guess you can pick me up. I'll let you know when I'm on my way."

"You've got yourself a deal," he said.

"Castle!" Harper's voice rang out behind me.

I hurried off the phone, stowed it away, and spun to face her. From a distance, she was a vague, blurry outline just outside the prison doors. Still, I called, "Did they find it?"

"They found it!" She jammed her fists into the air. "And it's got blood on it!"

"Did we get a warrant?" I asked.

"We did! We're arresting the son of a bitch in the morning!"

Chapter 29

Within the hour, we were on our way home. I napped along the way, which helped with the exhaustion. It was almost 11 by the time we made it to my car. Sam and Bentley were already waiting for us.

They exchanged a few pleasantries, but we were all exhausted. The two of them hadn't gotten the best rest either. Still, Bentley greeted me with a smile, a big hug, and a gentle kiss on my forehead. Sam drove his own truck home, and Bentley drove my Subaru.

As we pulled out of Harper's driveway, Bentley said, "It was a long day, but a good day, I hear."

"A victory in my book." Stifling a yawn, I stretched my arms overhead. They couldn't reach far in the small car, but it was something. "I knew from the moment I met the guy he was dirty. I just didn't realize *how* dirty. I still don't have all the details, not really, but the rest is for the FBI to handle."

"How dirty was he?" Bentley asked, looking both ways before we crossed the four-way intersection. "I know about the murder, but what else?"

"I'm not sure, actually. Something to do with drugs? I think his properties are sort of used as warehouses. Wouldn't be surprised if he's on Simeon's books," I said. Bentley laughed. "But it's ironic, considering how I started on this case."

"That you put your own customer away? Definitely ironic."

"Yeah, but he deserves it."

"Obviously," Bentley said. "But how do you leverage that?"

I stifled another yawn. "What do you mean?"

"I don't know." His expression was hard to decipher. His tone was lighthearted, and his eyes lacked the intense grief that had been so present in them lately. Something wan still lingered. "I don't know, it's just something I think about a lot. Not just for you, but for me too. Everything I did for the Lawsons, it always felt dirty. But working with Simeon doesn't. Then I feel like a hypocrite. Do you go through that?"

While I understood the thought process there, no. "Not really. I get why you would though."

"Yeah?" He glanced from the road to me. "How so?"

"Working with drug dealers, working for them, by society standards is inherently bad. But I don't see it that way."

I couldn't tell if he scoffed or laughed. "You see no moral issue with drug dealers?"

"I think it depends on the drug dealer." A shrug. "In my eyes, Simeon is no different than someone who owns and manages a vineyard or a beer brewery."

"That's quite a statement coming from an ex-cop."

"Guess so, huh?" I chuckled. "I guess it's complicated. I don't think drugs are a good thing. Most of the time, anyway. Not when it becomes full-blown addiction. Not when people are ruining their lives for substance. But I also know that alcohol affects the same brain receptors as heroin. When I was doing pills, I acted like it was somehow better than banging dope, but in the brain, it's the same thing."

"Yeah, I agree." The streetlights flickered across his face as we accelerated onto the highway. "But if not for the drug dealers, people wouldn't ruin their lives over the drugs."

"Sure they would. They just wouldn't get the drugs from the dealer. They would get some Sudafed and make their own meth. Or they would go to the doctor, ask for an ADHD test, answer all of the questions accordingly, and get prescribed Adderall. And if they couldn't, they would take their kid in, answer the questions accordingly so that their kid could get it prescribed and then steal the kid's script. Then they're getting it legally, and they're still getting high, but there's no drug dealer around anymore. Because prohibition doesn't work. Just like it didn't work in the thirties."

Laughing, he shook his head.

I bumped my elbow into his, chuckling too. "What?"

"You think meth and heroin should be legal?"

"It basically is already. All cops do is bust sellers. Unless someone's violent, stealing to get money for drugs, or driving under the influence, we usually let them go."

"And you think that's okay? That we just let this shit go on in our world?"

"I think criminalizing addiction helps no one. Alcoholics get more help and are less demonized in society because their drug of choice is legal. If other addictions weren't so stigmatized, they'd be safer for people who are going to do it anyway, fewer people would die from overdosing, and it'd take the power out of the hands of people like Brandon and Simeon."

"But you just said that you don't look at Simeon and Brandon the same."

"I don't. But that's because of the way they conduct business."

"Elaborate?"

"Simeon only hurts people when his hand is forced," I said. "If he's worried someone's going to snitch on him. If somebody hurts or kills one of his guys. Otherwise, he's actually a pretty productive member of society. He pays his taxes. He offers small, interest-free loans to people who need them. He helped me find a serial killer."

"Ah." Bentley nodded slowly. "But Brandon killed for greed. The woman had done nothing to no one, and he still killed her."

"Exactly. And I'm sure you see working for Simeon versus the Lawsons the same way," I said. "Even though what Simeon does is illegal, he has a moral compass. The Lawsons don't. They forced a girl who wasn't even of age it into sexual slavery."

Bentley winced.

Shit. "I'm sorry. I know it's a touchy subject and everything—"

"No, you're right." His voice was a bit softer, a bit sadder. "That's what they did. And you're right. Morally, it's a different level. They're all bad, but they're different levels of bad."

At least we were on the same page. "But to answer your question, that's how I leverage it."

A deep breath. "It makes sense."

Hopefully, it would help him sleep better at night.

* * *

IT WAS A LITTLE MORE THAN ANOTHER HOUR'S DRIVE HOME, BUT I managed to stay awake through it. By the time we arrived, all I could do was let Tempest out to pee. After telling Sam bye, then kissing Bentley good night, I went inside, dropped onto my bed, and fell fast asleep.

That was a little after 1 a.m. so when I awoke to a text at 9:30, I was rested up well enough. Even though I probably could've slept for a whole twenty-four hours to make up for the night I'd missed, there was no going back to sleep after I opened the text.

A multimedia message from Harper. When it loaded, I smiled.

Brandon Adams, sitting silently in the backseat of a cruiser. He didn't look at the camera. Just sat there with a clenched jaw, gazing ahead.

The message below it read, *We found a shit ton of drugs in the basement of that gas station. Since Brandon's the only one with the key, he's getting charged with it. Plus a few illegal guns in his safe. We found one of his cooked books too. Looks like we're getting him for money laundering.*

I figured it was best I didn't call you before we went. Don't want your witness getting compromised.

In other words, she didn't want the other officers, detectives, and agents to tie together that Olivia was the arsonist. I appreciated that.

I texted back, *Good call. Looks like he's having a shit day though.*

Assuming she had a fair deal of paperwork to get done, I went about my day. Tempest had been quite the trooper the last few days, so she deserved a good breakfast. Kibble with wet food on top.

After two days without a shower, I was disgusting. That was next on the list of priorities. My knee wasn't happy with the lack of attention I'd given it over the last few days. So I took a bath instead of a shower. The hot water helped my muscles relax.

By the time I was finished, Harper texted back, *It's about damn time.*

I responded with, *Amen.*

Once I got dressed, I took Tempest outside again to do her business. Bentley was already walking to his car with a suitcase. We greeted one another, and he explained that Grace was still asleep, but noticed me limping. He suggested we do our exercises and take a quick walk before we got on the road. No matter how anxious I was to wrap up Daisy's case, I wouldn't be much good to anyone after a four-hour drive if I didn't take care of my body first.

So I agreed. By the time we got back, Grace was awake. Not only awake, but dressed and ready to go.

Who was I to argue?

We loaded into my car, since it had more seats than Bentley's, and set off. About an hour into our drive, we stopped for breakfast at a diner beside the highway. As soon as we paid the bill, we were in the car again. We stopped one more time to use the restroom. Somehow, we still made it to our destination by three-thirty.

And as soon as we pulled up, I understood why Mr. Deluca let Daisy go in here.

This wasn't a top-of-the-line library. Not an old, beautiful building with gargoyles and stained glass. Just a little box on the edge of a small town, surrounded by pothole-ridden roads. A train raced by across the street, chugging loudly against the metal tracks. On the other side of it, birds chirped in the high treetops.

Since it was at the edge of town, there were no cameras outside. Only a few businesses, too, all of which were run down. A car repair shop stood across from the entrance, but there were no lights inside. A few buildings down on that same street, a liquor store was on the corner. Between the two, though, only old buildings with bars on the windows. Pieces of trash floated down the cement between them like tumbleweeds in an old western.

"So much for Amish people," Grace muttered in the backseat.

"I do want to stop at that Amish grocery store we drove past on the way back," Bentley said, unbuckling his seatbelt.

"We might be in Amish country, but this isn't an Amish town." I unbuckled my seatbelt as well. "Looks a lot like an inner city, doesn't it?"

"Sure does," Grace said under her breath. "You're bringing Tempest in, right? In case she's able to catch a scent?"

"That's the plan." Taking another gulp from my energy drink, I opened the passenger side door. "Where did you put the T-shirt of Daisy's?"

"It's in a Ziploc in the trunk." Bentley got out of the car behind me. "You want me to grab it?"

"Not yet." Opening the back seat for Tempest and grabbing her leash, I looked at the glass double doors to the library. "Just wanted to make sure we have it."

Grace said something, but it didn't register. I was too busy scanning the street for cameras. There was one at the end, down at the liquor store, but it wasn't aimed in this direction. I didn't see any others, but there were a few small shops on the adjacent street. When we were done, I could go talk to all the shop owners and see if there were any hidden ones.

It was possible the one at the liquor store had caught something. The GPS had taken us down that road to get to this one. The road to my left was one way. Still, I could look in that vicinity for a security camera that may have caught Mr. Deluca on film, but that wasn't so important.

If he had taken that road, rather than the one that went through town past the liquor store, it may have suggested he knew this area. That could help me in narrowing down who he was.

"Maddie." Grace snapped her fingers in front of my face.

"Don't do that," Bentley said. "It's very rude."

"You've done it," Grace shot back.

"Yeah, but she's rude to me too. It's a give-and-take. You're a kid. You don't get to be rude. Especially not considering everything she's doing for us."

Grace rolled her eyes.

I chuckled. "Sorry. Were you saying something?"

"Yeah. You ready to go in?"

Chapter 30

If only these walls could talk.

As we passed through those double glass doors, that was the only thing I thought.

Daisy had been in this very room only a week ago. She had walked on these Berber carpets. She had breathed in the scent of paper bound between hardcovers. She had touched one of those keyboards at the computer center in the corner. She had looked at these white walls, covered in posters about stopping the banning of books, donating to your local libraries, book clubs, local events, and these walls had stared back at her.

If only they could talk.

The checkout desk was off to the right. The librarian wasn't sitting at it but rustling sounded from the room behind it.

That was okay. I wanted to talk to the librarian, but that wasn't why I was here.

Grace was five steps ahead of me, beelining to the door with a sign that read "Restrooms." Bentley slowed his pace to stay at my side.

As much as I wished I could walk at Grace's speed, I didn't mind that she was ahead of me. This was her win. She'd found that message, if it even was a message. God, how I hoped it was.

When she reached the door, she yanked it open and held it for me. Bentley fell back, since this was the women's restroom and all.

Together, we walked inside.

It looked as I'd expected. Old, dingy linoleum floors, two chipped pedestal sinks, and three aged pink stalls. A drop ceiling hung above us. The paint in here may have been white once, but it was an odd shade of stained cream now.

Grace darted to the stall on the left end. I went into the other.

Squatting was no easy task, so I bent down to look behind the toilet. To my disappointment, it was only that. An old toilet with nothing stashed behind it. After reaching into my pocket and finding a few pairs of gloves, I pulled one on. Then I checked beneath the mildew-covered toilet brush in the corner. Nothing there either.

There weren't many other places to look. Still, I checked. I checked the feminine hygiene waste bin, as disgusting as that was. Even leafed through every discarded item. Gagged along the way, but a job was a job.

When that came out fruitless, after changing my gloves, I squinted inside the toilet paper holder. It was one of those massive black ones that held a toilet paper roll bigger than my head. At first glance, there was nothing to see. But I knew how to pick a lock, and there was one on the top. After finding my multitool attachment on my key ring, I did just that. Then I opened the container and pulled out the ginormous roll of toilet paper.

Still nothing.

It wasn't a modern public restroom toilet. Rather than the commercial build with the handle practically made to flush with your foot, it was a standard residential toilet. Meaning there was a tank.

Grabbing hold of its edges, I carefully lifted it onto the toilet seat. Couldn't exactly call myself a home improvement expert, but everything looked in order. There was nothing out of the ordinary.

"You got anything down there, kid?" I asked.

"Don't you think I would've told you if I did?" she snapped.

"Hey, don't yell at me." Returning the lid onto the tank of the toilet, I straightened up. "I was just checking."

Grace let out a long, low groan. "I don't understand. What could she have meant then? Third stall. This has to be what she was talking about, right? That's all that makes sense."

Stepping backward into the bathroom so I could look at all three, I sighed slowly. "She may have left something in here that the janitor found."

"Great." Grace crossed her arms against her chest. "That's exactly what I want to hear right now, Maddie."

"It could be a good thing. The janitor may have found it and left it in a lost and found or something." Squinting over the three stalls that took up the entire wall, I focused carefully. "Did you check the toilet paper dispenser?"

"Opened it up and everything," Grace said.

"Back of the toilet?"

"Yep. Nada."

"The pad waste bin?"

She gestured to the gloves around her fingers.

"Dammit," I said under my breath. In the distance, a hum sounded. A draft moved through. "Is there an air return in that stall?"

Grace hooked a thumb toward the left, referencing the one on the wall by the sink.

"Shit." Crossing my arms, I stared at the three stalls a moment longer.

Daisy was smart. She knew the waste bins would've gotten changed daily. The same went for the toilet paper. As soon as it ran out, someone would fill a backup.

If this was something she wanted us to find, she would've left it somewhere people wouldn't think to look. Something that wasn't maintained. Somewhere stationary.

"The drop ceiling," I said, hurrying back into the stall. "Go stand on the toilet and lift up the drop ceiling tile."

Grace gasped. "That's genius."

I sure as hell hoped so.

Gripping the top of the stall, I used it for stability to pull myself up onto the toilet. Carefully, I lifted the drop ceiling tile over my head onto the tile behind it. Dust, debris, and mouse crap rained down around me. Cursing under my breath, I found my phone in my pocket. I clicked on the flashlight, shined it inside, and rolled onto the tips of my toes to see better.

Plenty of dust, debris, and mouse shit, but nothing that looked intentional. Maybe—

"Oh, my God." Grace yanked my attention in her direction. Holding her phone as a flashlight, light blaring in my eyes, she held something up. "Do you think this is it?"

Again, I grasped the stall for stability to step down. "Wait until I'm not blinded."

A thump sounded as Grace hopped down from the toilet. "Seriously. This could mean something, couldn't it? I don't know if it's hers, but why else would this be up there?"

As my eyes adjusted, it became clear. A plastic bag with a label that read *Nature's Pantry*. Inside was a large piece of cloth, like a shirt or something of the sort.

Grace started to tear it open.

"No, no, no," I said. "Set it down. Put gloves on."

"Oh, right." With caution, Grace lowered the bag to the linoleum floor. She waited for me to hand her a new pair of gloves.

We put on a new pair together, then lowered ourselves to the floor.

She let me do the honors. Which was probably best since I had experience handling evidence.

I untied the handles. Inside was a large gray sweater. As slowly as possible, I lifted it from the bag.

A click sounded.

A piece of black plastic lay on the floor.

My heart stopped.

"Is that what I think it is?" Grace asked.

Still holding the sweater up with one hand, I lifted the piece of plastic with the other. My heart skipped with excitement. A smile came to my lips. "If you were gonna say a flash drive, the answer is yes."

* * *

Maddie's story continues in ***Field of Bones***, coming soon!
amazon.com/dp/B0D8WDNYLY

Want a free copy of the Maddie Castle prequel novella? Sign up for my newsletter and download a copy today:
https://liquidmind.media/maddie-castle-newsletter-signup-1/

Join the L.T. Ryan private reader's group on Facebook here:
https://www.facebook.com/groups/1727449564174357

Love Maddie? Noble? Cassie? Hatch? Get your very own L.T. Ryan merchandise today! Click the link below to find coffee mugs, t-shirts, and even signed copies of your favorite thrillers! https://ltryan.ink/EvG_

The Maddie Castle Series

The Handler

Tracking Justice

Hunting Grounds

Vanished Trails

Smoldering Lies

Field of Bones (Coming Soon)

Want a free copy of the Maddie Castle prequel novella? Sign up for my newsletter and download a copy today:

https://liquidmind.media/maddie-castle-newsletter-signup-1/

Love Maddie? Noble? Cassie? Hatch? Get your very own L.T. Ryan merchandise today! Click the link below to find coffee mugs, t-shirts, and even signed copies of your favorite thrillers! https://ltryan.ink/EvG_

Also by L.T. RYAN

Find All of L.T. Ryan's Books on Amazon Today!

The Jack Noble Series

The Recruit (free)

The First Deception (Prequel 1)

Noble Beginnings

A Deadly Distance

Ripple Effect (Bear Logan)

Thin Line

Noble Intentions

When Dead in Greece

Noble Retribution

Noble Betrayal

Never Go Home

Beyond Betrayal (Clarissa Abbot)

Noble Judgment

Never Cry Mercy

Deadline

End Game

Noble Ultimatum

Noble Legend

Noble Revenge

Never Look Back (Coming Soon)

Bear Logan Series

Ripple Effect

Blowback

Take Down

Deep State

Bear & Mandy Logan Series

Close to Home

Under the Surface

The Last Stop

Over the Edge

Between the Lies (Coming Soon)

Rachel Hatch Series

Drift

Downburst

Fever Burn

Smoke Signal

Firewalk

Whitewater

Aftershock

Whirlwind

Tsunami

Fastrope

Sidewinder (Coming Soon)

Mitch Tanner Series

The Depth of Darkness

Into The Darkness

Deliver Us From Darkness

Cassie Quinn Series

Path of Bones

Whisper of Bones

Symphony of Bones

Etched in Shadow

Concealed in Shadow

Betrayed in Shadow

Born from Ashes

Blake Brier Series

Unmasked

Unleashed

Uncharted

Drawpoint

Contrail

Detachment

Clear

Quarry (Coming Soon)

Dalton Savage Series

Savage Grounds

Scorched Earth

Cold Sky

The Frost Killer (Coming Soon)

Maddie Castle Series

The Handler

Tracking Justice

Hunting Grounds

Vanished Trails (Coming Soon)

Affliction Z Series

Affliction Z: Patient Zero

Affliction Z: Abandoned Hope

Affliction Z: Descended in Blood

Affliction Z : Fractured Part 1

Affliction Z: Fractured Part 2 (Fall 2021)

Receive a free copy of The Recruit. Visit:

https://ltryan.com/jack-noble-newsletter-signup-1

About the Author

L.T. RYAN is a *Wall Street Journal*, *USA Today*, and Amazon best-selling author of several mysteries and thrillers, including the *Wall Street Journal* bestselling Jack Noble and Rachel Hatch series. With over eight million books sold, when he's not penning his next adventure, L.T. enjoys traveling, hiking, riding his Peloton,, and spending time with his wife, daughter and four dogs at their home in central Virginia.

* Sign up for his newsletter to hear the latest goings on and receive some free content ➜ https://ltryan.com/jack-noble-newsletter-signup-1
* Join LT's private readers' group ➜ https://www.facebook.com/groups/1727449564174357
* Follow on Instagram ➜ @ltryanauthor
* Visit the website ➜ https://ltryan.com
* Get merch ➜ https://ltryan.shop
* Send an email ➜ contact@ltryan.com
* Find on Goodreads ➜ http://www.goodreads.com/author/show/6151659.L_T_Ryan

***

C.R. GRAY goes by a lot of names, but the most know her as Charlie, a fantasy romance author who's finally diving into the genre she's always wanted to write in - mystery and thriller. She's from a small town outside of Pittsburgh and hopes she does her city justice in the books she works on!

If she isn't writing, she's chasing after her three adorable, but incredibly stubborn, puppers - who may or may not have some of the same bad behaviors as Tempest in the Maddie Castle series. When she isn't writing, she's watching Criminal Minds or binge reading a Kathy Reichs or Kelley Armstrong novel for the millionth time. (They never get old!)

Made in the USA
Middletown, DE
28 August 2024